The Unraveling

of Abby Settel

To Bette,
A dear friend,

Sylvia May

The Unraveling

of Abby Settel

by

Sylvia May

Turquoise Morning Press
Turquoise Morning, LLC
www.turquoisemorningpress.com

Turquoise Morning, LLC
P.O. Box 43958
Louisville, KY 40253-0958

The Unraveling of Abby Settel
Copyright © 2011, Sylvia May
Trade Paperback ISBN: 9781935817956
Digital ISBN: 9781935817963

Editor, Wendy Williams

Trade Paperback release, August 2011
Digital Release, August 2011

Turquoise Morning Press
www.turquoisemorningpress.com

Dedication

For Richard

Acknowledgments

This book was completed with the support and generous help of many people.

Thanks to my first critique group—Sara Rupnik, Barbara Pedrotty, Lenette Howard, and James Cotter—for inspiring me to write the story in the first place, reading early drafts, and your continuing friendship. Thank you to Sally Honenberger and Jenn Stanley for your insightful suggestions. For helping me to grow as a writer, I am grateful to Patricia Westerhof, Susan Cockerton, Deb Serraville, Dawn Boshcoff, and Brian Henry. For your close reading and belief in the project, I thank Judy Garden, Paulette Brooks, Julie Surian, and the readers in my Waterloo book club.

Though this is a work of fiction, parts of it were inspired by an actual group called *Moving On After Moving In* founded by Susan Miller and guided by Edith Parks and Paula Nelson in Richmond, VA while I resided there. Susan Miller identified the concept of MAD (Moving Affective Disorder).

Thank you to my agent, Dawn Dowdle of Blue Ridge Literary Agency for continuing to believe in Abby. I appreciate the work of Wendy Williams, my editor, and Kim Jacobs of Turquoise Morning Press.

Finally, thank you to Richard, Eric, Lindsay, Stuart, and Jake for continuing to make my life an adventure.

Unravel:

1. To take apart; undo
2. To free from complication or difficulty; make plain or clear

Modern Language Association (MLA): "unravel." Dictionary.com Unabridged (v 1.1). Random House, Inc. 26 Nov. 2008. <Dictionary.com http://dictionary.reference.com/browse/unravel>.

Lost

"Another circumstance tormented me in those days: that no one resembled me and that I resembled no one else. 'I am alone and they are every one,' I thought."

~ Fyodor Dostoyevsky

*"Sometimes when I'm lonely
Don't know why,
Keep thinkin' I won't be lonely
By and By."*

~ Langston Hughes "Hope"

Chapter One

Autumn
Richmond, Virginia

Abby gripped the steering wheel. Where on earth was she? The houses on the street were dilapidated, their paint peeling and roof shingles curling. And gardens that, instead of flowers, were piles of dirt and weeds. A rusted car with tireless wheels was parked on a patchy lawn. Farther down the street stood a warehouse, its windows dark squares of cracked glass. A group of men, boys really, leaned against it smoking, watching her with eyes barely visible from under baseball caps.

"Yo!" one of them called. Another one tipped his hat and shouted something she couldn't understand.

Her stomach clenched and she clicked the lock button. The people at Peter's office had warned her to avoid certain parts of the city. This must be one of them. She averted her gaze from the boys, hoping not to draw more attention in her shiny red Honda.

She glanced around frantically, looking for a place to turn around, puzzling over how she ended up on this street. She cursed this new life in which she never knew how to get anywhere. Three weeks ago she wouldn't have lost her way. Then she knew how to get to places, knew how to live her life. Now she continuously questioned herself. Where to go. What to wear. How to behave. Being lost in this dubious neighbourhood was only fitting, since she was lost in her uncertain life.

A splash of dark pink caught her eye, incongruous with the surroundings. A large crape myrtle stood in a yard surrounded by a small white wood fence, its crinkled flowers bursting from the smooth green foliage. The house looked more cared for than the rest, despite the big confederate flag hanging in the front window. At least the windows were intact and a pot of purple petunias decorated the porch.

As she pulled into the driveway and shifted into reverse, the front door to the house opened. A tall man wearing jeans and a muscle shirt stepped outside. His head was shaved and shiny and his shirt stretched over defined chest muscles. Tattoos decorated his thick muscular arms. He held something in one hand. Was that a gun? She tightened her hand on the stick shift and her foot jumped off the clutch. The car lurched forward and stalled. The man strode toward her. She froze.

He stopped at her window.

Lowering her head, she turned the ignition. It just clicked.

"Watcha want?" His voice was muffled through the glass.

She gripped the key, afraid to move. Out of the corner of her eye, she saw him raise his arm, the one with the gun. She flinched and squeezed her eyes shut. Her heart pounded in her ears. This was the end. She would be shot in Richmond, Virginia, on a street whose name she didn't even know. At the hands of a stranger. She would die lost.

A tap sounded on the window.

Opening her eyes, she veered her gaze toward him, trying not to turn her head. His raised hand held a sprinkler nozzle, gray handle, black spout, and he was using it to rap against the glass. What a fool she was.

With a shaking finger, she pushed the window button and opened a one-inch gap of air. "I need to get to I-

195." She hoped her unsteady voice didn't betray her misguided fear.

He pointed the nozzle in the direction from which she'd come. "195? Ova theya. Two blocks." His southern drawl stretched the words.

"Thank you." Pushing her foot on the clutch as far down as it would go, she turned the ignition again. The engine rumbled, and she backed out of the driveway.

Her racing heart didn't slow until she saw the green signs indicating the entrance to 195. Limp with relief she pulled off to the side and took out her cell phone. With hands still trembling, she pushed three on the speed-dial. Peter's voice spoke on the voice-mail, assuring her he'd return her call as soon as possible.

Her throat tightened and she plucked at her slacks. "Peter? It's me, Abby. I...I..." she faltered. What could she say? *I was lost and scared? I need you here?* She shut the phone and cradled it in her hand.

The silence in the car was suffocating. Vehicles whooshed past her onto the highway. She flipped the phone, open and closed, open and closed. What should she do next? She couldn't face going to that meeting now, but the last place she wanted to be was the apartment. The emptiness of those three rooms closed in on her day after day, with its blandness of color, its atmosphere of transience. It fed her desolation the way moisture nourishes rust.

She shook her head. Today wasn't supposed to be like this. Today, for the first time in weeks, she'd awakened with purpose. She'd gotten out of bed early. She'd showered and dressed before Peter finished shaving. She'd hummed while making the bed, *Feelin' Groovy* of all things. And she'd made coffee, set out breakfast.

In her normal life she completed these ordinary tasks almost without thinking. But this wasn't her normal life. In this life she stayed in bed while Peter shaved and showered, dragging herself out from under the covers to wave him off to work. He'd leave without breakfast, without coffee even.

"I'll pick up something at the office," he'd say, aiming a concerned look her way before walking out the door.

But after yesterday she knew things had to change. Yesterday Hanna yelled at her on the phone.

"What's the matter with you, Mom? Isn't it bad enough that you moved so far away from me? Do you have to become a zombie too? Get out there. Do something."

She couldn't explain to Hanna how difficult "doing something" had become. How living in this city where she knew no one, had no life, paralyzed her. How untethered she felt from the person she used to be, as if she'd left herself behind in Canada and was marooned here as a stranger.

A daughter should be able to look up to her mother. So today Abby was going to be different. She would get out there and do something.

She made a list while Peter was in the shower and was cutting a banana into her yogurt when he came in the kitchen. He smelled of shaving cream and soap. His hair was damp, combed with his part too low the way it always was, and he wore a shirt starched crisp by the cleaners, pale blue the color of his eyes.

He sniffed and a surprised look crossed his face. "You made coffee?"

She nodded and smiled. He poured himself a cup and slid into the chair across from her. He shook granola into his bowl.

"You seem happy today." He said it almost like a question as if uncertain he'd pegged her mood correctly.

"I've got plans. See, I even made a list."

"That sounds like the Abby I know. What's on your agenda?"

"First the Social Security office. Then a hair appointment." With her fingers she combed through her ragged locks, thinking how she last had it cut nine weeks ago. Back home. "And I'm going to that Lost in Transition meeting."

"That's good. You'll meet people there. Will you go to the bank?"

"Oh right. I'll try to get the transfer arranged this aft." She added it to her list. Drinking the last of her coffee, she took her dishes to the sink. "Okay, I'm off."

They went out the door together. They used to do that before, in their normal life. Both with briefcases in hand, Hanna leaving with them, backpack slung over one shoulder. When Ben lived at home, he'd head out at the same time too. She smiled at the snapshot in her mind, the four of them all jumbled together at the door, putting on coats and shoes, each going their separate ways, finally to converge together again at the dinner table.

Not anymore. Now Ben and Hanna lived a thousand kilometers away and Peter went off to work while she stayed in the apartment.

"Have a great day, Abs." Peter kissed her as she stood by her car groping for keys in her bag. "It's good to see you so upbeat." He didn't add "for a change," although she knew he thought it. He was right. It was good to feel upbeat for a change.

Then he was off. The trees glowed green in the early morning sun and their pink blossoms looked fresh. She marvelled that here trees were still in bloom. It was almost October. Back home in Ontario, colored and dying leaves would be falling, and the days would be gray and cold. Certainly no flowering trees.

At the highway exit she remembered the MapQuest directions she'd left sitting on the printer tray in the apartment. Damn. She tried to recall the route: I-64 to I-195, then onto Laburnum.

****

The waiting room of the Social Security office was filled with people, mostly seniors with gray hair and canes. In one corner sat a Latino family—mother, father, two noisy boys munching on granola bars, and a baby casting his large brown eyes around the room. Was the family new to the country the way she was? Why were they all at this office?

A burly man with a flash of gray in his black hair leaned against the window. His blue jean overalls stretched across his belly. He smiled at her as she came in, his teeth gleaming white in his dark face. She smiled back and then scanned the counters, puzzled about where to go since there was no free wicket. She read the signs: Retirement, Disability, Survivors, Other. She assumed the last was her. Other.

She'd barely taken a step when the man in overalls moved forward.

"Ma'am?" he said in a deep voice with a thick drawl. He waved a slip of paper. "You hafta take a number."

"Oh." Her cheeks grew hot. "Thanks." She followed his pointing finger to a dispenser by the door and pulled out a paper tag. Number twenty-eight. Already so high. She was glad she hadn't taken the time to go back for the MapQuest directions.

She sat down on a hard plastic chair, faded red and surprisingly comfortable. Clutching her purse on her lap she looked around, wishing she'd thought to bring a book. Her old self wouldn't have gone anywhere without a book in her bag.

It felt strange sitting in this waiting room with all these unrecognizable people. She looked at her watch. If she still lived in Waterloo, she'd be readying herself to give a lecture, greeting students as they took their seats.

Not anymore.

She glanced at the woman beside her, a tiny thing leaning her bony hands like claws on a blue cane, wearing a purple knit suit, gray hair permed into tight curls. The woman's frailty reminded Abby of her mother, although her mother would never wear a purple pantsuit.

She checked the forms she'd completed last night and wondered how long she'd have to wait before her number was called. Hopefully there'd be enough time to phone Ben.

With the phone ringing in her ear, she tried to remember how many weeks it had been since she'd spoken to her son. He didn't answer when she called and she kept leaving messages to which he didn't respond. Almost twenty, he was pushing his independence, keeping to a minimum his contact with his family. But she worried about him, certain he was still on a troubled path.

To her right, the father in grimy work boots played peek-a-boo with his baby. The baby had chocolate on his face and he giggled uproariously, his chubby cheeks jiggling. Ben's recorded voice came through the phone.

She opened her mouth to leave yet another message when a digital voice informed her there was no more room in the mailbox. What was up with him? Didn't he check his messages? She snapped the phone shut, frustration and worry trickling into her mood.

"Twenty-eight. Window three."

Throwing her phone into her bag, she jumped up.

"I'd like to apply for a Social Security number, please."

"Identification?" The woman had a bosom big enough to set a teacup on. Abby took her passport out of her bag. The woman brought it close to her face.

"This is a TD visa. Your husband here on a TN?"

"Yes. He's already got his Social Security number. I was told if I filled in these forms I could get one too."

"Nope. You're here as a dependent and have no status on your own."

"But I'm a legal resident here." Abby tried to keep the annoyance out of her voice. "Surely I can get a Social Security card."

"Sorry, ma'am." The woman looked at her as if she expected her to move along.

"But..." Deflated, she jammed the forms and passport into her bag and walked out, willing herself not to cry.

Getting behind the wheel, she threw her purse onto the seat. It was so frustrating to be identified as only a dependent. She, Abby Settel, was significant back in Canada, smart, educated, a university professor. But here she was a non-person.

She shook her head to redirect her thoughts and drove out of the lot. After five minutes on the road, five minutes of deep breathing and resettling her mind, Abby realized she had no idea where she was going. She pulled the car to the side, thinking about the printed directions in the apartment, wishing she'd taken the time to go back to get them.

Twisting around in her seat, she scanned buildings along the street. No beauty shops. And she could no longer see the parking lot she'd just left. No signs for 195 either. She must have turned the wrong way out of the driveway.

Five after nine; she was late for her appointment. She ran a hand through her hair. If she were still in Waterloo, she'd be on her way to Debbie, who'd been cutting her hair for fifteen years. Debbie would slot her in no matter how late she was. Would this new hairdresser?

But there was no point in trying to find the place now. She should go straight to the Lost in Transition meeting. At least complete something on her list. If she drove the other way, she'd get on the highway and find the church where the meeting was held. She was pretty sure she knew where that was.

As she turned the corner, her cell phone rang. Ben? She answered in a voice that tried to let him know she was glad to hear from him but annoyed it hadn't been sooner.

"Mom. Are you out doing stuff?"

Not Ben. Hanna. Abby tried not to sound disappointed. She was happy to hear from Hanna too. "Yes, as a matter of fact. I'm on my way to a meeting."

"Good for you. Guess what? Our trio's been picked to play in a concert. I just found out."

"That's great. Congratulations, sweetie."

"Will you be able to come? It's next Saturday."

Abby shook her head. How could she go? She was here in Richmond. It was ridiculous to drive twelve hours to go to a two-hour concert. "Uh, I'm not sure. Let me think about it and I'll let you know, okay?"

"But I want someone from our family to be there."

"I know you do. Maybe Ben…"

"Ben! He never answers my calls. I haven't talked to him since you left."

"Oh." Abby again wondered why Ben never answered his phone.

"So you and Dad'll think about coming?"

"I'll talk to…"

"Gotta get to class. Bye."

The silence from the phone settled in Abby's ear. What kind of mother was she, not to go to her daughter's first university concert? Not to be available to figure out what was up with her son? A month ago, in her old life, her normal life, she'd be there for her kids. She would be on top of things. Now everything was out of control.

It was like an odd déjà vu, remembering how less than a half hour ago she had sat in the car with the phone in her hand, feeling frustrated and upset. Here she sat again, phone in her hand, barely recovered from her fright of that big man with the sprinkler nozzle.

A sprinkler nozzle, for God's sake! What was the matter with her?

She stared at the entrance to the highway. She would go to that meeting. She'd prove to Peter and Hanna, and to herself, that she could figure out this new life of hers. Get back in charge of things.

Throwing the cell phone on the seat beside her, she flicked the turn signal and looked over her shoulder as she eased into the traffic.

Chapter Two

She found a parking space on the street a block away from the church and maneuvered into it smoothly, nestling between a blue van and a black SUV. A small thrill of satisfaction coursed through her at her parking skills and it chased away the residual uncertainty from having been lost earlier.

This neighbourhood was very different—large red brick houses with slate roofs, beautiful gardens, green manicured lawns, shrubs trimmed into unnatural shapes. The faint hum of a lawn mower mingled with birdsong, and she could smell freshly cut grass. Sun dappled through the trees. Autumn was so green in Richmond, as if it were still summer.

She stared up at the building, struck by the size of the church complexes in Richmond. They were more like campuses and there seemed to be one on almost every other block. This one was red brick, surrounded by tall trees and pretty gardens of purple and white. It looked to be a welcoming place despite its size and its four different entries. She approached the door with a notice taped to it: Welcome to Lost in Transition.

Inside, her footsteps were muffled on the carpeted halls. Following signs with arrows, she arrived at an open door and hesitated. Voices bounced around her. Sunlight streamed through large windows on the opposite wall and settled on a circle of chairs. A young woman jiggled a baby wearing a yellow romper on her lap. Chatting by a refreshment table stood a cluster of women, some standing silent, sipping from Styrofoam cups. Close to Abby two women were talking. One had her arm around the shoulders of the other who was wringing a tissue in her hands. Her voice projected over the din of the room.

"…my eleventh move in twenty years." The woman was sobbing. "I'm having a really tough time. We're so far away from my kids. Our house is too small, and…."

Abby pulled back. She didn't want to get stuck in a roomful of crying women. Maybe she didn't need this support group. Support groups were for people who couldn't make decisions on their own, who didn't know how to do things. That wasn't her.

A dark-haired woman strode in her direction, smiling. Abby bolted. Passing a sign indicating the washroom she ducked in, leaning her back against the door, breathing hard. No one else came in. She washed her hands and stared at the mirror, not sure who was staring back.

Stepping out, she glanced back in the direction of the meeting. The hall was empty. Distant voices floated toward her. It would be easy to just leave.

She walked back to the meeting room and looked in.

The women were now sitting in the circle. One of them was speaking.

"…moved here a few months before me. We got to talking and decided to start this group. Y'all know that moving can be a real strain, and Patty and I wanted a support group for people like us. So here we are."

The drawl that drew out her words caught Abby off guard. And that y'all. It happened every time. Her conversations with the few people she encountered lulled her into thinking this place was just like home. Then she'd hear someone say something with that southern intonation and bam, she'd again realize she was in a foreign place.

She glanced around the room. Not one familiar face. Still, wasn't she a stranger too? To them? To herself?

Swallowing her nervousness, she stepped in. The woman who was speaking noticed her and gestured her hand toward the circle. "Hello. Please join us." She stood and pulled in an empty chair. Those sitting shifted theirs to the side, making space for Abby in the circle. She lowered herself into the seat.

The woman smiled at her. "I'm Ellen. We were just introducing ourselves and telling how we came to move here. Have you been in Richmond long?"

Feeling everyone's eyes upon her, Abby flushed.

"About three weeks."

She sensed nods, heard whispers. *She's really new.*

The woman next to her leaned in. "What's your name, hon?" she asked in a gravelly voice. Her dark hair was very short and blue-rimmed glasses framed her eyes. A nametag stuck to her shirt read ANNE M. in thick uppercase letters. The faint aroma of cigarettes wafted from her.

"Abby. Abby Settel."

"Hi, Abby," Ellen said. "Welcome to Lost in Transition." She returned to her chair. "Chris, I think it's your turn."

A woman sitting beside Abby spoke in a shaky voice.

"I'm Chris. I moved here from Wisconsin."

Abby realized Chris was the woman she'd heard crying earlier. Her red-rimmed eyes had deep circles under them and she held a wad of tissues between her hands.

"I'm having a lot of trouble coping..." Chris's voice faltered and she broke down sobbing.

Abby shifted in her seat and twisted the button on her sweater. How could this help, exposing your emotions to a group of strangers? She worried she might cry next.

A Kleenex box was passed down the circle toward Chris, who pulled out a tissue and blew her nose. The room was quiet.

Ellen spoke. "It'll get better. We all go through these kinds of feelings."

At her words, Abby felt a strange relief knowing she wasn't the only one whose emotions were a mess.

Ellen continued. "This is a safe place to cry. But hopefully we can help you get to a point where you're not crying anymore. Who's next?"

Abby scanned the faces. She hoped they weren't expecting her to speak just because she sat next to Chris.

"My name's Holly." The woman on the other side of Chris spoke. "We moved here in June from Chicago. We were happy about the move. Carl got a promotion. And we really like Richmond. The weather's great and I love my house, my garden." She smiled. "Our kids are in their twenties and didn't move with us, but Carl and I are enjoying that. Sort of like a second honeymoon. But it's hard to meet new people. That's why I'm here."

Abby felt a stirring of envy. Why didn't she feel the way Holly did? She missed her kids so much she ached. Maybe Holly didn't. Maybe Holly hated her life before moving here.

The baby on the lap of the woman next to Holly reached up and grabbed for Holly's hair. Abby wished she were sitting beside the baby, wanting to hold him. The baby's mother pulled back his hand and stood him on her lap.

"I'm Mandy and this is Josh. He's four months old. We moved here from Buffalo in April." She giggled. "I like the weather here too, even though the summer was really hot! But it gets kind of lonely not knowing anyone." She turned her head toward the woman beside her, as if she knew the routine.

The woman smiled and said, "Ellen already told you my name's Patty. My husband David and I came here from Germany about a year and a half ago. It's our third move. In Germany I got involved with a Lost in Transition program and it helped me understand the emotions I went through each time. Because even though every move was exciting, it was also pretty tough. I was six months pregnant when I moved here and it was really hard not to have my mom close by. After Belle was born last November, Ellen and I," she grinned and made eye contact with Ellen. "We decided to start our own Lost in Transition class here. The idea was started by someone just like us who moved around a lot and wanted to help women who were experiencing the pressures of relocating, a condition we call Moving Affective Disorder. MAD."

Abby sat back, struck by the revelation. That's what she was suffering from. Before coming to Richmond, she had no idea what an emotional impact moving would have on her. She thought she'd adjust easily, that it'd be an adventure. Didn't people move all the time and thrive? Some in much worse circumstances than hers—displaced, deported, seeking refuge. Compared to that, Abby's situation was rosy. Yet still she felt traumatized.

Patty continued. "Our program loosely follows the same structure, exploring the different stages and how to move forward." She shrugged. "Sorry, guess that was a long introduction." She looked at the woman next to her. "Your turn. Finally."

The women were young and old. Some new to the group, others had been coming for months. Most were sad. One woman ranted because she was anxious about the crime statistics for Richmond and then burst into tears. Abby remembered the fear she herself had felt earlier that morning, lost in that horrible neighbourhood. Another woman who seemed to be Abby's age was recently divorced and had come to Richmond on her own to start fresh. Abby was stunned by the bravery of her decision. A younger woman was upset about her children's school. A gray-haired woman had moved alone across the country to be close to her grandchildren, only to find they had no time for her.

As Abby's turn came closer, she began feeling anxious. Would she cry? She didn't want to expose too much about herself to these people she didn't know. Maybe she shouldn't be here.

A quiet halting voice pulled Abby from her musings.

"My name Li-Juan." A thin Asian woman was struggling to express herself. "I move China one month. I no…English." Tears ran down her cheeks, but she continued. "Tree chi'dren. I…" she waved her hand around the circle. "No understand. Talk too fast." She covered her face with her hands. The woman to her right put her arm around her shoulder. Anne M., on her other side, patted her knee.

"Aw, honey," Anne M.'s gravelly voice was surprisingly soothing. "We'll try to talk slower."

All of a sudden Abby felt ashamed of the indulgent self-pity she'd been wallowing in these past weeks. This poor woman was in a completely foreign place and couldn't even speak the language. It made her own situation seem trivial, and her discomfort became stronger.

Beside her, Anne M. leaned forward and started talking. That meant Abby was next. "My name's Anne. I moved from California two months ago, even though my husband came here four months before that. Everything that's happened since then makes me mad and upset. My kids hate it here. My husband's being a jerk, only thinking about himself, and I don't feel connected to anything. I feel this close," she held up her hand with the thumb and forefinger touching, "to taking the kids back to San Jose without him. I've been coming here to see if you could talk me out of it." She laughed hoarsely. "Not happening so far."

She sat back, then glanced at Abby. "Your turn, hon."

Abby folded her hands. She knew she should look up, make eye contact, but was afraid if she did, she'd lose her composure. She gazed at her intertwined fingers.

"I'm Abby, and I moved here with my husband three weeks ago from Canada." Her heart felt like it was beating through her sweater. "I...this move was hard because..." She swallowed. "We had to leave our kids; they're eighteen and twenty. And my parents who just moved to a nursing home. And..." Her voice quivered. She cleared her throat. "And my job. I'm here on a spousal visa so I'm not allowed to work, and I feel..." She sat back, mortified. She couldn't stop her tears. The Kleenex box was thrust into her lap. She stared at it and sniffled, rallied herself to finish. "I feel like I've lost myself. Like I'm disconnected from everything I used to be." She pulled out a tissue, wiped her nose.

Once more silence enveloped the room. Ellen spoke in a quiet voice.

"We're glad you came, Abby. That's a very common feeling among all of us. We all feel lost at first."

Abby kept her eyes down, looking at the soggy tissue in her hands. She felt, rather than saw, the nods of agreement. Humiliation flooded through her. How could she have exposed herself like this to these women she didn't know? She needed to get away from them. She didn't want to be here any more. She wanted to go back to the apartment where she could cry without anyone seeing.

Ellen continued with more energy. "Today we're going to talk about dealing with what you've left behind, how to put it in a special place in our hearts so we can move forward..."

Abby scraped back the chair. "I'm sorry. I just remembered I have an appointment." She grabbed her purse from the back of her chair and hurried out of the room.

In the solitary cocoon of her Honda, she let loose and wept, at the same time berating herself. Where was her strength? How had she become so adrift? She thought longingly of the life she'd left, recalling last spring, that day seven months ago when Peter announced he'd lost his job. That's when it all began, the unraveling of the threads that knit her life together.

Unraveling

*"An adventure is only an inconvenience rightly considered.
An inconvenience is only an adventure wrongly considered."*
~ G. K. Chesterton

*"Any real change implies the breakup of the world as one has
always known it, the loss of all that gave one an identity, the end of
safety."*
~ James Baldwin

Chapter Three

Spring (Seven Months Before)
Waterloo, Ontario

Lulled by the monotony of chopping vegetables for the stir-fry, Abby only half listened, letting her mind work through her to-do list. Hanna, who sat at the table ostensibly doing homework, entertained her mother with a monologue on her expectations of university life. The repetitive chop-chop of Abby's knife provided a background to Hanna's litany, in harmony with Norah Jones singing through the speakers. Abby felt surrounded by an atmosphere of ease and tranquillity.

A gust of fresh air and the slam of a door announced Peter's arrival, disturbing the calmness in which she and Hanna were immersed. When Abby responded to his greeting, she became acutely aware of an anxiety that simmered beneath his cheerful entry.

"Brr. I can't believe how cold it still is. And at the beginning of April too." He rubbed his hands. "But it warms me up to see my two girls."

He stepped behind Abby and kissed the back of her neck, startling her, and causing her to slice the carrot too thick. She thought she heard him whisper, "We have to talk." But when he didn't wait for a response and strode over to Hanna, she wasn't sure.

"Hi, kiddo." He leaned his hands on the table. "Have you come down from the clouds yet?"

Abby was puzzled. Not by his question to Hanna—because since Hanna received her university acceptance yesterday she seemed to barely touch the ground—but by the nervous energy he exhibited in his greetings.

Trying to draw his attention, Abby said, "Not that I can tell."

"Well, I'm excited." Hanna gathered her books. "I can't believe I got early acceptance in the music program I wanted." She began to lay out the plates and cutlery that were stacked on the table beside her. "Is supper almost ready? I need to leave for rehearsal in an hour."

Abby splashed oil into the wok and turned on the burner. "Give me about fifteen minutes and I'll have it on the table."

"Great, I'll go change." Peter bounced on his feet and nodded his head at Abby in the direction of upstairs as if indicating she should follow, but she ignored the gesture and took the marinating chicken out of the fridge. Surely he could see she needed to start cooking. If he wanted to talk to her, why didn't he just say so?

During dinner, his conversation darted from one topic to another: Ben's arrival on Friday, Abby's parents' increasing neediness, Hanna's upcoming concert, the essays Abby had to grade, Grandma and Pops coming for Easter dinner, the snow piles that still hadn't melted at the end of the driveway. The questions came non-stop, and more than once Hanna exchanged mystified glances with Abby, who was getting increasingly uneasy as the meal progressed.

"Dad!" Hanna put her hand on his arm. "Slow down. What's going on with you?"

"What do you mean? Nothing's going on."

"You're acting a little hyper."

Abby nodded. "I have to agree."

"Yeah? I drank a couple of coffees at a late meeting today. Guess they weren't decaffeinated."

"Huh." Hanna didn't seem satisfied. "Was work okay?"

"Oh, work was just work. You know."

And then Abby knew. Or was fairly certain she knew. Something in the way he said the word work, something in his voice. For weeks he'd been worrying about the company's bottom line and the future of his job. Something must have happened. Yet surely he'd tell them, wouldn't he? She listened to Hanna lecture him about drinking coffee in the afternoon. Maybe he didn't want to alarm Hanna. That must be why he'd whispered so quietly, and why he'd wanted Abby to follow him upstairs. All at once she felt guilty for ignoring his signals.

When Hanna finally excused herself, Peter stood and began clearing dishes. "As soon as she's gone we have to talk."

"Is it about your job?" Abby asked, still eating her apple.

"Yes, they've decid—" He looked over his shoulder and startled when he saw Hanna running downstairs. "Wait 'til she's gone," he whispered as he carried plates to the counter.

The stir-fry sat heavy in Abby's stomach. The bit of apple she was chewing was tasteless.

"I'm off." Hanna hoisted her knapsack. "Is it okay if I meet Jason for a coffee after rehearsal? I promise I won't be late."

"Sure." Peter responded almost too quickly. "Be home by ten."

"I will. See ya."

When the door clicked shut, Abby perched on the edge of her chair. "So tell me. What's happened?" She gripped the edge of the table, adrenaline coursing through her.

Peter sat down across from her and leaned forward, lacing his fingers together.

"I'm going to lose my job. The company's decided to contract out the work I do."

Her stomach somersaulted. "Oh my god."

"It's not official yet. Frank is meeting with the board tomorrow. But their approval is just a formality. My position's going to be defunct." He leaned back shaking his head.

She stood and took dishes to the sink, the plates clattering in her trembling hands.

He picked up an empty water glass, turning it round and round.

"Frank says they really don't want to let me go, but he can't see a better way to cut back. Unfortunately, I have to agree with him."

"How can you say that?" She wiped the counter, rubbing so hard she thought she might take surface off. "This is your job you're talking about."

"I'm realistic. Remember it was one of the options I suggested in my report? I know what the company needs to do in order to survive, and it's my job to do what's best for the company."

"That's very magnanimous of you." A stab of anger cut into her. "How does that fit with what's best for you? Or your family?"

He shrugged. "It's business, not abou…"

"What about our bills? And the kids' university tuitions? What's this going to do to our finances?"

"Obviously I'll get another job. And severance. We'll be fine." He sounded vexed.

She filled the kettle with water. "How will we tell the kids?"

"Don't say anything to Hanna yet. We should wait until it's official. Ben's coming home on Friday. We can tell them both then."

"It'll ruin their weekend."

"I know. Happy Easter, huh?"

She stared at him. "Don't tell them you were instrumental in the decision." Though she didn't intend it, her tone was bitter.

"Obviously I wish there was another way, Abs. I don't want to go. I've been with Hearth Financial forever."

"Almost nineteen years."

"Right." He banged the glass on the table. "You know, it does tick me off that they chose this option so quickly. I've helped them through a lot of bad times. I know it's illogical of me to think this, but it's almost as if they want me to leave."

Abby softened. This wasn't easy for him and her agitation wasn't helping. "Peter, your thoughts are all over the place. Think about the times you felt frustrated with stuff going on there. Won't it be good to get away from that?"

"Yeah. But I'd hoped to stay on for another six years, get my golden handshake and leave with a smile on my face. Even though I doubt Hearth will survive that long."

"We've talked for years about the possibility of you looking for another job." She remembered him sharing dreams and wishes for change. And she'd encouraged him, knowing it would be good for him, anticipating exciting adventures for herself and the kids.

"Yeah, but I never acted on it."

"You know what's hard about this?" She brought a pot of mint tea to the table and poured the aromatic brew into mugs, handing one to him. "This isn't really your choice, even though it changes your life. It's being forced on you and that means it's out of your control." She shook her head. Out of hers too.

"I guess you're right. I'll just have to work the job search so I am in control." He blew steam off his tea. "I wonder how I'll do that."

Abby warmed her hands around her mug. "I'm sure you'll find something else without any problem. You've got lots of experience and there are other finance companies here and in Toronto."

"I don't know. Maybe I could do some consulting. I was looking at some of the recruiter sites on the Internet today. There isn't much in Canada. A few prospects in the States though."

A wave of apprehension washed over her. Did she want to move to the U.S.? They'd have to leave the kids. And her position at the university. It had taken her years to establish her wonderful part-time teaching schedule. If they had to move what would she do?

Still, Peter hadn't been happy at work for a long time so this could be a good thing for him. In fact, it could be exciting for him. For both of them.

Her thoughts were a confused jumble of apprehension and excitement, uncertainty and expectation. Their life would definitely change. But how much of a change did she want? Would she even have a say?

She shook her head, as if to disperse those ideas. Peter would find a job close by. Life wouldn't change all that much. She needed to believe that.

They were into their second pot of tea when Hanna came home. She joined them at the table, full of stories about the orchestra conductor and the percussionist's mistimed entries. Her presence cheered the atmosphere, and when they all went upstairs to bed Abby felt lighter. Perhaps things would turn out all right.

****

She threw her legs over the side of the bed and sat up. Wiping the sweat off her forehead, she billowed her nightgown. Heat emanated from her like an oven. Every night hot flashes woke her up like an alarm. She squinted at the red numbers on the clock. Just after two. Yawning, she shuffled into the bathroom and a sudden dread clutched at her. Peter was losing his job. What would happen to them? They were no closer to knowing, even though they'd talked for hours before sleeping.

She turned on the faucet to fill her glass and in the dim glow of the nightlight stared into the mirror. Wide-awake and anxious, she felt the stillness of the early hours pressing on her. There would be so many complications if they had to move for a new job. How could they keep track of Ben? Where would Hanna go for relief from residence life? How would Abby be able to care for her mom and dad?

She thought back to her visit with her parents the previous day. Walking into their house, she noted not for the first time how badly it needed cleaning. The rooms smelled musty and of cat. She quietly disinfected the bathroom before using it, but her mother wouldn't let her vacuum the dust balls on the floors. Yellow Post-it notes were stuck on walls and cupboards. *Is the iron off? Hang up keys. Take pills.* Abby was relieved her parents had found a system to stay on top of things; at the same time she was distressed by the need for it.

The sight of her father unsettled her; he seemed to have deteriorated since the previous week. When she arrived, he was sitting at the kitchen table, staring at his hands. Gray bristles lay in disarray on his head, as if he'd forgotten to comb his hair.

"Hi, Dad," she'd greeted him loudly, knowing he had trouble hearing.

He looked up. "Hi, Abby. Have you seen Max? He's gone."

"Gone?" She bent to kiss him. "What do you mean?"

"He's not gone, Nick." Her mother was filling the kettle with water. Another yellow note was stuck to the fan hood above the stove. "I told you I let him out this morning while you were getting dressed. Do you want some tea, Abby?"

"Yes, please. Dad, I'll look outside and see if I can find him." She opened the back door and before she could lean out, a black cat ran into the house.

"Here, Max." She crouched down. The cat walked over to her and she stroked his back. He nudged his head on her knee and purred loudly, his tail wrapping around her leg. She didn't really like cats, even though they'd always had one when she was growing up. Rather, her father had always had a cat. When she was a little girl, she used to believe he loved his cats more than her. He certainly gave them more of his attention. Things hadn't changed much.

"Hey, you little rascal." Her father stood and leaned down. He shook Max's head back and forth. "What are you doing, eh?" At his loud voice the cat sprang away and ran down the hall.

"Let's sit down, Dad. Mom's making tea. Do you want a cookie?" Abby opened the tin she'd brought. When he took a bite, crumbs stuck to the bristles on his chin. His eyes were watery and there were seams on the outside of his sweater. Her father had become a dishevelled old man.

"Dad, you've got your sweater on inside out. Do you want to fix it?" She touched his arm.

He looked down at himself. "Huh?"

"Oh, Abby, just leave him be. He likes it that way." Her mother took the whistling kettle off the stove and poured steaming water into the teapot.

"See that note, Abby?" Her mother pointed to the Post-it above the stove as she turned the burner off. "It reminds me to turn the stove off."

"I noticed a few of those around."

"Marie Wilson said we should do that. She writes notes about everything she forgets and it helps her remember. Now we do it too." She swirled the teapot around. "You have to always warm the pot before you make tea."

"I know, Mom, you tell me every time."

When Abby took mugs out of the cupboard, she found their handles sticky. Inside of one of them, a hardened layer of sugar was stuck on the bottom. In the fridge the sugar bowl sat on the shelf beside the milk carton.

Opening the milk she jerked away from the smell, wondering if her parents had noticed it was sour. Surely they hadn't been drinking it. Her anxiety about her parents escalated. This situation couldn't go on. She needed to do something.

"You'll have to have tea without milk today." She poured it down the sink. "We'll get some fresh milk when we go to the grocery store."

"I made a list somewhere." Her mother rose from her chair.

"You can get it in a minute, Mom. Let's have our tea."

"But I don't know where the list is."

Her father raised his head. "You made a list in the kitchen. A kitchen list."

"Yes, but where is it?" Her mother raised her eyes to the ceiling and frowned.

"We'll look for it after we have our tea, Mom. And if we can't find it we'll go through the cupboards and see what you need, okay? Let's just visit for a while." She sipped her tea, scalding her tongue. "So how are things this week?"

"Can't complain," her mother said. Her eyes glistened with tears. She blinked a few times and started again. "Marie and Tom Wilson came on Tuesday."

"Mom, are you all ri..."

"Marie knits with me." Her mother shook her head, her lips forming a feeble smile.

"Tom and I play euchre, but he cheats," her father interrupted.

"I'm sure he doesn't cheat, Dad."

"Yeah, he wins all the time."

"And your Aunt Josie brought us a shepherd's pie on Saturday." Her mother nibbled on a cookie. "She gave us a new puzzle, too."

"That was nice of her."

Her mother touched Abby's arm. "Soon we'll be able to work in the garden. Did you see the bulbs coming up in the front?"

"I did. It won't be long before your tulips and daffodils are blooming." She fiddled with her teaspoon. "Do you think you'll be able to manage all the work in the garden this year?"

"Of course we will."

"But it might be nice to have some help. Have you thought any more about what I suggested last week? That we get someone in to do some of the housework for you? At least the heavy cleaning. I left that phone number to call, remember?"

"I can clean my own house." Her mother's voice rose.

"Mom…"

She huffed. "I don't want to talk about it.

So they didn't. Throughout the visit, while grocery shopping, while eating lunch, while working on the jigsaw puzzle on the dining room table, Abby's mother wavered between unexplained tears and obstinacy about her independence.

After Abby's father had gone for a nap, her mother, in a rare moment of candidness, mentioned his decline.

"Your father…" she began, shaking her head.

Abby became more alert. Her mother hardly ever discussed her husband. "Is he okay?"

"He's just..." she shrugged. "not such good company. And I get lonely."

Abby took her mother's hand. It was soft and wrinkled. Veins were visible through the translucent skin and brown spots dotted the surface. She caressed it. "You and Dad could move into a seniors' residence closer to us. You'd have lots of company in a place like that."

"We want to stay here, in our home." Her mother pulled back her hand. "You just want to put us away somewhere so you don't have to worry about us."

"Mom, you know that's not true." Abby would worry about them no matter where they were. "We want what's best for you. And Dad is getting hard to manage."

"We manage just fine."

Yet Abby knew they didn't. In the darkness of her bathroom, she drank some water and put the empty glass on the counter. Whether they moved away or not, she would have to do something about her parents.

She walked through the darkness toward Hanna's room. Opening the door a crack, she smiled at the lump under Hanna's blankets. Her beautiful lively daughter. What would she say to the news about her father's job and the possibility they might have to move away?

Across the hall Ben's room was tidy, his bed made ready for his arrival. Leaning her head on the doorframe, she replayed their phone conversation in her mind, with his troubling news about his grades and vague references to something he needed to tell them.

Sighing, she turned and shuffled along the dark hall that was her path through this black night of uncertainties. Stopping at the threshold, she listened to Peter's breathing. A wave of affection swelled in her. It could be exciting to start somewhere new with him, the way it was when they first married and moved here. Maybe there was a positive side to all this too.

She groped her way back to the now cold nest she had left and sat gently on the bed, trying not to disturb Peter. She slid under the covers and lowered her head on the pillow.

"Can't sleep either?" Peter's voice rose up through the blackness.

"No. Too much on my mind, I guess. Thinking about your job. The kids. About everything."

"Yeah, me too," he rolled over to face her. "I'm thinking about all the phone calls I have to make. Like Mike, to see if he can use a partner for his consulting work. It's a small company, though, so I'm not too optimistic. I'll call a couple of recruiters too. I have to update my resume..." He moved toward Abby and stroked her arm. "Hey. How are you doing with all of this?"

"Honestly? There's a part of me that's excited about the prospect of this change." She rolled over to face him. "I mean, you've been at your job for almost twenty years. We've lived in this house just as long. I kind of like the idea that we're going to shake things up." She sat up and hugged her knees. "Sometimes my life is so full of responsibilities I feel as if I'm on a fast moving train and just want to get off. The kids. Mom and Dad. My job. The library board. Sometimes even my friends. I feel like I have no time for myself, much less the two of us. Some days I just want to run away and escape everything."

He sat up too. "You think my getting a new job somewhere else will help you do that?"

"I don't know. I'd still worry about the kids. And my parents. But a change might be good." She clutched the end of her nightgown in her hands, wringing the fabric into a spiral. "Don't you think?"

"I guess. But my mind can't go there right now. I'm too stressed about what I'm dealing with this minute. I can't believe I'm being forced to leave a job where I've spent more time than at home. Some of the people I work with are like family." He exhaled loudly. "And where will I find another job at my level? I'm fifty-four years old. I'd love to retire, but with two kids in university, we can't afford to do that. I suppose consulting is an option but I don't know if there's enough money in it."

She nodded. "I'm also terrified. We've built this life here and it's a good life. Why would I want it to change? I hope we don't have to move." She stood up and smoothed her nightgown, then climbed back into bed and sat facing him. "My feelings are all mixed. Weird, huh?"

"I don't know, Abby. Remember that thing I read once? About how a groove can also be a rut? It's all in how you look at it."

"Yeah. I guess the way I feel about my life depends on the day." She laid her head back on the pillow and stayed quiet for a while, staring into the night. Her eyes had adjusted to the darkness and she could make out the ghostly shapes of the dresser and the chair with Peter's clothes hanging over it.

Peter twisted back and puffed his pillow. "You know, we can look at this as a bad thing that throws our life into upheaval or we can see it in a positive light and think of it as an adventure."

"Right. Some adventure." She sat up again. "Not to change the subject, but what do you suppose is up with Ben? That phone call."

"Who knows? He has to figure out what he wants in life. We can only push him so much."

"I know." She laid her head on his chest. "But he also needs help." She twirled a few of his chest hairs.

"Abs," he traced light circles on her back. "I'm sure things will be fine."

"I hope so."

His hands slid down along her spine, fingers fluttering faintly across her skin. Their lips met and they drew together. As she snuggled beside him, the darkness in the room seemed filled with disquiet. They held each other, seeking solace against the unknown by molding themselves into each other's familiar curves.

Chapter Four

The morning broke through Abby's consciousness while it was still dark. She opened her eyes and sat up, feeling strangely energetic as she put on her sweatsuit. Quietly she crept down the stairs. Filling a glass with water at the kitchen sink she peered through the window at the thermometer mounted outside, illuminated by the patio lamp. It was still cold, weather for hat and mittens.

As she stepped out, the crisp predawn air brushed her face. The quietness of the neighbourhood settled on her shoulders like a shawl and the moon shone low in the sky. Street lamps cast a friendly glow on the sidewalk. She stopped in front of Diana's house and stamped her feet to scare away the chill. The door opened and Diana stepped out of the house, wearing yellow mittens and earmuffs.

"Good morning," Abby greeted her friend.

"Speak for yourself." Diana looked at her through half opened eyes. "It's a good thing we do this together because without you I'd never get myself out of bed this early, much less out on the street."

"But you always feel very virtuous when we're done. Which way?"

"I don't care." Diana turned left.

"Okay, that way." Their breath came out in small clouds, dissipating into the darkness. "What are you so grumpy about?"

Diana kept her eyes on the sidewalk. "Nothing. I'm just not a morning person, as I keep telling you."

"Okay." Abby walked faster. "Let's pick up the pace. It's a beautiful morning."

The sky was starting to lighten at the horizon. In the park, a cluster of trees was silhouetted against velvety amethyst and a star shone white in the deep navy of the sky.

"Why are you so perky this early in the morning?" Diana was breathing hard.

"I don't really know. I'm actually kind of stressed."

"Why? What's up?"

Abby cleared her throat. She may just as well blurt it out. "Peter's losing his job. We might have to move."

"Oh, my gosh!" Diana stopped. "Did you expect this?"

Abby took her arm, propelling her forward. She explained to Diana what Peter had said about changes at Hearth Financial and told her about Peter's fear that he wouldn't find a job in Canada. About her own unease precipitated by the possibility they'd have to leave everything and everyone she loved. Then she described the inexplicable anticipation she felt about it all.

"Mostly I'm afraid of what it will do to us and our lives. Because it occurs to me that my life here defines who I am. Being Ben and Hanna's mother, an English professor. Secretary of the library board. Book club member." She nudged Diana. "Your friend."

"Darn right. You can't move. I'd miss you too much. Surely Peter will be able to find something in Toronto. He could commute."

"I don't know. He doesn't seem to think there's much in Ontario."

"Hmph."

"Anyway, when I think about moving, about leaving everything I know, I wonder who I will be?" She took the mittens off her sweaty hands.

"Oh, Abby." Diana touched her shoulder. "You know you'll still be those things. And you'll replace what you do here with other pursuits. You'll just redefine yourself, be the same you but with new layers."

Abby nodded. She liked the sound of that, liked the idea that living somewhere else might transform her into a new version of herself.

Diana sniffed. "But hopefully you won't have to go anywhere. How will I survive without my best friend?"

They stopped walking. Abby's narrative had taken them all the way to the stark black building of the Perimeter Institute. She looked toward Erb Street and the downtown core of this city she loved. The streetlights still glowed although the sky was brightening. A few lighted windows were scattered on the dark office buildings and the Seagram barrel stack cast odd shadows on the pavement. A yellow glow lit Alma's Coffee Shop from the inside, spotlighting a man sitting at the counter by the window. Small mounds of leftover snow lined the edge of the curbs and clustered on the unused train tracks. On the tree branches there were shadows of buds, the promise of green.

"Wow. We've gone far."

Diana looked toward the park trail. "Yeah. We should head back."

Abby turned and took long steps into the park. Diana matched her strides and for a while they walked without speaking. Abby focused on her breathing, their footfalls the only sounds she heard. The brightening sky highlighted cumulus clouds in pink and the stars had disappeared. The moon was still visible, a trespasser in the lighter sky.

"Is Ben coming home for Easter?" Diana's question was like a contrapuntal entry over their rhythmic steps.

"Uh huh, he arrives by bus tomorrow."

"Are things going better?"

"Not really." Abby's stomach knotted. "When he called to tell us about the bus he dropped the bombshell that he's failing two of his courses and barely passing the others. If he doesn't pass his exams, he'll be kicked out of the program for good."

"Oh, no. He was so determined to do better this time. What happened? Too much partying again?"

"According to him that's not why, but he didn't give a reason. He only said that now he knows what to do and for us not to worry. He'll tell us about it this weekend and just wanted to give us a heads up." She dug into her pocket for a tissue and blew her nose. "Do you believe it? A heads up?"

"It's hard to imagine, isn't it? He was such a good student in high school."

"Yeah. Sometimes his stupidity makes me so mad. He squandered his first year, and now he's doing it again." Abby sniffed. "Damn, why do I cry so easily?"

Diana hugged her. "Because you're worried about him. Because your life's turning upside down. You're allowed to cry."

"But I was feeling so good when we started."

"Well, I can't explain that."

"Let's talk about something else." Abby stepped forward again. "How's your mom?"

"Doing much better. She got a clean bill of health from her surgeon. You should have heard her at his office yesterday. She was her usual demanding self."

"That's great."

"Or not." Diana smiled. "I was kind of hoping this scare would have mellowed her, but it hasn't. At dinner last night she was telling us all what to do again. Good old Mom. How'd your visit with your parents go yesterday?"

"The usual. My mom tries hard to be a good hostess—as if she needs to be with me—but things are getting hard for her. I tried to talk them into hiring a cleaner but they're so determined to be independent."

Finding it more difficult to talk she slowed her pace. "They refuse to have someone in the house. They absolutely won't discuss moving to assisted living. I don't know what to do about them. Especially with my dad deteriorating the way he is."

"Maybe you should get him assessed. Remember Stan's mom? She started having trouble just like your dad and then was diagnosed with Alzheimer's."

"You don't think Dad has Alzheimer's, do you?"

"I don't know. It could be lots of things. All I'm saying is you should probably get him to see somebody."

"I guess I'll have a chat with their doctor and try to set something up." She stopped suddenly. "What if I have to move away? I'm the only family they have."

"What about your cousins and aunt?"

"I couldn't ask them to take on the responsibility of Mom and Dad. My aunt's old too and my cousins need to look after her."

"Well, cross that bridge when you come to it. You may not move."

"Right." She inhaled deeply. "It's all too much isn't it? As if I don't have enough to deal with."

"Well, we are in the sandwich generation."

"Ha." Abby smiled ruefully. "This sure isn't how I expected my midlife crisis to play out."

"Yeah. No red sports car for Abby. Just one crisis after another."

****

When Abby arrived at her house the sun was up and the air was starting to warm. She smiled at the sight of small tips of green poking through the dirty crystallized snow that covered patches of the garden.

Picking the newspaper off the stoop, she let herself in the door. Peter's voice bellowed "Born to be Wild" in the shower. Hanna's clock radio was blaring, but there was no sound of movement from her room or her bathroom. Abby started up the stairs to rouse her daughter then changed her mind. Hanna needed to be responsible for herself, and if that meant she arrived at school late, so be it.

Instead, Abby went to the kitchen and started the coffee. She set the table for breakfast, then counted out vitamins: three white calcium tablets, a yellow "cholesterol-smart" vitamin for Peter, an orange women's vitamin for Hanna, and a green "weight-smart" one for herself. Really. Did they need this rainbow of supplements?

At the top of the stairs, she listened to the quiet down the hall and walked to Hanna's room. She rapped on the door.

"Hanna. Are you up?"

"Yeah." Barely a whisper came through the door.

"You have an early rehearsal before school today."

In a more alert voice, Hanna called, "Okay, I'm sitting up."

"Good."

In her bedroom, Abby straightened the tousled bedclothes and went into the bathroom. The shower was off and a steamy, soapy smell hung in the air.

"That coffee smells good." Peter stood naked, staring in the mirror.

"It'll be ready by the time you get downstairs."

"See how gray my eyebrows are getting?" He wiggled them at her. "They're almost white."

"I've noticed that. And look how gray your chest hairs are." She stroked them and kissed him. "You're still looking pretty good for an old man, though."

Peter grabbed her hands and brought them to his lips. "An unemployed old man. I wonder who will hire a guy my age." He walked into the bedroom. "What's on your agenda today?"

"Teach my classes, then office hours." She turned on the shower.

"Oh, yeah. Takeout Wednesday," but the rest of his words were lost to her as she stepped into the streaming water.

****

As she blow-dried her hair, she stared at her eyes in the mirror. Did they reflect the anxiety she felt about Peter's job? Or excitement for the possibilities? Her brown eyes gazed back at her, telling her nothing. She redirected the left side of her hair that was flipping the wrong way. Unsuccessful, she gave it one more stroke with the brush and headed downstairs, relieved to hear the drone of Hanna's dryer down the hall.

In the kitchen Peter read the newspaper while absently spooning granola into his mouth. "The Leafs lost again last night," he said between crunches.

"Surprise, surprise." She poured herself a cup of coffee and sat down. "The crocuses are coming up in the garden. They're still pretty small, but they're there. Spring is definitely on the way."

"Yup," he replied absent-mindedly. He looked up. "The board meeting's at noon today."

Her hand jerked as she stirred granola into her yogurt. "At least we know it's coming." She wondered if anyone could really be prepared for something like this.

He folded the paper over. "Here's a job in Bermuda I could apply for."

Bermuda! A wiggle of excitement tickled in her belly. "Really? That would be interesting. How much does it pay?" She leaned forward to see.

Footsteps sounded on the stairs. Quickly Abby reached for a different section of the paper and began turning its pages.

Hanna walked into the kitchen exuding energy. Her blonde hair was pulled up into a clip, tendrils escaping at the sides. The hue of her eyes seemed to spill into her sea green sweater and her hands clutched the ends of its long sleeves. "Good morning, parents. Anyone interested in giving me a ride to school?"

Peter sipped his coffee. "I'm leaving in about five minutes. Will you be ready then?"

"Sure. I'll take a granola bar and apple to eat in the car."

Abby stared at her. "At least drink your orange juice and take your vitamins."

"I'll be fine, Mom." She went to the cupboard. "Stop worrying so much."

Chapter Five

Abby looked up from the papers she was grading to watch Hanna working the mixer in the icing. She savoured the coziness of the atmosphere: the chocolaty smell of brownies, Bach flute sonatas playing on the CD player, rays from the lowering sun warming the room. If they moved away, would she ever have days like this again? She rubbed her forehead, pushing her angst about Peter's job into a hidden corner of her mind. She'd managed to do that for most of the day while they prepared for Easter and for Ben's arrival; cleaning, baking Ben's favourite raisin-nut cookies, hollowing out eggshells to paint. As if their life wasn't about to be shaken up.

"It'll be great to have everyone here, with Grandma and Pops on Sunday." Hanna banged the beaters on the side of the bowl. "Wanna lick?" She handed one to her mother.

"Thanks." Abby savoured the sweet chocolate. "I love having the whole family together. These times will happen less and less, won't they? With you a soon-to-be-independent university student."

Hanna grinned. "Yeah, but I'll still come home to do laundry every week."

Abby returned a half-hearted smile. Hanna walked over to the sink and started to clean up the counter. "What time is Ben coming?"

"His bus gets in at five." She checked her watch. "I'm leaving in a half hour. Want to come?"

"Yeah, I can't wait to see him. When we IM'd last week, he said he's got something to tell us. And he talked about a girl."

"Really?" Abby's eyes widened in surprise. "He's been in touch with you?"

"Well, just last Friday. I finally caught him on instant messaging. Usually he doesn't answer but this time he did." She closed the dishwasher. "Hey, do you want me to set up your laptop so you can chat with him too?"

"That'd be great." Abby took off her reading glasses. "He's got a girlfriend? I haven't heard from him at all, other than that phone call this week to figure out the bus."

"He's been kind of weird. Hardly ever answers my texts or on the computer even though he's always online."

"Maybe he's preoccupied." Abby's insides clenched, a familiar sensation she experienced whenever she worried about her misdirected son. "I think he's been having problems with some of his classes."

"Again? He's being so stupid."

"I wonder if there's something else going on with him. What did he say about the girl?"

"He only mentioned that she was sitting at the computer with him. But he wouldn't even tell me her name. I tried to goad him into saying more but he didn't."

Abby wondered if the girl was a distraction causing him to fall behind in his schoolwork. "Did he tell you anything about school?"

"Not really. Only that it sucks." Hanna took a knife from the drawer. "I wish he'd get it together and stop messing around."

"Me too." Abby hadn't realized Hanna had these same concerns about Ben. "On the phone he said he's figured things out so we shouldn't worry. I wonder what he meant by that." She clicked the end of her pen. "He didn't say much more. Maybe you can talk to him while he's here and find out what's up, why he's so incommunicado."

Hanna chuckled. "Good word, Mom. Guess I can try."

Should Abby put this burden on Hanna? Wasn't that a parent's job? "Or we can. You just focus on having a good visit with your brother. That's your assignment this weekend." *And*, she added silently, *deal with your dad's news.*

"Also bake brownies," Hanna laughed as she cut the brownies into squares and put them on a plate.

"And what a good job you've done. We'll have them for dessert tonight with ice cream." Abby shoved papers into her briefcase and went to the fridge. She held out a casserole dish. "Voila. Cannelloni for supper. Let's make the salad and set the table so dinner will be ready when we get home with Ben."

****

They arrived at the station a minute before the bus was due to arrive. Walking into the building, they headed for the glass doors at the back. Their footsteps echoed in the chilly terminal. People stood waiting. Murmurs of conversation scattered around the room.

"I'm glad I won't have to come home on the bus when I'm in university," Hanna said, peering around the doorway at the terminal bays.

"I'm sure it adds to the adventure for Ben." Abby didn't want to think about how to respond to her daughter's comment, considering the precarious circumstance of where home might end up being.

Hanna pointed to headlights approaching. "There it is, I think."

An announcement over the intercom confirmed that the bus arriving was indeed the one from North Bay carrying Ben home. They went outside as it pulled up to the terminal. Its door opened and a pair of feet in high-heeled boots appeared at the top of the steps, bringing down a girl with blue spiky hair wearing tight leather pants and a short furry jacket. Behind her, a mother with a baby in a front carrier who was holding the hand of a little boy climbed slowly down the steps. An old man with a knitted Canadian Tire hat on his head stopped at the bottom and held his hand out for an old woman, also wearing a knitted Canadian Tire hat. Then, finally, Ben. Wearing his green duffle coat, iPod buds in his ears, and his hair sticking out every which way. He needed a haircut.

"Ben," Hanna called out. He turned and smiled, pulled down the ear buds.

"Hanna. Mom." He walked over. "Good to see you."

"You too, Ben." Abby reached up to tousle his hair. He ducked away. "You look good."

"Gotta get my stuff." He and Hanna walked over to where the bus driver was emptying the baggage compartment. Ben picked up his hockey bag and slung it over his shoulder. Abby wondered if he'd packed his clothes in that, but then Hanna picked up a gym bag.

Ben started for the exit ahead of them. "I brought my hockey stuff home, Mom. Since hockey season is over. It needs washing."

Hanna wrinkled her nose. "Phew. You're not kidding."

In the car Ben quietly answered Hanna's questions about residence, his hockey playoffs, and the snow that was still on the ground in North Bay. Although he was somewhat taciturn, he seemed fine. Abby sighed with relief. She wondered how his exams were going. She'd better not ask. It might change the companionable atmosphere in the car. And Peter should be part of that conversation.

"Tell Mom about your girlfriend," Hanna teased.

"Julie's not my girlfriend. We just hang out sometimes."

"That's how it starts Benny Boy," Abby said as she turned the car into the driveway. She suddenly thought about having to tell them the news about Peter's job and a sliver of unease wormed its way into her good mood. She shook it off as they walked into the house, inhaling the garlicky, cheesy aroma of cannelloni in the oven.

"Something smells good. I'm starving." Ben dropped his bags and headed for the kitchen. "Hey, Dad, we're home."

Stepping over the bags, Abby called out. "Ben, put your hockey stuff into the laundry room first, okay?"

As Ben went to pick it up, Peter came through the door. He hugged Ben and looked at Abby, his eyes questioning hers. She smiled and shrugged.

Releasing Ben, he scanned his face. "How are you doing?"

"I'm good." Ben shifted his eyes. He turned to Hanna, poking her in the side.

"Hey, Hanna Banana."

Hanna squirmed away. "Don't do that! Grow up."

"Come on, guys." Peter kissed Hanna on the cheek. "I bet you've missed your brother."

"Yeah, right."

"I think this reunion calls for some wine," Peter said, opening the door to the basement. "I have a nice Chianti that'll go great with cannelloni."

"That means we'll need wine glasses on the table. Ben, could you get them?" Abby put the hot casserole dish on the table and began to toss the salad. "It's so good to have the family together."

"Yeah, it is." Ben brought the wine glasses and looked at Hanna. "You want some, right?" Hanna nodded, avoiding her mother's gaze. Abby raised her eyebrows but Ben just shrugged. "So, Hanna, what have you been up to?"

"If you'd read my e-mails, you'd know. Why don't you ever answer them?"

"Too busy, I guess. Sorry."

Abby glanced at Ben as she put the salad bowl in the center of the table.

"Swamped with school work?"

"You could say that." He sat down and picked up his empty wine glass, turning it in his hands.

Hanna sipped her water. "What about IM? You're almost always on but you never answer."

"Abby, can you help me?" Peter called from the basement. "I can't seem to find that Chianti."

Irritation niggled at Abby and she decided to ignore him. She didn't want to leave this conversation.

"Abby?" Peter called again.

She rolled her eyes at Hanna and Ben. "I'll be right back."

At the bottom of the stairs, Peter stood holding a wine bottle. Abby pointed to it. "I thought you called me down to help you find it."

"Sh. I just wanted to talk to you for a minute." He was whispering. "We need a plan for telling the kids about my job. Do you think we should tell them as soon as we sit down?"

She sucked in a breath. "I don't know. What do you think?" She tried to match his tone in volume, but nervous energy turned it into a breathy version of her normal voice.

"Quiet, Abby. We don't want the kids to hear us."

"Sorry." She murmured more quietly. "Let's wait until dessert. That way we can catch up on the kids' news before having to deal with it. And," she smiled, "give the wine a chance to mellow them."

"Good idea." He apparently missed the wine joke. "You go up first."

"No. Let's go up together. It'll look more natural."

****

Ben and Hanna tucked into the food with enthusiasm, hardly stopping to answer the questions Abby posed in her attempts to get a dialogue started. Peter ate quietly, his mind seeming to be somewhere other than at the table. As their appetites were sated, they became more animated. Hanna told a tale about her eccentric physics teacher. Peter shared a funny story about a dog in the office. Abby talked about the Post-it notes stuck all over Grandma and Pop's house. Ben sat quiet. He smiled at appropriate times but contributed nothing to the conversation. This unsettled Abby. He was usually the one with the stories, the one who made them double over with laughter or sit back in amazement. She wondered what had happened to change him.

Ben scooped the last crust of melted cheese out of the casserole dish. "I guess there won't be any leftovers for lunch tomorrow," he said, putting the last bite into his mouth.

Abby rose from the table. "Time for dessert." Her heart beat faster as she thought about the discussion that was to follow.

Peter stood. "I'll help you." He began to gather plates.

"Wait. I'll get the dessert." Hanna jumped up. "I made it, after all."

"She did. You guys are in for a treat." Abby reached for the kettle. "I'll make tea to go with it."

In the midst of all the activity there was little opportunity for Peter and Abby to confer on how to present the topic of Peter's job loss. They could do little else than make eye contact. Finally they were all back at the table with a brownie topped with ice cream and a mug of tea in front of them. Peter cleared his throat.

"I have some important news to share with you." He looked at the kids in turn and then locked eyes with Abby. "I have to find a new job because I'm losing my position at Hearth Financial"

"What? You're being fired?" Ben sat up straight.

"Not fired, really. More like being phased out."

"But you're a vice president there." Hanna looked bewildered. "They can't do that."

"Yes, they can. It's actually a good move for the company, Hanna." Peter had sunk in his chair and now he sat straighter. "And for me, too. I'm looking at it as a positive change, like an adventure. I think it will be good to try something new, break out of my rut so to speak. And I'll get a severance package to help the transition to a new job." He sounded as if he was convincing himself.

Ben and Hanna stared intently at Peter. Their desserts were almost untouched, the ice cream melting, creating white puddles around the brownies.

Abby expelled her breath. She hadn't realized she'd been holding it until just then and wondered how much time had passed since she'd breathed. "Dad will try hard to find a job around here," she said.

Hanna put down the fork she'd been holding. "What do you mean? Why wouldn't he find a job here?"

"Well," Peter shrugged. "It's very possible we'll have to move. I've been exploring the options and it looks like it'll be tough to find a job in Waterloo or Toronto."

Wanting to quell the panic rising in Hanna's eyes, Abby said, "You'll be in university residence in September, Hanna, so you'll stay in Waterloo no matter what. You won't be living at home for most of the year anyway. And nothing is definite yet. Only that Dad has to find a new job."

"Wow." Ben leaned back. "Dad not working at Hearth Financial. That's weird. You've always worked there." He glanced around the kitchen. "I can't imagine not coming home to this place."

"Yeah." Hanna joined in. "You can't sell this house. It's the only home we've ever lived in."

"Hey, guys," Peter said, obviously trying to keep his voice calm. "Let's not jump the gun here."

"Yes, we don't know yet that we'll have to move." Abby tried to ease the tension hovering around the table. "Dad needs to find a job first."

"Actually, I think I'm cool about it." Ben's tone was strangely nonchalant. "Parents do what they do. I'm on my own anyway, Hanna, and in a couple of months you'll be too. What does it matter?"

"How can you say that, Ben?" Hanna was indignant. "It matters. It's our home."

"Of course it matters, Hanna." Abby touched Hanna's hand. "I'm sure it's important to Ben, but it's good that he can have an accepting attitude about it. Let's take this one step at a time."

"Right." Peter stuck his fork into a piece of brownie. "For now, all you need to deal with is the fact that I'll be looking for a new job. I finish at Hearth in August and it's only April so we've got months to get our heads wrapped around this." He took a bite and chewed deliberately. A strained silence hovered over the table. "Hanna, this brownie is delicious."

"Glad you like it, Dad." She stood, scraping her chair. "May I please be excused?" Her cheeks flushed red.

"Hanna, please sit down." Abby didn't want her leaving the table upset. "I know this is distressing news. It's not how we want things. But everything will work out." She stroked Hanna's arm.

Hanna lowered herself back to the chair, wiping the heels of her hands over her eyes. "Do you think you'll have trouble finding another job?" she asked in a quiet voice.

"Maybe you could retire," Ben suggested.

"Not likely, with two university tuitions to cover."

Ben mumbled something and Abby's ears perked. "What's that, Ben?"

"Nothing. Sorry."

Peter cleared his throat. "I don't think I'll have trouble. It'll just be a matter of finding something that'll suit me in a location that will suit your mother and me. Suit all of us."

"And if nothing else comes up you could work at Home Depot." Abby grinned, hoping she sounded light-hearted.

"Yeah, Dad, that'd be perfect. You'd love working with all those tools." Ben pushed his plate away. "And you'd look good in that orange apron."

Peter smiled. "So, Hanna, did you tell your brother about your acceptance at WLU?" Peter's abrupt change of subject startled Abby.

"Ben already knows. I texted him the news."

"Yeah. Pretty cool, Hanna Banana," Ben said without inflection.

"Stop calling me that. Benjie." Hanna tossed her napkin at him.

"Hey."

"Come on, guys." Abby wondered if they would ever stop their juvenile teasing of each other. "Cut it out." She stood and began stacking the dishes. "Dad and I'll clean up the kitchen. Ben, you go put your hockey gear in the washer."

"Maybe Hanna can be a dear sister and do that while I take my stuff to my room."

"No way. Not that stinky stuff." Hanna ran upstairs. Ben followed. Peter took glasses to the sink.

"That went better than I expected," he said.

"I guess it went okay. Hanna was pretty upset, though." She put dishes into the dishwasher. "Ben's response was a bit odd, don't you think? He wasn't too troubled by it. Something's going on with him. We need to find out what's up."

"Well, maybe he really is okay with it. He's almost twenty." He took up the trash bag and tied its ends. "But it's true he wasn't his usual self tonight. Something *is* going on." He went to the garage with the trash. She closed the dishwasher and filled the sink with soapy water, worrying about how she'd be able to help everyone cope with the change that was besetting them.

****

The house was quiet when she returned from the grocery store the next morning. The aroma of fresh coffee tickled her nostrils. Hanna sat painting eggs at the kitchen table wearing her pajamas. Abby marvelled at the fact that she'd be going to university in the fall. In pink polka-dot flannel she looked like a grade-schooler.

"Morning, Hanna. It's nice to see you up before noon on a Saturday." Abby put the last of the groceries on the counter. "That coffee smells good."

"Yeah, I made a fresh pot after Dad took the last cup."

"Where is Dad?"

"In the basement."

Abby pulled out a bakery bag. "Want a croissant?"

"Thanks." Hanna took one of the golden rolls and broke a piece off. Flakes of the pastry fluttered to the table. "I've got a rehearsal at the church at twelve. With Emily. We're playing at the eleven o'clock service tomorrow."

"Oh, that's right." Abby picked up a hollow egg that was dyed blue. Hanna had painted a tiny house with flowers on it and clouds in the sky. "This is cute."

"Thanks. It's supposed to represent our home. That we might lose." She looked pointedly at Abby and then sighed. "This might be the last time I'll paint eggs in this kitchen."

"That's a little dramatic." Abby handed her the egg.

"I guess." Hanna smiled sheepishly and looked at the egg, turning it slowly. "This is kind of cheesy. What I really want is to paint one like those Ukrainian eggs, but mine never turn out right." She put it down and picked up a pale yellow eggshell. "Mom, what's going to happen about Dad's job?"

"Really, I don't know. He'll look for a new position and when he's offered one he likes he'll take it. Obviously he wants to find something close to here, but he might not." She pulled a bag of apples out of the grocery bag. "We can't know what's going to happen. But Hanna," she put her arm around her daughter's shoulders, "no matter what happens, your home is where we are."

"Talk about cheesy, Mom. Home is where the heart is?"

Abby kissed the top of Hanna's head and went back to the groceries. "As cliché as that is, yes. Your home is with the people you love. But let's cross that bridge when we come to it." She placed oranges into the fruit basket. "Right now we need to be supportive of Dad. This is a tough time for him. He's been working at Hearth Financial for many years. The people he works with are almost like family to him."

"I know. But it'll be hard on all of us, though."

Abby wanted badly to tell Hanna how emotional she'd been since she heard the news. She wanted to describe how uncertain she felt about what would happen to the family, her own life, her job, her network of friends. And how scared she was that she wouldn't be able to hold things together for everyone. Instead she said, "Yes, it will be hard. But I know we'll get through it just fine."

Hanna made a few strokes on the egg with her brush. "There are too many changes happening in the family, Mom."

"Well, life is all about change, Hanna." She took a flowered mug out of the cupboard, poured herself some coffee and sat down. "For sure some changes are unexpected and unwanted. But there are good ones, too. Like you going to WLU." She glanced up at the clock. "If you're going to be at the church by twelve, you'd better get ready. It's eleven fifteen."

"Oh my god!" Hanna put down the egg she was painting. "I'll clean up when I get back this afternoon, okay?" She scraped back her chair and ran upstairs.

The egg wobbled and slowly rolled toward Abby. She picked it up and put it into an empty slot in the carton.

Peter walked through the basement door. "I thought I heard your voice." He kissed her and held up his empty mug. "Any coffee left?"

"There's lots. Hanna made a fresh pot. I'll put a salad together for lunch in a few minutes."

"Has Hanna left for the church yet?" He poured coffee into his mug, which was black and had white letters on it that read *#1 Dad*. Ten-year-old Ben had given it to him for Father's Day. Amazing it was still around.

"She's getting ready. Has Ben made an appearance yet?"

"I don't think so. It's time he got up, though." He walked toward the basement door. "You wanna get him out of bed?"

She shrugged. "Sure."

****

After Hanna left for the church, she laid a tray with a glass of juice, a cup of coffee, and a croissant. She took a jar of cherry jam from the cupboard and placed it on the tray with a spoon. As an afterthought, she put Hanna's blue egg with the house into an eggcup and added it to the tray. Carrying it upstairs, she knocked on Ben's door.

"Ben? Are you awake? Can I come in?"

She heard a mumble and, deciding to interpret it as a yes, pushed open the door. A small opening between the curtains sent a shaft of sun into the dark room. The smell of sleep hung in the air, stale and thick.

"I've brought you breakfast in bed. How's that for being pampered?" She set the tray on the bedside table. She didn't understand how he could still be asleep this late in the day. Opening the curtains, she lifted the window an inch. Ben pulled the bedcovers over his face.

"Mom." He stretched the word over two syllables.

"Come on, Ben. It's noon. Time to get up." She tried to keep impatience out of her voice. "Look. Here's coffee, orange juice. A fresh croissant with cherry jam." She pulled the blanket away and kissed him on the cheek. "Oh, rough beard." She rubbed his chin. "It's nice to have you home." She perched on the end of the bed.

He sat up and yawned, then picked up the orange juice and drank it all. He lay back on the pillow.

"Nothing like orange juice to shake out the sleepies." Abby wondered if her cheerfulness sounded forced. It felt forced. She just wanted to shake Ben out of his detached attitude.

Ben rolled his eyes and broke the croissant in half. He put a spoonful of cherry jam on it.

She took Hanna's egg and held it up. "Hanna's been painting eggs. Look, isn't this cute? It's our house."

He grunted and she reined in her annoyance.

"Ben." She picked at the bedspread. "Your dad and I are worried about you. You seem preoccupied and distracted. And disconnected from us. Is something wrong?"

"No, Mom. I'm fine."

"You don't seem fine to me." More like a person I don't know, she thought. "You said on the phone that you had something to tell us. Can you enlighten me as to what that might be?" As the question left her lips, she realized she should have waited for Peter before beginning this discussion.

"I'm just making some decisions about my life, Mom. I guess that's why I seem preoccupied to you."

A bud of apprehension blossomed in her gut. "What kind of decisions."

"Well, school for instance. I'm quitting. I'm not going to write any of my exams."

"What do you mean not write your exams? You'll lose your year." She clenched her fists and the egg in her hand crumbled into bits. Startled, she looked at it and shook the coloured pieces of shell onto the tray. He couldn't possibly consider another wasted year as a good option.

"I don't care about my year. There's no point. I wouldn't pass anyway. I've hardly gone to class all term." He brushed flakes of croissant off of his chest.

"You haven't been going to class?" Heat flushed her cheeks. She remembered the commitment he'd made to them when they agreed to support his return to school. Apparently it meant nothing. "What have you been doing instead?"

"You know. Stuff."

"No, I don't know." She was an inept mother. She should know. "Is this about that girl? What's her name, Julie?"

He made a face. "This has nothing to do with her. This is about me."

"Is this what you meant when you said on the phone that you were giving us a heads up?"

"Sort of. Anyway, it doesn't matter now. I'm moving into a house with a bunch of guys next week."

"A house? What are you talking about? Where?" She jumped up and went to the other side of the bed, staring down at him.

"In Toronto. Near Queen Street. I forget the exact address."

"Toronto?"

"Yeah. And I've got a job."

"A job?" She was sounding like an imbecile, parroting everything back to him. She folded her arms in front of her chest. "What kind of job?"

"Uh, at a Starbucks. Around the corner from the house."

"How did you arrange all this from North Bay? When did you put this together?" It didn't make sense to her.

"My friend Wes has a brother in Toronto and we went down there to stay with him for a couple of weeks. Two of his roommates were moving out so we decided to take their rooms. And then I found the job. It's what I want to do, Mom."

A couple of weeks? Ben had left school to go to Toronto for a couple of weeks? And he did this without letting them know? She sighed and sat back on the bed. "This is what you wanted to tell us."

"Yeah." He sipped his coffee. "I was going to last night, but with Dad's news I figured it wasn't a good time. I was going to ask you and Dad if I could take my bed and stuff. If you could help me move."

"But what about your life plan?" She reached her arm toward him, then thought better of it and pulled back. "I get that you don't want to study kinesiology any more. But what do you want to do with yourself? What about a career? Starbucks is just a temporary job, right?" Her dreams for her son were shattering. He was throwing away his opportunities, ignoring his potential.

"I'll figure it out, Mom. For now, I'm doing what I want to do."

"But…" Her eyes were hot. A lump lodged in her throat. Anger and distress, fear and frustration all jumbled together inside of her. The phone rang in the hall. Ignoring it, she swallowed. "Ben, we need to discuss this decision of yours with Dad."

Another ring. Come on, Peter, she pleaded silently, answer it.

"What's to talk about, Mom? I've made my decision."

The phone stopped partway through the third ring. She exhaled. Be practical. Don't push him away with emotion.

"Ben, this is a major decision. Have you worked out a budget? Can you afford to live on what you're going to earn at Starbucks? Because if you're going to do this you'll have to support yourself." She knew that's what Peter would say.

"Yes, Mom. I know what I'm doing. The rent is cheap, especially for Toronto."

Ben's eyes were aloof, distant. His hair was flattened on one side and sticking up at the top. His night beard looked unkempt. She wondered when her little boy had become this man she didn't know.

Peter called up the stairs. "Abby?" His voice sounded urgent. She went to the top of the stairs.

"Up here."

"You'd better take the phone. It's your dad. Something's happened."

Chapter Six

She sped along Highway 401 barely registering the landscape whipping by. Driving as if on autopilot, she turned off the radio, needing the quiet to organize her tangled thoughts.

Less than an hour ago her weekend had derailed. The image of her family pulling together in the face of Peter's job loss was burst apart. Ben's revelations had shaken her. She hadn't had a chance to digest his words or discuss them with Peter.

That phone call. When Peter ran up the stairs holding the phone in the air, she almost collided with him as she rushed down to meet him.

"It's your dad. Something's happened," he said. "I can't make out what he's saying. Something about your mom, Easter baskets, the basement. I think she's hurt."

She grabbed the phone. "Dad? What's happened?"

"Is that Abby? Peter? Who?"

"Dad, it's Abby. What's happened to Mom?"

"She found the Easter baskets. But she fell. She can't get up. She's crying."

"She fell?" She put her hand on the banister to steady herself. "Where?"

"She's lying down there. Calling me. Crying."

Abby could see it in her mind. Her mom prostrate on the floor reaching for him. Her father helplessly looking on. "Did you phone 911?"

"No, I phoned you."

"Okay, Dad." She took a deep breath to try to calm her shaking voice. "We'll call 911 and get an ambulance over there." She glanced at Peter, who was already taking his cell phone out of his pocket. "Is Mom able to talk? Can you hand her the phone?"

"She's in the basement. I'll try." She heard him grunting and then huffing and puffing.

"Dad," she called into the mouthpiece. She didn't want him to fall too, unsteady as he was. "Dad. Don't go down the stairs." But he didn't answer. Peter huddled over his cell, talking quietly into it. Her mouth was dry. She held the phone tightly to her ear. Something clattered, then a shuffling noise, and her mother's trembling voice came on the line.

"Abby?"

"Mom?"

A shaky breath. A sob. A sniff. "Abby?"

"I'm here, Mom. Tell me how you are. Where do you hurt? What happened?" Too many questions at once, Abby knew.

"I fell...the stairs. I...can't get up." Her intake of breath shuddered through the phone. "My side hurts...my arm. It's...hard to...breathe."

"Oh, Mom. Stay still. We're getting help. Peter's called 911." She looked at Peter, who was nodding to her. "An ambulance will be there really soon. And we'll come too, right away."

"Don't hang up, Abby."

"Okay, Mom. I'll stay on the phone until the ambulance gets there. I'm here, okay?"

She kept the phone to her ear, prattling on about who knew what, just to keep her mother distracted. She talked to her while walking down the stairs to the kitchen and pacing around the room. She calmed her mother while trying to control her own panic, at the same time discussing with Peter which of them should go to Woodstock. She wedged the phone in her neck as she gathered her purse and jacket and put on her shoes. When the paramedics arrived, they told her they had control of the situation and would take her mother to the Woodstock Hospital. Finally she hung up the phone.

Now she was driving to the hospital. Peter stayed behind and would tell Hanna what happened. Ben had heard of course, hovering quietly at the top of the stairs, but Hanna would come home full of life and then have to face this. Abby knew this would distress Hanna. She hoped Peter would be able to reassure her. Maybe Ben would help him tell the news. Ben. She wondered if he'd tell Peter about quitting school.

Abby pushed Ben's troubles to the back of her mind and thought about her mom. Had she broken anything? Would she need to be admitted? Abby's father wouldn't be able to cope at home without her mom. Maybe they should bring him home to Waterloo. Thinking about all the possible scenarios overwhelmed her.

She couldn't believe her bad luck. Tears distorted her view of the road. Not now, damn it. She sniffed loudly, wiping at her eyes. Something was happening to her stable existence, her good karma, as if her life was being ripped asunder. She berated herself—these crises were happening to other people, not to her. It wasn't all about her.

Still, she was the one bearing the brunt of it all. She needed to stay strong for everyone else but didn't know how when she felt so engulfed by everything. She railed aloud into the silence of the car.

The miles passed quickly. Her exit came into sight and she began to think about what she'd find at the hospital. After she'd hung up the phone, she'd called her cousin Christina, who had assured Abby she'd meet her parents at the hospital. How would her dad be with Christina?

Hopefully her mother wasn't in too much pain and she hadn't had to wait too long before she was seen;

Abby knew all too well how emergency rooms worked. Her mother was probably frightened too.

When she finally pulled into the parking lot, adrenaline was shooting through her. She parked crookedly, noticing the rear bumper hanging over the painted line when she slammed the car door. She hesitated, wondering briefly if she should straighten it, then ran to the building. She inhaled gulps of air as she stopped and waited for the ER doors to slide open.

Inside she scanned the people in chairs, not recognizing anyone. But on the other side of the intake desk, she spotted her father sitting quietly with his head down, between Christina and Aunt Josie. Her mother wasn't in sight. She walked toward them and Christina rose from her seat.

"Abby." She gave her a loose hug. "You made really good time getting here."

"Yeah, I guess I wasn't paying too much attention to the speed limit. How's Mom? Where is she?" She bent over her father and hugged him. "Hi, Dad. You okay?"

"They brought Frieda here, but she's gone." He looked up at Abby, his eyes wet with tears.

She grabbed Christina's forearm. "Gone?"

"No, Abby, she's not gone." Aunt Josie patted her father's hand. "Nick, she's getting x-rays, remember? The doctor thinks she's broken some bones and wants to make sure."

"Didn't anyone go with her?" Abby asked. Surely the hospital would have allowed someone to accompany a frightened old woman to the lab.

"They told us to wait here," Christina shrugged. "So we stayed with Uncle Nick."

Anger flashed through Abby. Christina should have insisted on going with her. Abby held her breath, trying to settle her agitation. Getting angry wouldn't help. She exhaled. "I'll see if I can find her. Thanks, you two, for being here."

"Oh, it's nothing, dear." Aunt Josie smiled up at her. "She's my sister, you know."

"Yeah, no problem, Abby. I'm just glad we were able to help." Christina returned to her seat. "We'll stay here with Uncle Nick while you go find out about your mom."

Abby turned to her father and spoke louder. "I'm going to find Mom, okay, Dad?"

He raised his head. "Huh?"

Aunt Josie waved her hand in the direction of the hallway. "You go, Abby. He'll be fine."

At the intake desk she spoke to the receptionist, then the triage nurse, and then an intern wheeling a gurney on which a frail, white-haired man slept open-mouthed. Finally she found the x-ray department. Her mother lay on a bed parked in a hall outside of a waiting area filled with people. Through the bars of the raised sides she looked small under the white covers, and pitiful. Her cheeks were bright red spots and her face scrunched in pain. Her eyes were closed. On one side of her forehead was a large bruise, and the arm that lay on top of the covers was mottled with purple splotches. Abby stopped mid-stride. She'd never seen her mother look so vulnerable.

"Mom?" She whispered, afraid of startling her.

Her mother opened her eyes and slowly turned to face her. "Oh, Abby." Tears brimmed from her eyes and rolled down the sides of her face onto the bed. "What have I done?"

"What do you mean, Mom?" Abby found a tissue in her purse. Moving close to the bed, she dabbed at her mother's tears.

"I fell and broke my hip. Now who will look after your father?" She grimaced as she took a breath. Her brow furrowed. "It hurts, Abby."

"Oh, Mom. Don't worry about Dad right now. Let's get you feeling better. Have they taken x-rays yet? Did they give you anything for the pain?"

A brisk male voice behind her broke into their muted conversation. "Mrs. Baker?"

Abby turned. "I'm Mrs. Baker's daughter."

"I need to take your mother to be x-rayed." He looked behind Abby to her mother. "Ready, Mrs. Baker?"

Abby put her hand on her mother's. "Can I go with her?"

"Only to the door. You can wait outside and be with her again as soon as she's done." With a clack, he unclipped the brakes with his foot and began wheeling the bed down the hall. Abby walked beside it, helping to steer.

"I'll be right near you, Mom."

Her mother twisted her head then winced. "I'm glad you're here."

"I wouldn't be anywhere else."

****

Hours later she left her mother, bandaged and sedated, sleeping in what would be her bed for the foreseeable future. In the cafeteria, Abby bought a coffee and sat down at a table. Her dad had gone home with Aunt Josie earlier and Abby knew she should pick him up but couldn't find the energy to do so.

It seemed strange to be drinking coffee when it was dinnertime. She sipped and looked around, not really seeing her surroundings. What now? The doctor had told her that a broken hip usually meant the end of independent living for someone her mother's age. Abby knew her father couldn't take care of her mother. Suddenly the issue of what to do about her parents had escalated and she needed to make decisions quickly. Randomly she leafed through the papers and brochures about assisted living and government support programs they'd given her.

She flipped open her cell phone. Her third call to Peter in twice as many hours. Or was it her fourth?

"She's finally in a room and will probably have to stay in the hospital for a few weeks," she said to Peter's hello.

"How's she coping?"

"Not too good." Abby steadied her voice. "Right now she's sleeping. Apparently she's had a mild concussion too. Can you believe it? Broken hip. Fractured rib. Broken arm."

"That must have been quite a tumble. I wonder how far up the stairs she was when she fell."

"All to get some stupid Easter baskets!"

"I guess we're going to have to figure some things out for your parents sooner than expected, huh?"

"Yes." But I don't want to do that right now, Abby thought, staring at the pile of papers. "Peter, I think I'll bring Dad home for the night. Can you make up the spare bed?"

"No problem."

"How are the kids? Are they coping all right?"

"They seem to be taking it in stride. Hanna's a bit weepy, but she's toughing it out. We've ordered pizza. I'm guessing you'll eat before you get back here."

"Yeah, I'm going to pick up Dad from Aunt Josie's. I may get something there. Honestly, I don't know how I would have managed if she and Christina hadn't been around. I should probably go there right now and take him off her hands."

"Hey, babe? I love you."

"Yeah, love you too. I'll call before I leave Woodstock, okay?"

"Don't worry about us. We're doing fine. Just take care of your dad."

As she flipped the phone shut, she realized that despite all the calls she'd had with Peter today, she hadn't discussed Ben. And since Peter hadn't said anything either, Ben must not have told him his plans.

They needed to talk to Ben before he went back to North Bay on Monday. Was he even planning to return there? She wondered when he wanted to move. Somehow they had to fit that conversation into this weekend. Easter weekend. And there was that leg of lamb in the fridge.

Her mind was zapping all over the place. Time to go. She drained the last of her coffee and tossed the cup into the trash. The brochures she stashed into her purse.

The cold air outside startled her and she zipped up her jacket. Spending time in the hospital was like being in another world; a world where one's concept of time altered, where other people made decisions about you, where the air and light were different, and even voices sounded different. She felt as if she'd been away from the real world for a long time.

****

When she parked in Aunt Josie's driveway, dusk had settled and it was almost dark. The door opened to her knock and she immediately felt warmth and comfort flowing out to her. Yellow light framed Aunt Josie in the doorway and sounds from the TV were in the background, something with applause. Aromas of stew and cinnamony apple wafted out the door.

"Abby." Aunt Josie, with her hug, somehow maneuvered Abby inside. "Did Frieda settle in all right?"

"She was sleeping when I left. She's going to have a tough time." Abby looked toward the living room and saw her father sitting in the chair facing the TV. "I'll get Dad out of your way now."

"Eat something first. You didn't have anything yet, did you?"

Abby shook her head.

"Your father is fine for the time being. He's watching Jeopardy."

In the kitchen a place was set for her—plate, cutlery, a glass of milk, a basket of sliced bread, butter. Aunt Josie lifted the lid off the pot on the stove. "I've got some nice stew for you."

Abby was surprised at how hungry she suddenly felt. The stew was delicious. Chunks of beef spiced and garlicky, pieces of carrot, celery, onion, potatoes, a peppery gravy for dipping the bread in. She ate with gusto.

Her aunt sat across from her and laced her fingers together. "Abby, I want to talk to you about your father."

"I know what you're going to say." Abby downed her glass of milk. "That was delicious. Thank you so much."

"Do you have room for dessert?"

"Always."

Aunt Josie pulled a dish out of the oven and scooped apple crisp into a bowl. "I knew your father was getting forgetful, and sometimes he acted like a child. Your mother has been telling me things. But having him here for so many hours today I see that he's a very confused man."

"I know. I've been thinking that too. But Mom hasn't really told me very much. I think she's afraid we'll put her away in a home with him."

"Well, my dear, none of us old people want to be put away."

"I didn't mean it like it sounded. It's just that..." She spooned some of the apple crisp into her mouth. It was scrumptious; cinnamony, tart, buttery.

"Listen, Abby. I think he is too much for your mother to handle, especially now. She's going to be laid up for a long time because of this fall. She may never get on her feet again."

"She might. She'll go to physiotherapy, and the...."

"Abby," her aunt interrupted, "you need to be realistic. Even if your mother becomes mobile again, your father is too much for her. He needs special care."

Abby put her spoon down and slumped in her chair. "You're right. I've been thinking the same thing for weeks but have been avoiding it." She looked sheepishly at her aunt. "I guess I can't avoid it any more, can I?"

Chapter Seven

Abby finished wrapping the lamb, trying to think of recipes for the leftovers. The roast had hardly been touched. They'd be eating lamb all week.

Peter walked into the kitchen and began counting off on his fingers. "Your dad is settled in bed. Hanna's promised to stay upstairs. And Ben's waiting in the living room. You ready?"

Abby nodded and followed Peter. Ben sat hunched in a chair, as if he were awaiting trial.

"Hey, Ben." Abby touched his shoulder.

Peter took the seat directly across from their son and leaned forward, resting his elbows on his knees. "All right, Ben. Explain yourself. What's going on with school?"

"Nothing's going on. Literally." Ben shrugged. "I just don't like it. It's boring and I'm not motivated to do the work, so I don't. It's better I quit now than waste my time and your money."

"But what about the money we've already invested in your tuition and residence?" Peter's eyes radiated indignation. "And our agreement when you went back to school this year? We won't support you failing your year."

"I'll pay you back." Ben rolled his eyes as he spoke. "Just keep track of what I owe you."

Peter inhaled deeply, obviously trying to calm himself. "But you know if you pass your courses you won't owe us. In fact, if you make an effort and complete this year, you'll always have that under your belt. And it'll be easier to return to school if you want to do that later."

Ben snorted. "No chance of that."

Abby couldn't keep silent any longer. "Ben. You could be a bit more respectful." Realizing her fists were clenched, she unfurled them.

"Right. Sorry." Ben gave the appearance of being contrite. Abby wondered what he was really thinking.

Peter sat back in his chair. "I guess if Ben wants to try something different while he figures out what to do with his life, then we have to accept that."

"But we both think he's making a mistake!" Abby couldn't believe Peter's rapid acquiescence. "He…"

"Abby," Peter's eyes bored into hers. "Ben has the right to choose his own path, as long as," he looked directly at Ben, "he understands that he's financially responsible for himself while he's doing it."

"I know that." Ben looked defensive. "I'm not asking you to support me."

"Okay then. When do you want us to help you move your stuff?"

****

Ben's new home in Toronto was a detached house set up as a multi-room rental. From the outside it appeared clean and tidy. Obviously someone maintained the exterior and the yard.

However, the inside was very different; dirty floors, peeling paint, and it had an odd smell. Three boys around Ben's age greeted them at the door. They were polite and shook hands when introduced. While Peter and the boys moved boxes and furniture down the narrow stairs to Ben's room in the basement, Abby toured the house with Hanna. She was encouraged when she saw a chore schedule posted on the fridge but then caught sight of stacks of dirty dishes in the sink and boxes filled with empty beer bottles piled high in a corner. Hanna's nose wrinkled as she walked around and Abby tried very hard to make positive comments for her sake. But the filthy sate of the bathroom struck them both speechless. Their eyes met; they obviously felt the same disgust. How could Ben want to live in this place? Peter came up behind them and whispered in Abby's ear. "It's Ben's life, Ben's home. Let it go." He was right of course. She closed her eyes and left the bathroom.

Ben's room was clean, though it had only one small window high up near the ceiling making it dim and cheerless. But Ben was happy with it. Once they set up the furniture and his computer, his enthusiasm filled the space.

"When the boxes are unpacked, it'll feel just like home." He grinned.

Abby was encouraged to see him so upbeat but couldn't help herself. "Make sure you give that bathroom a good cleaning, Ben."

He rolled his eyes and said in an exasperated tone, "Mom, stop worrying." He led them out then, through the rec room past a large round table on which lay decks of cards and poker chips, past a washer and dryer, and up the wooden steps to the front hall.

"See you guys." He appeared eager for them to leave. "Thanks for your help."

"Have a good life, Ben." Hanna punched him lightly in the arm and ran outside. "Keep in touch," she called over her shoulder as she climbed into the car.

Peter patted him on the back and shook his hand, then pulled him into a hug. "Good luck, Ben. Know that we're here for you if you need anything."

"Bye, Benny Boy. Good luck with all this." Abby hugged him tight and kissed his cheek. "We love you." Then without looking back, she stepped outside, not wanting him to see the expression on her face that would show she didn't believe in him.

"Love you too. Bye."

Peter put his arm across her shoulder and they walked down the porch steps together. At the bottom they both turned to wave but Ben had already shut the door.

In the car Hanna announced that Ben was crazy, put her headset on her ears, and fiddled with her iPod. Abby looked at Peter.

"I guess he's truly out of the nest, huh?"

"He may fly back in." He flicked the turn signal and checked his blind spot. "He'll probably find out this isn't the answer."

She took a tissue from her bag and blew her nose. "It's so hard to let go when I know he's making a mistake." Hearing music from Hanna's ear buds, she turned. Hanna had her nose buried in a book.

"Hanna, it's too loud."

Hanna continued reading so Abby reached back and touched her knee. That succeeded in getting her attention, so Abby mouthed the word "loud" and pointed to her ears. Hanna adjusted the volume and returned to her book.

Once they were on the highway, Peter carried on a monologue, as if he were trying to convince himself as much as Abby that Ben would be all right. "He'll learn soon enough that earning minimum wage isn't what he'll want for his life. He'll decide to go back to school eventually. He's a smart kid who can do so much more and he knows it."

Abby was trying to settle her own mind and didn't respond, not that Peter needed any response. And really, she didn't know why this was upsetting her so much. Ben was young. He had many years to figure things out. She should just stop fretting and let him grow up in his own way. Yet deep down, her mother-heart knew things were amiss.

****

The Unraveling of Abby Settel   83

Abby's anxieties continuously wove themselves into the fabric of her thoughts. Peter's job situation was the warp, uncertainty about Ben the weft, and her parents a fraying thread intertwined throughout. It all affected her concentration and she found it increasingly difficult to focus on the tasks of daily life. Meal preparation became arduous, and she served takeout for dinner more often than cooking it. Her progress on the final exams slowed. She stared at students' essays on her desk, not reading them. She gazed at the television unaware of what she was watching.

While she spiraled into ineffectiveness, Peter's frame of mind seemingly shifted to one of enthusiasm and anticipation.

"How do you feel about Vancouver?" he'd ask when he came home from work. "Or Los Angeles? Or Barbados?"

There seemed to be job possibilities everywhere but in Waterloo. Peter was energized by the job search and appeared unaware of Abby's discombobulation. Nonetheless, some of Peter's attitude infected her and, despite everything, she felt an unexpected stirring of excitement.

She was in her office at the university working on the exam for her Children's Lit course when she was interrupted by a knock on her open door. Her department head stood in the doorway.

"Abby, Sharon tells me she hasn't received your signed contract for the spring term yet. You are going to teach that detective fiction course for us, aren't you? And the short story one?"

"Oh my gosh, Gerald. I forgot all about it. I have it right here in my briefcase." She shuffled through sheets of paper. "I'll sign it right now." She walked over and handed him the contract. "I'm so sorry."

Gerald looked into her face. "Everything all right?"

"Yes, of course. Why do you ask?"

"It's not like you to forget this." He held up the papers she'd handed him. "You seem a little..." he looked up at the ceiling as if searching for the right word, "distracted?"

"Life is just, ah, full right now." Should she tell him Peter lost his job? That they might have to move? No, it was too soon. Nothing was definite. She needn't jeopardize her position here just because Peter's future at Hearth Financial was non-existent.

"Kids okay?"

"They are. Hanna received early acceptance into the music program at WLU. She's pretty excited about it. I'm just the proud mom."

"And Ben?"

"Oh, he's taking some time off school and is working in Toronto. He's doing all right." Wishing she could believe that, she looked at her hands and twisted her rings.

"Okay." He waved her contract in the air. "I'll let you get back to work. Exam time is upon us."

Abby plopped back into her chair. How could she have forgotten to sign the contract? She closed her eyes and rubbed her temples.

Turning back to her computer screen, she tried to pick up where she'd stopped. In Kenneth Grahame's *Wind in the Willows* and E. B. White's *Charlotte's Web*, compare... Compare what? She couldn't remember what she'd been trying to get at. Shaking her head, she closed her laptop. It was impossible to focus now. Time to go home.

She drove along University Ave., replaying her conversation with Gerald and reliving her embarrassment. Automatically, she pulled into the parking lot of the Wok-In Takeout and then realized it was too early to pick up dinner. If she brought home spring rolls now, they'd be cold and soggy by the time Hanna and Peter came home. She should cook tonight. Maybe that would get her out of her funk.

****

At the grocery store Abby pushed her cart around aimlessly, unable to come up with an idea. She grabbed cans of soup and boxes of instant dinners, ashamed about putting them in her cart. She hoped she wouldn't run into anyone she knew.

Pondering a choice between a vegetable or meat lasagna at the freezer, she was startled by a voice behind her.

"Abby Settel! How are you?" A small, athletic looking woman approached her. "I haven't seen you for ages. How are your kids doing?"

"Oh, hi." Abby maneuvered herself to block the view of the contents in her cart. Recognizing the woman's face, she couldn't remember her name. Where did she know her from? The university? Hockey? The kids' schools?

"We're visiting family here. You know, we so enjoy living in Toronto we hardly ever make it back to Waterloo. Weird, huh, being so close?"

"I guess so." Abby tried to sound chipper like the woman. "Um, I've forgotten, how long has it been since you moved?"

"Now let's see, it must be about seven, no eight years. Our kids are both in university now and we left when they were still in junior high. You know Andrew's in his third year at Queens and Laura is in first year at UBC. Imagine her being so far away." The woman shook her head. "Hard to believe how the time goes. Can you believe our boys are almost twenty? How's Ben? Did he ever get into the junior As? He was quite the hockey player."

Ah, thought Abby, she's a hockey mom. What was her name?

"Actually, Ben was playing for Nipissing U but he's taking some time off school to try a few other things. Hockey's still his first love, though." She wondered if that were true. "And Hanna's just been accepted into the music program at WLU. For flute."

"Oh that's great. Laura's studying fine art. Andrew has completely given up hockey. It's good to hear Ben's still playing. We always expected him to go far. What position?"

"Well, he's um..." Abby's throat constricted and she was unable to form any more words. Damn. What was wrong with her? She blinked a few times and clutched the cart handle tightly.

The woman brought her face closer to Abby's. "Oh my God, Abby, is he all right?"

"Yes. No. It's just that..." Abby rooted around in her purse for a tissue and tried to steady her voice. "Ben's fine." She blew her nose. "It was great to see you, um, say hi to the family."

"Okay, Abby. You take care."

She knew the woman was watching her as she wheeled her cart down the aisle. She must think she was crazy. Leaving her shopping cart at the end of the freezer aisle, Abby ran out of the store mortified by her meltdown.

****

In the end she decided on spaghetti for dinner, vegetarian spaghetti because there was no meat in the house. Peter arrived home as she was filling a pot with water. Walking into the kitchen, he picked up the mail.

"Hey, Abs, I have an update," he said, reaching for the jar of sauce she was struggling to open. "Here, let me get that."

"About a job somewhere?" Abby took back the opened jar. "Thanks."

"Not exactly. Frank and I worked out what I'll need to do to ease the transition at the office. We set the official date for my last day of work and they've finalized the details of my severance. It's a good package, Abby."

She plopped the sauce into a pot and stirred as she turned on the burner. "How can anything be a good package if it means losing your job?" She directed her gaze at him, challenge in her eyes.

"All I meant is that the payout is generous and will keep us going until I find something else. I'll keep our benefits for a year, too." He shrugged. "It's better than being booted out with nothing."

"You're right. Sorry." She went back to stirring the sauce. "When's your last day?"

"Officially it's August eighteenth, but I'll take my vacation time at the end so I'm actually finishing July twenty-eighth. Cool, huh? Now I just have to find a new position somewhere." He came up behind her and put his hands around her waist. "Maybe we can take a holiday between jobs."

"Maybe, but I can't go anywhere until my term marks are in. That's the beginning of Aug..." Her throat tightened and she swallowed. Turning around, she stared at him, tears blurring his face. He held her and stroked her hair.

"Honey, things will be okay." His sympathy made her cry more, as if his love dissolved the floodgates of her control. Her shoulders shook and he pulled her closer. "Did you have a bad day?"

"No. J-just everything..." She closed her eyes. "I don't know what's wrong with me. I cry all the time." She extricated herself and went into the bathroom. Looking in the mirror at her face blotchy from crying, her eyes red-rimmed and wet, she admonished herself. "You are pathetic."

Chapter Eight

Summer
Waterloo, Ontario

Abby merged the car into the highway traffic, happy to be with Hanna and anticipating a good day together. She was trying hard to not let her worries overshadow the brightness of her mood; in fact, she'd decided to adopt a new philosophy. Live in the now. And right now she was driving to Toronto with her daughter.

"Have you thought about what color dress you want?" She glanced at Hanna fiddling with the radio.

"I'm hoping to get a blue one. Emily said Carol's Classics has a whole rack of dresses in different shades of blue. She saw one dress that's perfect for me. I hope they still have it and I can find it."

"What's Emily's dress like?"

"Oh, Mom, it's gorgeous. It's pale yellow and has tiny flowers embroidered around the edge, and these pretty little straps, and the skirt is long and sleek. I hope I get one just as nice." She pulled out a magazine. "Thanks for taking me to Toronto."

"Your prom is pretty special and you need a special dress for it. If Emily says Carol's Classics is the place to go, then I'm all for checking it out. Besides, I've been looking forward to this. It's been a while since we've shopped for clothes together." Abby smiled at Hanna. She had another reason for going to Toronto. "And we can drop in on Ben while we're there."

"Yeah, that'd be cool. I haven't talked to him in ages." Hanna opened her magazine and sang along with the radio.

Neither had Abby. In fact, he hadn't been in contact since his move to Toronto almost two months ago. He didn't answer his phone or respond to messages left on his voice mail. He didn't reply to e-mails. She'd taken to staying logged on to her instant messaging whenever she worked on the computer to see if Ben was online. He often was, but never replied to her *Hey, Ben, are you there?* Peter thought he was trying to prove something before he'd contact them.

"He's showing us he can be completely independent, that he doesn't need his parents," Peter would theorize. "I read an article in MacLean's that said lots of young adults behave like this when they're first on their own. It's all about establishing their independence or something. It's normal." Abby wasn't so sure.

Now she was determined to see Ben. When Hanna had asked about a shopping trip to Toronto she readily agreed, realizing it provided a perfect opportunity to visit her wayward son.

"Hanna," she pointed to her purse. "Why don't you try calling Ben to tell him we're coming. Just hit number five."

Hanna held the cell phone to her ear. "It's his voice mail. Should I leave a message?"

"No. If he's not home, he's probably at work. We'll go to Starbucks to see him."

"I wonder how Ben likes his new life."

"Me too." Abby tried to picture him at an espresso machine foaming milk. She could imagine him being very methodical about measuring the amount of coffee and getting the milk to just the right temperature. He might actually be good at his job. "Once we find your dress we may be able to take Ben out for lunch."

"Yeah, there are some funky restaurants on Queen Street near his Starbucks. I remember seeing them when we helped him move."

"He does live in an interesting part of Toronto."
And one that let loose all kinds of worries in a mother's
imagination. Abby remembered being unnerved as they
drove through the area when they moved Ben. Head
shops and "alternative lifestyle" stores next to boutiques
and vegan restaurants. Angry looking young people
standing in doorways, dressed in black, their eyes
rimmed and hair spiked, sharp hardware piercing their
lips, noses, and eyebrows. Homeless teens begging on
the sidewalk.

She shook her head. Live in the now, she reminded
herself. Stop worrying about Ben. Right now this trip
was for Hanna.

Carol's Classics was far from Ben's neighborhood. It
was on a side street just off Bloor Street not far from
Holt Renfrew's. It was a wonderful shop, filled with
dream dresses of all colors and fabrics and styles.
Hanna's face lit up when they walked in the door and she
headed directly for a rack that had an array of blues
hanging from it. Abby looked around and thought with
longing of the girl she'd been at eighteen. She would
have loved to get her prom dress in a store like this.
Instead she'd sewn hers from fabric her grandmother
had given her. The fabric had seemed pretty enough on
the bolt; pink rosettes intertwined with pale green
tendrils. But when the dress was sewn, Abby thought it
looked more like upholstery. Grandma painstakingly
helped her to gather the puff sleeves to give even fullness
to both and she was so proud of the end result that
Abby didn't have the heart to tell her how much she
disliked the dress.

"She looks like a princess," Grandma said to Abby's
mother, who agreed with shining eyes.

"We can put little pink roses in her hair. And Abby," her mother stroked one sleeve, "you can wear my
green shawl that matches the green in the dress."

Abby remembered staring at herself in the mirror, thinking the sleeves were too puffy and the waist too high. All during dinner at The Steakhouse, she tugged her dress down. But then when her date, Fred Landson, finally got up the courage to tell her how beautiful she was and kissed her, she forgot all about the dress and danced in his arms all night. She smiled at the memory.

"Mom, look at this one," Hanna called. She draped a periwinkle gown in front of her. "I think it's the one Emily described to me."

"It is very pretty," she said, looking at the price tag. It cost less than she expected, making it even more attractive. "And it suits you. I love the color." She fingered another dress on the rack. "Why don't you find a few different ones to try on to compare?"

"I will." Hanna put the dress over her arm and began to inspect the others. "Hey, Mom, why don't you try some on too? Just for fun."

Abby thought about trying to squeeze her almost fifty-year-old body into these dresses that were made to flatter young, nubile figures. Perhaps if she were ten pounds lighter? She shook her head. She couldn't begin to imagine how her rounded belly and padded hips would look in these sleek, slinky gowns. She laughed aloud at the picture in her mind. "I'd look like one of Cinderella's stepsisters. No, this is your shopping trip, sweetie. I'll just hand you dresses and give you my opinion."

While Hanna was in the dressing room, Abby thought back to Ben's prom night. He and five other boys in his class had rented tuxedos and a limo and they'd gone as a group. He announced the next day that he had an awesome time. "It was great being a free spirit at the prom," he said. "You can dance and hang out with lots of different people." She wondered if Ben was enjoying being a free spirit here in Toronto.

Stop, she admonished herself. This is about Hanna. Stop thinking about Ben. She called to the door of Hanna's dressing room. "How's it going, Hanna?"

"Almost ready. Be right out."

Abby glanced at a mother-daughter pair arguing over a dress with a very low-cut bodice. Hanna was so different from Ben. She and Jason had been dating since the beginning of eleventh grade and it didn't appear that either of them had any thoughts about changing that.

"Here I come."

Hanna stepped through the doorway and Abby caught her breath. Her daughter looked ethereal. Delicate straps caressed Hanna's shoulders and the bodice of the dress followed the curves of her figure, modestly accentuating her youthful breasts. The fabric flowed along the lines of her slender waist and cascaded from her slim hips into folds that seemed like blue mist.

"Oh, Hanna, you look incredible." She wondered how her little girl could so suddenly have been transformed into this stunning young woman.

"I think it's a pretty amazing dress too, Mom. Should I get it?"

It was that easy. Hanna tried on other dresses, but they kept coming back to that first one.

"You know what you like," the saleswoman said when they paid for the dress. "This dress is you and you knew it when you first took it off the rack."

"Do you think Jason will like it, Mom?"

"He'll love the dress. You're going to look so beautiful on prom night."

Hanna giggled. "I know."

They bought shoes in the shop next door and then Abby couldn't resist buying Hanna a pretty silver necklace with earrings to match from a vendor on the street. They walked along Bloor Street with their bags, arms linked. Hanna announced, "I'm ready for a latte."

Abby laughed. "Right. Off to Ben's Starbucks then. Maybe he'll make us our coffees."

As they climbed in the car, the dark clouds of worry that Abby had been keeping at bay began to infiltrate the lightness of their morning. She was nervous about what she might find out about Ben, and wondered if he'd be glad to see them or annoyed they'd come unannounced. Maybe he'd feel they were invading his space, interfering with his life. She tried to decide whether she should act happy and unconcerned when she saw him. Maybe she should let him know they were upset about his silence, make him feel guilty and question his commitment to his family.

Abby exhaled. For certain she was over-thinking.

Starbuck's buzzed with activity. Swooshing steamers, ringing registers, and a polyphony of conversations peppered the atmosphere. Abby and Hanna nudged their way through a group of people gathered at the entrance.

Hanna stared up at the board with the list of coffees. "Mom, can I have a Venti Latte?"

"Sure. Do you see Ben anywhere?" Abby stood on her toes to see if she could spot Ben behind the counter.

"Nope. He's not at the registers." Hanna pointed to the bakery counter. "I don't see him over there either. I can't tell if he's by the coffee machines, though. This place is crazy."

"You're not kidding." Abby stretched her neck to look over the heads of the people in front of her.

When they finally stood at the counter, she'd still not seen Ben. Behind the cash register stood a pretty young girl with long dark hair that had fluorescent pink streaks shooting through it.

"What can I get you?" she asked. Abby could see a little silver ball pierced into her tongue. How did that not drive her crazy?

"A Venti Latte, please. And," Abby handed her a five. She leaned closer, "I was wondering, could you tell me if Ben is scheduled to work today?"

The girl wrote something on an empty cup and set it over to one side. "Who?"

"Ben. Ben Settel. He works here."

"I'm sorry, I don't know any Ben." She handed Abby her change and looked at the person behind her. "Can I help you?"

Abby stood still, holding her coins. A seedling of dread was taking root.

"Mom?" Hanna touched her arm. "She's probably new here. Let's ask that guy who's making the coffee. He looks older so maybe he's the manager."

Abby followed her daughter to the end of the counter and listened as she asked about Ben, knowing what the answer would be.

"No, we don't have anyone named Ben working here."

Hanna persisted. "He only started a couple of months ago. Are you sure?"

"Yes. Sorry."

Of course it was true. Ben did not work here. He probably never had. Abby had known something was off. "Hanna, let's go."

"Nobody here knows Ben. That doesn't make sense. He's supposed to work here."

She grabbed Hanna's arm. "Let's get out of here."

"I have to get my latte, Mom. Just a sec."

The wait for Hanna's coffee was interminable. Abby stood by the door, jangling her keys while she watched Hanna add five packets of sugar to her cup. Finally they were on the sidewalk.

"Where do you think Ben is, Mom?"

"I don't know." Abby turned in the direction of Ben's street. "Let's walk to his house. We'll leave the car parked."

"Do you think he works at a different Starbucks?"

Abby briefly let that nugget of hope sit in her mind then shook it from her head. "No, he pointed this one out when we moved him, remember?"

"What does it mean? He was lying about his job?"

"Apparently." Abby could barely get the word out. In the face of her anger, she felt fear. Her heart pounded in her ears.

"Mom, slow down." Hanna called from behind her. "I can't walk so fast with this coffee."

Abby stopped and waited for Hanna to catch up. "Hurry. I need to get there and find out what's going on."

When they arrived at the house, Abby was surprised to see how innocent it looked. Peaceful, even. It didn't match the bewilderment she felt. They climbed the steps and rang the doorbell. No sound came from within.

"Did the bell ring?" Hanna leaned to the side trying to look in a window.

Abby tried again, pushing the button deeply and holding it for a few seconds. A two-toned melody echoed inside.

"Yup, it works. Did you hear it that time?" Hanna straightened.

"Yes, but there doesn't seem to be anyone here." Abby knocked loudly on the door. No response. Hanna made a fist and banged three times.

"Anyone there?"

Nothing.

Abby started down the porch steps. "Let's look through Ben's window. Maybe he can't hear us down in the basement." They made their way to the back of the house, where Ben's window showed closed blinds. Abby climbed into the window well.

"Mom, you can't go in there."

"I certainly can. How else will I see through the window?" Her foot squashed something unidentifiable as she stepped closer to the window, but she hardly paid attention, merely shaking her foot as she crouched down. Looking in the hollow created by her hands, she peered through the grimy glass and tried to see between the slats of the blinds. Nothing. She knocked on the window. "Ben? Are you there?" She knew he wouldn't be. She knocked again, louder. "Ben?" Where was he?

"Can you see anything?"

"No, the blinds are closed. I don't think he's in there." She stood and reached her hand up to Hanna, who helped pull her out of the window well.

"I don't know where else to look for him." Abby brushed her shaking hands over her pant legs. "Any ideas?"

"No." Hanna put her hands on her hips. "Where can he be?"

"I don't know. Let's not panic." Abby paced back and forth. "Do you know anything about the boys he's living with?"

Hanna shook her head. "I don't know any more than you do, not even their last names."

Abby looked back at the house. "We could wait for him to come home." She turned and walked to the front of the house and sat down on the steps of the porch.

Hanna ran after her. "Mom, we can't just sit here. What if he doesn't come home for hours?"

"Maybe one of the other boys will."

"Or not."

"I have to do something, Hanna."

Hanna went to the sidewalk and looked up and down the street. Returning to the steps, she suggested, "Why don't we write him a note?"

"That's a good idea." Glad to finally have something tangible to do, Abby opened her handbag and searched inside it. "We'll stick it on the door." Pulling out a notepad, she rummaged in her bag again.

"What'll we say?"

"That we came by and could he please call us. Oh, here's my pen." Abby opened the notepad and began writing.

"He probably won't respond to it, Mom."

Abby knew Hanna was right. But she had to try. "I'll also write that we really need to speak to him."

"Yeah, ASAP. He's being stupid."

Abby looked up at Hanna. "I hope that being stupid is all he's doing."

Hanna shrugged. "Can we still go out for lunch?"

"I guess. We need to eat before heading home, don't we?" Abby didn't much feel like eating, though. Her stomach was clenched in a knot, leaving no room for nourishment.

They walked along the street in the direction of the car, Abby registering nothing she passed. When Hanna pointed out a small vegetarian restaurant, they went in. Hanna ordered a wrap with sprouts and chickpeas; Abby had black bean soup. It might have been delicious but she didn't notice, leaving more than half of it untouched. For Hanna's sake she tried to recapture the mood from their morning but could not overcome the angst she felt about Ben and kept looking out the window, hoping she'd see her son.

Hanna tried to come up with an explanation.

"Maybe he quit Starbucks because he got a really good job and wants to surprise us." Hanna's optimism pierced through Abby's uncertainty.

"Maybe. Why wait to tell us, though?" Abby wondered. "Why do you think he doesn't respond to any of our messages, Hanna?"

"I don't know." Hanna pulled a brown-coloured sprout from her wrap and placed it on her plate. "He's probably doing something he doesn't want us to know about."

"That's what I'm thinking too," Abby stirred her soup. It was dark and looked like thick chocolate. "What could he be doing?"

"I don't know. I don't think he's into drugs or anything."

"I hope not." Could they really know for sure?

On the drive home they were both silent. Hanna reclined the back of her seat and closed her eyes, falling asleep. Abby drove and fretted.

****

Peter was bringing in the lawnmower when Abby drove into the garage. He smiled and waved, walking over to open her door. Hanna stretched herself awake.

Peter leaned in and kissed Abby, exuding the scent of newly mown grass.

"Hey, how was your shopping trip? Did you find a dress?"

His question startled Abby. She'd forgotten that the purpose of their trip had been to get a dress for Hanna. Her thoughts had been taken over by Ben during the drive home. What might he be up to? Where might he be? What should they do about finding him? The shopping excursion with her daughter had faded to the background.

"We did, Dad. Wait 'til you see it." Hanna climbed out of the car. "It's awesome."

"Will you model it for me later?"

"Sure." Hanna took her bags out of the trunk and headed into the house. "I'll go put it on right now."

Peter shut the car door behind Abby and followed her inside. "Did you see Ben? How's he doing?"

"We went to see him but couldn't find him." She put her handbag on the kitchen counter. Anger overpowered her anxiety and her voice rose. "Apparently he's not working at Starbucks. Nobody there had heard of him."

"What?" Peter looked bewildered. "What do you mean?"

She described the visits to Starbucks and to Ben's house, her voice getting shakier as the story progressed. When she related what she'd written in the note, she wiped at her eyes in annoyance. "Where do you think he could be, Peter? Should we call in the police, do you think?"

"No, I don't think we need to do that yet. The Starbucks thing is something to worry about, but that's not for the police to deal with. And Ben doesn't live alone in that house so if something had happened to him we'd have heard. Maybe we should contact the parents of the other boys to try and track him down."

"But we don't know who they are."

"True. We can contact the landlord. He'll have at least one of their names on the lease."

Abby was relieved he'd come up with a solution. Her angst receded as he put his arms around her. He spoke into her ear. "We'll find Ben and get this straightened out. We'll straighten Ben out, too."

"What do you think, Dad?" Hanna walked into the kitchen, swishing the skirt of her new dress.

"Holy Hanna." Peter whistled.

"Dad."

"Honestly, Hanna, you look stunning. That is one beautiful dress. Jason will be wowed."

Hanna lifted her skirt and poked out a foot. "See my new shoes?" She leaned forward and held out the necklace around her neck. "And my jewels?"

"Very pretty. Your mother spoiled you." He hugged her.

"I know." She looked at Abby. "Thanks, Mom."

"Anything for you, my dear." Abby brought the phone book to the table. "Do we know the landlord's name?"

Hanna's smile vanished. "Are you talking about Ben?"

"Yes. Dad thought we could call the landlord to see if we can get his roommates' names."

"Abby, I have to think about how to find the landlord's information. I'm not sure we have it."

Abby slumped into a chair. "Okay," she said in a small voice.

"I have some good news." Peter pulled up another chair and positioned it facing her.

"What about?" Hanna sat on the table between them.

"Off the table, Hanna." Abby said then looked at Peter. "What good news."

"Chestnut Manor called. They have a place for your parents. We can move them this week. We'll go there tomorrow to check the room out and make the arrangements."

"Really? For both of them?"

"Yup. It's a couple's room on the assisted care floor. They call it a honeymoon suite."

"That is good news."

Hanna fingered her necklace. "So Pops can move out of that other place he hates? And be with Grandma again?"

"Yup. The place he's in is just a temporary respite facility. And I know Grandma will be happy to get out of the hospital, that's for sure." He looked at Abby. "Want some tea? Or maybe some wine?" He pointed to a bottle sitting on the counter. "I bought a bottle of Yellow Label."

"Oh, definitely wine." Abby pushed back her chair.

Hanna twirled around the room and stopped in front of Peter. "Dad, will they allow Max to move with Grandma and Pops? Or do we get to keep him here? Where is he, by the way?"

"I put him outside." Peter took a corkscrew out of the drawer. "I cleaned up one mess too many today. And to answer your question, Hanna, he can't go to Chestnut Manor with Grandma and Pops. They don't allow pets."

Abby took some cheese out of the fridge. "Hanna, you should take the dress off."

While Peter opened the wine, Abby nibbled on some cheese. She felt hungry even though it was only four. Taking crackers out of the cupboard, she considered her parents. She hoped they'd be happy about the move to Chestnut Manor and that being there would help her mother's recovery. It might be good for her dad too. Moving him to that temporary facility really upset him. And he missed his cat.

Her musings were interrupted by the phone ringing. Peter picked it up.

"Hey, Ben," Peter turned to face Abby, locking eyes with her. Abby froze. "We haven't heard from you for a while."

Abby's heart hammered in her ears. It took all the control she could muster to stop herself from grabbing the phone out of Peter's hand.

"Oh. Well, don't you check your voice mail or read your e-mails?" Peter was agitated. Abby whispered loudly, "What's he saying?"

Peter shook his head and looked down, breaking eye contact with Abby. "Why haven't you called before now? We've been worried."

She walked over to Peter and grabbed his elbow. "Ask him about Starbucks," she mouthed. He didn't respond. She grabbed a pen and a piece of paper and wrote *Starbucks job?*, putting it in front of Peter's face. He took it from her and nodded. She ran upstairs to the bedroom and picked up the extension.

"...my job and doing stuff with the guys in the house."

"Ben? Mom here." She cleared her throat. "Ben, why don't you answer us when we phone you, or IM you, or e-mail you."

"I was telling Dad. I've been busy with work and the guys. I read your e-mails; I just don't get around to answering them."

"Hanna and I went to your Starbucks today. Nobody there knew who you were."

"What? That's just weird."

"We asked two people and both of them said they hadn't heard of you." Her heart thumped. She could hear Peter breathing on the other phone.

"Who did you talk to?"

"Ben," Peter interjected. "Do you have a job there?"

"I told you I did," he said defensively.

"Then why didn't the people there know you?"

"I don't know. I'll find out who Mom talked to and straighten that out."

"Are you working tomorrow?" Abby said, sitting down on the bed. "Can you come home for a few days?"

Peter spoke up. "We have to go to Woodstock tomorrow, Abby, but I think it's a good idea for Ben to come home for a visit. When are you off next, Ben?"

"I can come home next weekend. Is that soon enough for you? What's up anyway?"

Abby didn't voice the accusations that formed in her mind. "Nothing's up. We just need to talk to you." She steadied herself. "So you can come on Saturday?"

"Yeah, okay. Can you pick me up?"

"I'll drive to Toronto in the morning," Peter said. "I'll be at your place at ten on Saturday. Okay?"

"Okay. Bye."

"Wait..." Abby wasn't ready to say good-bye to him. The phone clicked. "Bye, Ben. We love you," she said into the receiver.

Peter's voice came through the earpiece. "I think he hung up, honey."

"I know. I wanted to talk to him some more."

"Yeah, me too. We'll see him in a week. At least he called us."

"He did. Do you believe him about Starbucks?"

"It seems fishy to me." The phone started beeping. "Why don't you hang up and come down here. There's a glass of wine waiting for you."

Chapter Nine

She hadn't traveled in the backseat of a car for a long time. It gave her a different perspective. Instead of being surrounded front and side with the scenery passing by, her view of the road seemed two-dimensional, almost like having tunnel vision. Depending on which window she looked through, she saw smaller, different sections of the landscape.

She noticed a thinning patch on the back of Peter's head. Did he know he was starting to go bald? She leaned toward the front.

"I think you're going to like living in this place, Dad," she said, trying to sound excited.

Her father stiffly turned his head to look at her. "When can I go home, Abby?"

"You're going to your new home. Mom will be there, and…"

"But I want to go home. To my house. Where Max is."

Peter said, "Max is at our house, Nick. We're taking care of him for now." He touched Abby's hand, which was resting on his shoulder. "You're moving to Chestnut Manor because Frieda was hurt and she can't take care of you until she gets better. And you can't stay in your house by yourself."

"But I already stayed in a new place. Now you say I can't stay there so I want to go home."

"Dad," Abby tried to keep frustration out of her voice. "We went over this. You're going to live in Chestnut Manor with Mom. There will be people there who can take care of both of you. You can be together.

And it's nice there. You and Mom get to live in a honeymoon suite."

"Huh? Honeymoon? What's that?"

Peter glanced sideways at him and smiled. "It's what they call a couple's room. It's bigger than the usual room, so that you and Frieda can live there together."

"What about my house?"

"Your house is still your house." For now, reflected Abby. They should probably sell it soon. "Chestnut Manor is pretty close to the neighbourhood so it'll be easy for your friends to visit you."

Her father grunted.

"And we've moved some of your things to your new room so it'll feel just like your home."

"What things?"

"Let's see, your brown recliner, your TV, pictures, some of your magazines, your fishing trophies…" She thought about how she'd agonized over the choice of items that would give her parents the most sense of home. Her mother hadn't wanted to discuss it and her father was too confused to be of any help. It had taken four trips between her parents' house and Chestnut Manor before Abby was satisfied.

She needed her parents to feel at home in this place. It would be too difficult to move away if they weren't settled. Because the longer it was taking for Peter to find a job, the more Abby was convinced that she and Peter would be leaving Waterloo.

Her father shifted in his seat. "Can Max come too?"

"No, Dad," Abby shook her head. "Max can't live with you there."

"Then I don't want to go." He crossed his arms and turned his head sideways to look out the window.

"We can maybe bring Max to visit you sometimes," Abby said. She didn't know if a cat was allowed to visit

Chestnut Manor, but if she needed to lie to help her dad today, she would.

Her father didn't respond. He didn't move from his defensive stance. She put her hands on her lap and sat back. Peter caught her eyes in the rearview mirror and shook his head slightly.

"Won't it be nice to see Mom again?" She touched her father's shoulder. "You haven't seen her since the accident."

"My mom?"

"No Dad, my mom. Your Frieda."

"Ach, Frieda. Frieda's gone." He wiped his hand over his face.

"Dad. Frieda is not gone. She was hurt and has been in the hospital all this time. But she'll be with you at Chestnut Manor."

"Yeah? Frieda is fine?"

"We've been telling you." Abby eyes widened in exasperation as she again looked at Peter in the rearview mirror. "Mom...Frieda broke her hip and was in the hospital. Now she's ready to leave the hospital. She's in a wheelchair, but she's getting better."

"She's waiting for me at home?"

"At your new home in Chestnut Manor." Abby grimaced at Peter. He smiled at her encouragingly.

"Frieda and Max?"

Abby groaned.

Peter spoke up. "Why don't you wait and see how things are when we get there, Nick."

"Yeah, okay."

They didn't speak the rest of the way. Peter focused on his driving. Abby pressed her lips together to stop herself from saying something that would create more confusion for her dad who stared at the window in front of him.

Abby wondered how her mother was coping with the transport from the hospital. She hadn't wanted Abby to be a part of it.

"You take care of your father," she said. "I can manage on my own with the people from the hospital." Even in her diminished condition, she was obstinate and wouldn't listen to Abby's protests. "I'll meet you at the home and then I'll help your father settle in."

Abby was a little concerned when her mother added, "This is only temporary, anyway." Abby didn't respond to the comment and hoped that as time went by her parents would get so used to living at Chestnut Manor, they'd forget about moving back to their house.

Chestnut Manor was a large, yellow brick building with four floors of windows along the front. It was nestled in a forest of trees giving it the appearance of a cozy retreat. Or, Abby thought, something hidden away from the vital, active world.

She guided her father along the walk lined with red and white impatiens. Two women sat in wheelchairs on a brick patio near the entrance, the dappled sunlight casting speckles of shadows on their wrinkled faces. One wore a pink sweater and she looked up as they approached, breaking into a bright smile.

"Hi-hi," she said and nodded her head.

"Hi there," Abby pulled her father over to the woman, whispering in his ear. "Look, Dad, here's someone who might be a new friend." She turned to the woman. "This is my father, Nick Baker. He's moving here."

"Hi-hi." The woman cackled. "Hey diddle diddle."

"Huh?" Abby's father resisted and pulled back.

She let go of him and bent down to the woman. "It's a lovely day to be out, isn't it?"

The woman looked up and touched Abby's arm. She looked so sweet, so tiny, like a child in a grown-up's wheelchair. Her gold-rimmed glasses magnified her eyes, making them large blue glassy circles, and the softness of her pink sweater complemented the fluffiness of her snow-white hair.

"Hi-hi," she said again. "Hey diddle diddle."

Abby looked at the other woman, who stared vacantly at the grass. These two were not all there. Was she seeing her parents' future?

"Come on, Abby, Nick," Peter held the door open. "They're waiting for us."

In the foyer of the building, she passed more white-haired people sitting along the wall, some in wheelchairs, others on coloured vinyl padded chairs. They looked as if they were waiting for something. Like a bus.

Or life to be over.

Why was she thinking so negatively? This was a good seniors' residence and her parents would be well cared for. On the tour, they'd been shown lovely bright rooms, an activity center, an impressive dining hall, a library. Still, Abby hoped she'd never have to go to a place like this. It was depressing. All these old people with no future.

Her father shuffled along behind Peter. It was sad to see him so resigned, his strong will so diminished. How would he react when he saw his Frieda again?

At the end of the hall, the administrator came out of her office and shook Peter's hand. When they first met Janet Howe, Peter was impressed with her professional and caring approach. And her gorgeous looks. Today her shining black hair was pulled back in a chignon. Abby thought that's what it was called; she'd never been able to master the art of the hair bun. Mrs. Howe was wearing a tailored suit that looked identical to the one she'd worn the last time, except this one was navy instead of taupe. Wondering if the woman had a closet full of this style of suits in a subdued rainbow of colors, Abby hurried to catch up to them.

"Hi, Mrs. Howe, er, Janet. This is my dad, Nick Baker." Abby shook her hand.

"Yes, your husband introduced us." She smiled at Abby's father. "I was just telling Mr. Baker that his wife," she looked at Abby, "your mother, arrived about a half hour ago from the hospital. She's settling into the room. Shall we go there now?"

She held her elbow out to Abby's father, who smiled as he put his hand in the crook of it. She led him toward the elevator. "Now, Mr. Baker, you are on the second floor, in room 201."

"201. Yes."

Abby was amazed at how her father was cooperating. No talk of going home or having Max here. Janet Howe had obviously charmed him.

"What did she say to him?" Abby asked Peter.

"Nothing really. Just welcomed him. I guess he likes her. He did nudge me and whisper that she smells good." He squeezed her hand. "Let's be thankful for small blessings."

The room was to the right off the elevator. Its door was ajar. When Janet Howe pushed it open, Abby heard her mother exclaim. "Nick!"

"Frieda?" her father responded, a look of confusion in his eyes. He walked over to her wheelchair. "Frieda, I thought you were gone." He touched her cheek and slowly bent down to kiss her.

Frieda grabbed his arm. "Nick, Nick. I'm not ready to leave you yet."

Abby's parents looked into each other's faces. Her mother's eyes were shiny with tears and she stroked her husband's hand. Abby raised her hands to her heart and sighed, smiling.

"Is Max here?" Her father pulled away from Frieda and looked around the room.

"Max is your cat?" Janet Howe asked. "We can't have pets living here, Mr. Baker, but I notice that there's a photograph of a cat on the dresser. Is that Max?"

"Yes." He picked up the photograph and rubbed his fingers over it. "My Max."

"Mom," Abby approached the wheelchair. "How'd your move go?"

"Fine. The driver of the van was a nice man. He did a good job helping me."

Abby swept her arm. "What do you think of the room?"

"It's big. Good for my wheelchair." She pointed to the beds. "Look what pretty quilts they put on the beds."

"Mom, those are your quilts. You made them. I brought them here from the house." How could her mother not recognize these quilts that had taken her months to make?

"I made them?" She sounded amazed.

"Yes, and they're beautiful. They do make your room look homey, don't they?"

A bewildered expression crossed her face. "Homey? Abby, I…"

"Yes, Mom?" Abby crouched down to her eye level.

Her mother looked around the room. "Nothing. Never mind."

Peter's hand lightly brushed Abby's neck as he bent down in front of the wheelchair. "Have you had a tour of this place yet, Frieda?"

She shook her head.

"Your mother arrived less than a half hour ago," Janet Howe said, "so we haven't had a chance to take her around. And we thought it would be better if your parents toured the facility together."

"We can take you around, Mom." Abby touched her mother's shoulder and walked to the back of her wheelchair. "Come with us, Dad?"

Mrs. Howe cleared her throat. "Abby and Peter, I think it would be better if you let me show your parents the facilities. Your choice of course, but in my experience it would be best if you go now."

Abby was surprised. "Go?"

"We find that the resident's initial adjustment is better when they're on their own. Just for the first few hours while we orient them and help them settle. You, of course, are welcome back any time after that. In fact, why don't you join us for dinner this evening?"

"I don't think I'm comfortable leaving them alone so soon without anyone familiar around." Abby felt her parents both staring at her.

"I understand. But it will make this transition easier for them." She gestured toward the door. "I can walk you out."

"But..."

"Abby," Peter touched her arm. "I think we should go."

"Really?"

Peter nodded.

"Okay." Abby leaned down to her mother and hugged her. "Mom, we'll come back later and have dinner with you."

"Abby," her mother clutched Abby's arm and whispered in her ear. "I don't want to stay here." She sounded frightened.

"I'm sorry, Mom," Abby whispered back, uneasiness spearing her heart.

"I know your father needs this, but I don't want this."

Abby swallowed. "None of us want this, Mom. But we don't have a lot of choices. Why don't you give it a chance and we'll see how it goes. Okay?" She kissed her on the cheek. "I love you." Then she rose and hugged her father. "Bye, Dad. Peter and I are going now."

"Huh? Okay, bye."

They were quiet on the elevator down to the first floor. As they exited, Janet Howe spoke in an encouraging tone. "They're confused and displaced right now but that's normal." Her high heels clicked on the floor. "In a few weeks they'll get used to the routine and be much better."

A few weeks? Her parents would be feeling unhappy, or as Janet Howe said, "confused and displaced" for that long? Abby glanced back at the elevator. Peter put his arm around her shoulders and propelled her forward.

Sunlight poured in through the glass of the main entry. Handprints smudged the doors near the handles. Janet Howe stopped and pushed one side open.

"I'll look forward to seeing you at dinner tonight. Why don't you come by around four thirty?" She shook their hands. "You know we'll be in touch regularly to let you know how they are. And don't hesitate to call us. Or them," she added. "Any time."

They stepped outside and the door closed behind them.

"That's that," Peter said. He took Abby's hand. "Not too hard, was it?"

How could he say that? It was one of the most difficult things she'd ever done. "I feel so guilty for shoving them in here."

"Geez, Abby, we're not shoving them in here. This is a good place, and it's the best solution for them. For all of us. You know that. There's no reason for you to feel guilty."

"I know. But guilt isn't always logical." She stared down at the path as she followed Peter to the car.

Chapter Ten

Abby awakened feeling as if she were on fire. Her night sweats and hot flashes came more frequently of late. *Hurray for menopause*, she thought as she pushed the covers off and stretched her arms and legs over the whole width of the bed. She looked at the clock. Three twenty-seven—only twenty minutes since the last time she checked. Sliding to Peter's side, she hugged his pillow. She wondered how he was doing in his hotel room in Houston, wondered if he was lying awake at three in the morning worrying about his interview. She hoped he wouldn't like the job. Texas was too far away. And hot. She tried to imagine living there. Would Peter start wearing a Stetson and a leather bolo around his neck? Would they have a view of oil wells and cattle from the kitchen window?

She sat up. Tossing and turning and sweating in bed weren't helping her sleep. Maybe a cup of tea would help. She put on her slippers. The quiet in the dark house felt like a blanket. She walked softly down the stairs.

This was becoming a habit of hers, wandering around in the silent early hours of the morning, worrying herself into a black hole. But one eventually becomes used to the darkness in a black hole and more able to see things clearly. When would she be able to see things more clearly?

She shook off her negativity. Being awake at this time gave her extra time to get things done. That was a better way to view her night ramblings.

In the kitchen she turned on the light above the stove, casting a dim glow over the counter. As she filled the kettle, she was startled by a brush of fur against her leg. A meow broke through the silence.

"Hi, Max." Abby turned the burner on under the kettle and bent down to pick him up. Before she could touch him, he shot off, disappearing into the dining room. Poor Max. He was having a tough time adjusting to his new home. She'd made an appointment with the vet for the next day to see what could be done for Max. He'd become incontinent. On the carpet. On the couch. How could they take a cat with this problem to Houston, or wherever they ended up living?

The whistling of the kettle pierced her thoughts and she poured the steaming water into her mug, sighing. She was so tired.

She dipped the tea bag in and out of the water, in and out. At least her father had stopped asking about Max. That was a good thing. In fact, he seemed to have adjusted to the routine at Chestnut Manor quite well, although his demeanour had become flat. His eyes were resigned, his responses dull. As if he'd given up. She missed her gruff old dad.

Her mother was still fighting the change, though. They'd been there for three weeks and she was still talking about moving back home, still acting as if she'd soon be walking and then she'd pack up and leave. Poor Mom. Neither her doctor nor her physiotherapist was hopeful she'd ever be able to walk again; her bones weren't healing the way they should.

Abby put the mug on the table and sat down. She stared at the blackness through the window. Sometimes it was so hard to find the energy to keep everything going. To keep everyone's spirits up. Especially hers. She felt like such a fake staying positive for her parents when she just wanted to scoop them out of that place and bring them home. And being supportive of Peter's job search when really she just wanted to stay put in the life they had here.

Then there was Ben. His weekend visit home hadn't materialized. He'd left a message on their voice mail a few days after he'd phoned them, at a time he knew no one would be home.

"Hey, Dad, Mom, sorry, but something's come up. I won't be able to come home this weekend after all." His digitalized voice sounded upbeat, not apologetic. "I'll call you as soon as I have another free weekend." He hadn't yet. Once again they were playing a one-sided communication game with Ben—phone, e-mail, instant message— and he would remain silent.

She picked up her mug and walked over to the desk. Lifting the lid of her laptop, she pushed the power button.

"Please let him be on and answer," she pleaded as she waited for it to boot up. She opened the instant messaging window. Ben was online.

Hey Ben. What are you doing awake so early in the morning? she typed, then hit enter and waited. Nothing. If he was at his computer, he surely must have heard the beep telling him there was a message.

I couldn't sleep. Dad's in Texas for a job interview. What's up with you? She hit enter again. Still nothing. Maybe Ben wasn't there and he'd just left his computer on. Maybe...Abby couldn't think of another maybe.

I miss hearing from you, Ben, and I'm worried about you. Please answer. She sat and waited another five minutes for Ben to reply and then shut down the computer.

****

Driving home from the vet, Abby's thoughts were a jumble of confusion. About a cat!

"He's eighteen years old," Dr. Smythe had said. "And he's reacting to a trauma in his life. He's been torn away from a home that's familiar to him and put in strange surroundings. You can't expect him to behave normally. Unfortunately, once cats begin this type of behaviour, they don't stop." Then he'd suggested that the only viable solution was to put Max to sleep.

She hadn't wanted Max in the first place; now here was an opportunity to duck out of the responsibility of caring for him. Yet it seemed like a cruel copout. Hanna would be horrified to hear she was even considering such a decision. Thank goodness Abby's father had forgotten about Max. She couldn't imagine what his reaction might be.

Max meowed in his carrier.

"Yes, Max, I wouldn't even be contemplating your demise if you'd behave yourself." She reached through the wire door of the carrier and scratched behind his ear. He meowed again. "I sure don't need your problems on top of mine."

The sight of Peter's car in the garage shifted her mood, and she found herself smiling as she stepped out of the car. She'd missed him, she realized, even though he'd only been gone one night.

"Hey," he said, standing up from the kitchen table where he'd been typing on his computer.

"Welcome home. How was Texas?"

He walked over to her and kissed her. "Hot. I wasn't impressed with the job, so it's a no-go as far as I'm concerned. But I have other good news."

"Yeah?"

"Remember that job in Richmond I was telling you about? With Asset Credit Union?"

"Richmond, Virginia?"

"Yes. I had a phone interview with them just before I flew home and it went great. They want me to fly down there next week." He smiled, his eyes sparkling. "This could be it, Abs. The job sounds good. The company is expanding internationally and they've created a new position that is totally suited to my skill set."

"That's exciting." She kissed his cheek. "Richmond, Virginia, huh? How far away is that?"

"About a thousand kilometers from here. MapQuest says it's an eleven-hour drive. Remember when we drove to Myrtle Beach a few years ago? Richmond is about two-thirds that distance."

"Hm. So we could drive home from there." She grinned. "You know what Richmond makes me think of? *The Waltons.* On TV."

"What?"

"I remember John Boy coming down from Walton's Mountain to Richmond to work on the newspaper or something."

He laughed. "You're kidding."

"That show gave me an impression of green loveliness about Richmond." She looked up at the ceiling, searching her memory. "Or maybe that was Walton's Mountain. Anyway, Virginia sounds kind of appealing to me. At least more than Texas."

"Well, I'll find out how lovely and green Richmond is next week."

A meow came from the cat carrier and she bent to open its door. "We have to talk about Max." The cat rubbed against her legs.

"What did the vet say?"

"That the stress of his relocation is what's causing him to mess around the house. And there's nothing we can do about it."

"Hm."

"He suggested we have him put down. Do you believe that?"

"Sure. Max is pretty old."

"But he's also pretty healthy except for his arthritis. How can we end his life just to convenience us?"

"Are you talking about killing Max?" Hanna stood at the kitchen door.

Peter turned to her. "Not killing, Hanna, euthanizing."

"It's the same thing." Hanna spit out the words.

"Hanna."

"Can't the vet do anything for him?" Her voice was pleading.

Abby explained what the vet had said. Hanna's eyes glistened.

"But that's just cruel. How can a vet be so callous about a cat's life?"

"Aw, sweetie." Abby hugged her. She swallowed and looked at Peter.

Peter cleared his throat. "Hanna," he said, "the vet isn't a bad guy. He's just thinking about what's best for everyone, even Max. Max isn't living a very happy life right now."

The cat sniffed around Hanna's feet and she picked him up.

Abby spoke up. "And in this case, Dr. Smythe saw it as the best solution. I mean, I was complaining about the messes in the house. And Max is an old cat."

"But we're not going to do it are we? Pops will be devastated." Hanna pressed Max close to her and snuggled her face into his neck. Max squirmed, jumped out of her arms and ran out of the kitchen.

Abby was just about to say that Pops wouldn't even know what they were talking about when Peter put his arm around Hanna's shoulders and said, "Are you willing to clean up all his messes?"

Hanna wrinkled her nose.

He continued, "We also have to remember it's very likely that your mother and I will be moving. Should Max have to face the trauma of another move? That might be a crueler thing to do to him. You know Pops can't take him back, so where else would he go?"

"It sucks. Life sucks. Everybody's leaving me." Hanna's face flushed, and a tear trickled down one cheek.

"I know this is a tough time, Hanna." Peter rubbed her back. He bent his head to peer in her eyes. "But we love you."

"I know." Hanna pushed him away. She wiped her eyes and sniffed loudly. "Maybe Ben could take Max. That house already stinks."

Abby stroked the tear drying on Hanna's cheek. "I guess we can keep Max in the basement while we figure out what to do. At least his messes will be contained."

"Okay. We can bring his food and water dish down. And he can visit with us upstairs when we're there to keep an eye on him." Hanna looked at Abby. "Right?"

Abby nodded.

"I'll go find him." Hanna left the kitchen calling for Max.

Abby stared after her. "I guess we'll have to become the voice of doom for Max before everything is settled. That won't be easy."

"I know," Peter said. "I'll take him to get it done if you'd like."

"We'll figure it out when the time comes. For now you need to focus on your interview in Richmond."

Abby was uncertain what to hope for. Of course she wanted Peter to get a job that appealed to him. That was the most important thing. Richmond, Virginia. She liked the sound of the name. And it was south so it was bound to have a warmer climate. But a thousand kilometers away. Still, it was the closest location so far that was a real possibility. And it was driveable, close enough to come home if the kids or her parents needed her.

Different enough to feel exotic. Maybe she should wish for this to be the one.

She touched his arm. "If it's the job you want then you need to make sure you get it."

He pulled her to him and enveloped her in his arms. This, she thought. This is all that matters. To be with Peter. No matter where.

Chapter Eleven

When she arrived in the room, her father was sitting on the bed, staring at his shoes. Her mother sat at the little table in the corner with a pencil in her hand, a newspaper open in front of her.

"Hi, Mom and Dad." The door was ajar and had opened with her knock. "Look, I brought you a plant." She walked in and put the pot with yellow gerberas on the table.

"Abby." Her mother put her right hand on the wheel of her chair but couldn't seem to turn it. Her left arm lay unmoving on her lap.

Abby walked over to her and bent down. "How are you doing, Mom?" She kissed her cheek.

"Not so good, Abby. Not so good." Her eyes filled with tears. "I'm trying to do this jumble but I can't get the words."

Abby looked at the newspaper page her mother pointed to. Letters were penciled all over it. "Let me say hi to Dad and then I'll help you with it, okay?" She walked over to her father and touched his shoulder. "Hey, Dad."

He looked up. "Huh?"

"It's me, Abby. Your daughter."

"Oh." He pushed himself up. "Welcome. Would you like to take a seat?"

"I'm going to help Mom with her jumble. Want to sit with us?"

"Okay."

Abby moved her mother's wheelchair over to make room, then she and her father each took one of the two chairs at the table. Abby pulled the newspaper over.

"Let's see, m-i-a-n-l-a. Can I have your pencil, Mom?"

Almost immediately, Abby figured out that the word was animal. When she spelled out the letters of the next word, her mother lost interest. Instead she stroked Abby's arm. "It's so good to see you, Abby. Thank you for the nice flowers." She picked up the pot and buried her nose into a yellow bloom. Putting it back on the table, she said, "Did you go to our house?"

"No, not yet. I usually check on it after I visit here." Abby wanted to discuss selling the house and wondered when would be a good time. "Hey," she tried to sound enthusiastic. "Do you guys want to go for a drive? I can take you to the park. Or a store."

Her father looked panic-stricken. "No. I want to stay here."

"I want to go," her mother said. "But I don't like going in the car. It's too hard to get out of my wheel-chair."

"We'll just go for a walk, then. Dad, you can come for a walk with us, can't you? Around the garden? I'll stay right with you."

She went behind her mother's wheelchair and clicked off the brakes with her foot. "Come on, Dad."

He stayed in his chair and didn't look up. Why was he so lethargic? Was it his medication?

"Dad?" She walked over to him and took hold of his elbow. "Come on. Take my arm."

She maneuvered the wheelchair through the door. Placing her father's hand on one of the handles, she put her hand over his.

"You are a very nice girl," he said, as they walked to the elevator.

"Why, thank you, Dad."

Her mother turned her head back to look at her. "I don't think he knows who you are, Abby."

"Sure he does, don't you, Dad? I'm your daughter."

He nodded. "Yeah, you're a daughter."

Perhaps her mother was right.

In the foyer, they passed the row of people sitting along the wall. Every week Abby saw them and she'd dubbed them "the waiters." She smiled as they went by.

"Wouldn't you like to sit down here sometime, Mom?"

"No. I don't know why all these old people sit here by the door." She shook her head. "Sometimes I ask them but they don't tell me."

They walked along the asphalt paths under trees and through colorful gardens, stopping at the pond. Ducks swam on the water and two of them were quacking on the shore. A large gazebo with benches set in a circle was nestled among willow trees. Surprisingly on this sunny morning, there was no one in it. Perhaps it was too early in the day. Abby pushed the wheelchair up the short ramp. "Let's sit in here for a while."

Her father, who had let go of the chair handle, stood at the bottom of the ramp. He was looking at the ducks.

"Dad?"

He didn't answer. Abby put the brakes on her mother's chair and walked back down the ramp. "Want to sit in the gazebo with us?"

"No. I want to look at those, those, cackers."

"You mean the ducks?"

"Yeah, the ducks."

"Okay. Mom and I will be right here." Too bad they hadn't thought to bring bread so her father could feed the birds. She sat down beside her mother, watching her father as he tentatively ambled toward the pond.

"So how are things going, Mom?"

"Abby, I'm not good. Your father is so..." She stopped midsentence, looking at Abby with watery eyes.

"I know, Mom. He's going downhill fast. I wish we could do more for him."

Her mother took a tissue from her sleeve and wiped her eyes under her glasses. "And I'm not good. I forget things and get confused. And I have so much pain."

"Don't they give you pills for that, Mom?" She would check with the doctor. Maybe they needed to increase her mother's dosage.

"It doesn't help. The pills make me sleepy and mixed up." She looked forlornly at Abby. "Why is this happening to me?"

"I don't know, Mom. Sometimes bad things just happen." Really, there was no point in asking that question. Life didn't offer up reasons for sending you on detours. Look at her own situation. Why did Peter have to lose his job? Why was Ben such a worry? Why was she losing control of things? She looked over at her father. Talk about losing control. Her mom and dad growing old this way was awful and she couldn't do a thing to change it. "We have to take what life throws at us and do the best we can," she said.

"Sometimes I wish I was dead."

"Mom!" Abby recoiled from the thought. How could her mother think that? What would Abby do without her mother?

"But then who would take care of your father?"

"Mom, don't talk like that. And it's not only Dad who needs you. I do too. Think of how sad Hanna and Ben would be without you. We all still need you."

"Can you take us home with you? I miss you so much."

Abby shook her head and turned to look at her mother. "You know that wouldn't work, Mom. I can't take care of Dad and you the way you need it. The people here are nice, aren't they?"

"Yeah, nice." Her tone was sarcastic. She shook her head. "They aren't my family, Abby."

"I know." Her mom was still able to fuel her guilt. Yet Abby felt guilty even without her mother stoking it. She often asked herself how she could relegate the care of her parents to strangers when she was a healthy woman capable of doing so. They were her parents after all. She was shirking her duty. When her mother talked like this, she felt it even more.

"Maybe I could bring you home with me to visit for a few days."

"Really?" Her mother's face brightened. "And we could stay there?"

"For a few days. Then I'd have to bring you back here."

The light that had brightened her mother's eyes dimmed and she looked away. "I don't want to go away if I have to come back."

Abby sighed. Time to change the subject. "Hanna got a job as a lifeguard this summer, Mom. And she's teaching swimming lessons, too."

"That's nice. Hanna's such a nice girl. How's Ben?"

"Ben's fine, Mom. Still living in Toronto." *Doing who knows what.*

"Why is he living there?" Abby's mother asked this every week. She must sense that something was not quite right with Ben.

"You know why. He's got a job there." Abby didn't want to discuss Ben with her mother. She wouldn't understand. Even Abby didn't understand. "Peter's away on a trip right now, Mom, so Hanna and I are alone for a few days."

"What for? Where?"

"He's in Richmond, Virginia. For work." She should tell her about Peter losing his job. Abby had skirted around this news every time she visited her parents but hadn't yet told them. She wanted to wait until everything was settled and they knew exactly how things were going to change.

"Abby," her father called and waved his hands over the ducks. "These, these..." He sighed in exasperation. "They are funny."

"Are they?" She glanced up at her father standing beside the pond, several ducks surrounding his feet. "They are cute. Shall we try to find something to feed them?"

He shook his head and flapped his arms at the birds. Some flew away; others waddled quickly to the water.

"Look at Dad, Mom," Abby said, smiling. Her father, in his gangly way, began to chase the ducks then followed them into the water. She jumped up and ran towards him.

"Dad!" Stopping at the water's edge, she reached her arm out. Her father, walking in water up to his pant cuffs, turned around.

"It's wak...wer...wat...ah," he shook his head.

"Water. And it's wet," Abby said. "Come on, Dad."

He plodded toward Abby. She took his hand and pulled him out of the pond.

"Look, your shoes are soaked. Let's go in and change them, okay?"

"Okay."

"Then we can go to the café and get a cup of coffee." Hand in hand, they walked to the gazebo. "You want some coffee, Mom?"

"Coffee? I don't drink coffee anymore, Abby. Only tea."

"Sure, Mom, anything you want."

After tea, they went to the craft room where she and her mother painted with watercolors together and her father sat and stared at coloured pegs and boards. Abby ate lunch with her parents in a dining room filled with white-haired people slurping soup, chewing with open mouths, and crumbling food into their laps. When she left her mom and dad in the afternoon, they were in their room looking almost the same as when she arrived. Her father was sitting on the bed staring at his slippers. Her mother was at the table with a magazine in front of her. Abby said good-bye at their door and her mother waved, teary-eyed. This wasn't any way to live out their days, Abby thought in the quiet cube of the elevator. Sounding like Hanna, she told the universe it just wasn't fair.

****

Abby finished slicing the last of the biscotti and stood the cookies up on the cookie sheet. Carefully she carried it over to the oven. The phone rang, startling her, and three of the cookies fell over. Damn. She righted them and slowly put the cookie sheet in the oven.

"Hey, babe." Peter sounded happy. "Watcha doing?

"I've just put biscotti in the oven for book club to-night. How's Richmond?"

"Richmond's good. It's very warm. What kind of biscotti?"

Why was he asking about the cookies? She wanted to know about Richmond. "Almond apricot. Tell me about you. How'd the interviews go?"

"They went really well. This is a fantastic job, Abby. The people at Asset are great." His enthusiasm bubbled through the receiver. "They've essentially offered me the position, although we still have to negotiate a few things. I won't decide, though, until you have a chance to come here. See if you like Richmond."

Her mind darted. Even though Peter said he hadn't, his tone of voice told her he'd decided. A wave of apprehension washed over her, then anger. But why? There was no reason to feel angry with Peter. Her heart thudded in her ears. She was afraid to speak. Her silence hung over the phone.

After a minute Peter said quietly, "Of course, if you hate it, I'll keep looking." Then his voice perked up. "But I know you'll like it here. The weather is great and I've liked everything I've seen so far. There are awesome neighbourhoods, great houses. And," his voice softened, "it's very lovely and green."

His reference to Abby's own words mollified her, and a spark of anticipation unexpectedly lit her spirit. "Yeah? Tell me all about it."

"Why don't I wait until I'm home tomorrow. Then I'll tell you everything you want to know. Right now I've gotta run. They're taking me out for drinks in a few minutes. I just wanted to call to hear your voice. And tell you that this job is it. It's exciting, eh?"

"It is." She thought about her visit to Chestnut Manor that morning. "Peter?"

"Yes, babe."

"Do you think we could find a nursing home in Richmond for my parents? It would be so good if they could be close."

"That's not gonna happen, Abs. The whole issue of medical insurance is a biggy in the States. There's no OHIP here and it would cost us a fortune to cover them at their age with their health issues."

"Oh. Just thought I'd ask." Suddenly she felt bad for her earlier lack of enthusiasm. "I'm glad the interviews went so well," she added. "See you tomorrow. You'll be home in time for supper, right?"

****

She closed the door behind her friends, leaning her back against it. As usual, she'd had fun with her book club. The book choice, *Belonging* by Isabel Huggan, had provoked an interesting discussion. And it was an apt selection for Abby's situation; a story of relocating and a contemplation of home. But the group focused on the book for less than thirty minutes before veering off on a discussion of how it related to their own lives. Then, of course, the topic of Abby and Peter's inevitable move arose. Everyone was sympathetic about Peter's job loss, but each had differing opinions as to how he should approach the next step.

"I'm surprised he's looking outside of Ontario," Lynn had said. "I know if Mike lost his job, he would do anything so we could stay here."

"It's not that easy," Diana defended Peter. "If there isn't a job here, he doesn't have a lot of choices. Not everyone has the resources to start a business out of the blue."

"I think this will be a good thing for you guys," Gerty interjected, munching on a biscotti. "It's an exciting change for you. I insist on viewing it as positive. And you should too, Abby."

"But what about the kids?" Lynn protested.

"They'll be fine." Sharon said. Her three oldest had been out of the house for a few years and her youngest was off to university in the fall. "Hanna is moving out in September, anyway." She turned to Abby. "And you know they can call us any time."

"For anything," Gerty added. "We'll be their surrogate parents in Waterloo."

"Thanks, Sharon, Gerty. I really appreciate that," Abby said. "But I worry about taking away their home, their anchor."

"Pshaw." Sharon was always practical. "It's not like you're dying. You're still their parents and wherever you end up living will be their home too."

Abby wondered if that was true.

"But we'll sure miss you," Lynn said.

"We will." Diana put her arm around Abby's shoulders. "You have to continue to read along with the book club every month and definitely come back for our annual cottage weekend. You're still one of us, no matter where you live."

Abby smiled as she thought about her friends. She'd known them forever it seemed. They were like her family. She would miss them. Her smile faded. She pushed herself away from the door and began picking up wine glasses from the coffee table in the living room.

"Mom, guess what." Hanna shot down the stairs. "Jason is going to Windsor. How can he do that to me?"

"What do you mean?" Abby put down the glasses.

"Remember he was accepted at WLU? We were going to try to get in the same residence and everything. Now he gets this scholarship from Windsor and he's going there instead. Who goes to Windsor?" She plunked herself down on the couch. "How can he leave me like that?"

"Oh, Hanna." Abby sat down beside her. This was not necessarily a bad thing. Hanna and Jason were too young to be so serious anyway. "He's not doing this to you. He's taking advantage of the best opportunity offered to him."

"But what about me?"

"I'm sure you're still important to him. Did you talk about staying together long distance?"

"Well, yeah, but it won't be the same."

Abby knew that. It might even mean the end of it. She'd seen it happen often enough in her years of teaching university freshmen. They'd be at a different school from their boyfriend or girlfriend, in a different city, meeting new people, living a new life. When they went home on the long weekend at Thanksgiving, they'd break up. The "turkey dump," the students called it. Still, she wasn't going to tell Hanna about that. "Of course it won't be the same. But if the two of you want to stay together, I'm sure you'll figure out how to make it happen."

"Hmph. Do you believe it? First Dad loses his job, then Grandma breaks a bunch of bones and Pops start losing his mind, and Ben goes AWOL…"

Abby's heart did a double beat at the mention of Ben. "Hanna…"

"Then Max gets a death sentence, and now Jason decides to move hundreds of miles away. It's not fair. My life is falling apart."

"Your life is not falling apart." She knew what Hanna felt like, though. "In September you'll be turning a whole new page. Think of how excited you are about studying music at university. You'll have a great time in residence. Emily will be your roommate. And you'll meet all sorts of new friends too."

"I guess. But what about my friends who are going out of town? What about my family? And Jason?"

"Sweetie, you'll still keep your friends, the ones that matter anyway. And you know Dad and I will always be here for you. No matter what." Abby felt as if she was saying these words of encouragement to herself.

"How can you be here for me if you live somewhere else?" Hanna crossed her arms.

"I meant that you'll be able to call on us and we'll come running whenever you need us. We won't abandon our special girl." Abby wrapped Hanna in her arms and kissed the top of her head. "Come on. Help me clear up and I'll make you some hot chocolate to go with one of these biscotti."

****

Later, while she stood in her nightgown brushing her teeth, Abby looked in the mirror and saw the same expression of anxiety in her eyes that she'd seen in Hanna's. Poor Hanna. Abby didn't know what she could say that would ease the distress her daughter was feeling. How could she? She couldn't remove it from her own heart.

She spit in the sink and rinsed her toothbrush. She thought of Peter, having drinks with his new co-workers. Tomorrow he'd be home from Richmond and they'd start making plans. She knew they'd end up moving there. She couldn't imagine what she would see there that could make her say no to it, especially when Peter had such positive feelings about the job.

She put away her toothbrush and turned out the bathroom light. Crawling into bed, she wondered what it would be like to live in Richmond. She wondered what the people were like there, and if they all spoke with a southern accent. Were they racist? She'd heard things about the southern states, not all of it good. Maybe rednecks lived in Richmond. Maybe everyone owned a gun. She thought of an article she'd read about crime rates in the States where Richmond was cited as having one of the highest. That was scary. But with Peter being so positive about it, there must be good things too. Surely they'd be able to make friends. Peter said he liked the people at Asset. And with the warmer climate, she could have an amazing garden. She'd liked the houses she'd seen on the real estate Web sites this afternoon. But they didn't show anything about the communities. What would she do in Richmond, without her job, without her kids? She really didn't know much about the city. Tomorrow she'd Google it. Imagine. She was going to live in Virginia. How strange that would be. She turned off her light, wondering if she'd be able to sleep.

Chapter Twelve

"Want some help marking, Mom?" Hanna slid open the patio door, carrying two glasses of iced tea.

"Is that really what you want to spend your time doing on this beautiful afternoon?"

"Yup. All my friends are busy." Hanna sat down and picked up one of several red pens that were in Abby's open briefcase. "Besides, you know how I like marking."

"You're a strange girl, Hanna," Abby laughed. "But I'd appreciate the help. You can do the multiple choice questions."

She handed Hanna the answer key and sat back, taking a sip of her drink and looked around the garden. Through the maple tree the sun cast dappled shadows on the last few lilac flowers left on the bush. The peonies were ready to burst, ants busily crawling around the balls of the buds. From where she sat, Abby couldn't really distinguish the ants; the peony buds just looked like globes in motion. On the trellis, she saw hundreds of pale purple buds on the clematis. It would be stunning again this year. Max, sunning himself on the edge of the patio, stood and stretched, arching his back, and yawned. He sat down and eyed Hanna.

Abby put her glass down, the ice cubes clinking.

"Apparently they drink lots of iced tea in the south so I'd better get used to it," she said.

"Do you think you'll really move to Richmond, Mom?"

"I do, sweetie. Dad seemed pretty certain about getting the job." She sat forward and picked up her pen.

"For me, the best part is that it's close enough to drive here. So I'll be able to see you lots."

"It's a thousand kilometers away, Mom. Do you honestly believe you're going to do that very often?" Hanna stared disbelieving at her mother.

"Yes, as often as you need me to." Also, she thought, as often as I need me to.

They worked quietly for a while, each focusing on the papers in front of them. When Abby finished, she looked at her watch. "Dad should be home soon. His plane landed over an hour ago." She went to the hanging baskets and started deadheading the fuchsias.

"Can we eat dinner out here? I want to stay in the sun as much as possible to get my hair blonde."

Abby laughed, remembering how often she'd stayed in the sun for the same reason. Still did. "Do you want some lemon juice to spray on it? That's what I used to do." She ran her fingers through her darkening hair. Maybe she should start doing it again. "And yes, we can eat out here. I'm barbecuing anyway."

"What will we be barbecuing?" Peter's voice caused them both to turn to the door.

"Dad!" Hanna jumped up and hugged him. "Welcome home."

"I see my girls are working hard."

Abby put the pile of brown blossoms on the table. "Yes, my assistant and I have been getting these exams marked. But I think we've done enough for today." She kissed Peter and pulled him to a chair. "Sit down and tell us all about Richmond."

Peter smiled at Abby, his face expressing...what? Excitement? Anticipation?

"I didn't see anything in Richmond that would cause me to say no to this, Abby. I think you'll like it there."

"You do? What did you see that makes you say yes?"

"Yeah, Dad, what's Richmond like? Will I like it?"

Peter talked about the weather, about how the sun shone the whole time he was there, and how hot it was. He described the trees, how they were everywhere, and how tall they were, and the beautiful gardens he'd driven past, the pink and white trees that were in bloom.

"I don't know what kind they are, but they're gorgeous."

He told them that the old part of downtown had cobblestone streets and interesting shops and restaurants. That Richmond is right on the James River, its rapids running through the city. He described neighbourhoods he'd driven through.

"I don't think we'll have any trouble finding a house we like. And you two will love all the stores. Furthermore," he said, starting to sound a little like a tour guide, "Richmond is an hour away from the mountains, an hour and a half from the ocean, and two hours from Washington DC. It's a great location."

Abby had to agree; it sounded like a wonderful place to live. "So what's happening with the details then? Have you accepted the job?"

"Not officially. I want you to go there with me first. I was thinking we could go next week. If you can cancel your classes next Friday, then we could leave after your last class on Wednesday, drive down, and come back on Sunday. I've tentatively arranged to meet with them on that Friday."

"You wouldn't fly?" Hanna asked.

"Not this time. I think it would be good for us to get a feel for how the drive would go."

Abby smiled, feeling excited. A road trip to Richmond. Moving there. It might be an adventure. "I think I could arrange to cancel Friday's classes. How about you, Hanna?"

"I can't go, Mom. I have to work, and then on the weekend is our camping trip, remember?"

Yes, Abby remembered the camping trip. She wasn't thrilled with the idea of Hanna and Jason, with Emily and her boyfriend and a third couple, going camping on their own. But she and Peter had reluctantly agreed. After all, they were going to university in the fall.

"I think it's better that just your mother and I go, anyway, Hanna. At least this time."

Abby started gathering papers and putting them into her briefcase. She needed to process what she had just heard. "Peter, could you light the barbecue? I'm getting hungry."

As she slid the patio door open, the doorbell rang. Hanna ran past her to answer it. Abby wondered who would be coming by around suppertime and looked questioningly at Peter. He shrugged.

"Mom. Dad. It's Ben."

They hurried into the house. Hanna stood to one side holding the door open.

"Just come in, Ben," she said and then looked at Abby wide-eyed.

Ben stood on the porch, a gym bag slung over his shoulder. His face was pale, with deep shadows under his eyes.

"Ben." Abby embraced him. "Come in the house. You don't have to ring the doorbell."

He hesitated. "When you hear what I have to tell you, you may not want me to come in."

"Why? What are you talking about?"

"Nonsense," Peter put his arm around Ben's shoulders. "We're your family. This is your home. Just come in."

Abby stepped back, and together Peter and Ben came inside. She closed the door with shaking hands. Fear roiled in her gut. What could Ben possibly have to tell them that would make him think they wouldn't want him to come in?

"Dad's right, Ben. This is your home. We love you." She touched his arm. "What do you need to tell us?"

Ben's face flushed. "Mom, Dad, I really screwed up." He inhaled a trembling breath.

"Ben," Peter moved the strap of Ben's gym bag off his shoulder and lowered it to the ground. "Let's go into the living room."

Abby touched Hanna's arm and nodded her head in the direction of upstairs. Hanna opened her mouth to protest, but Abby shot her a look that stopped any sound. Hanna started up the steps.

Ben sat on the couch, his elbows on his knees, head in his hands. He swayed back and forth, making quiet weeping sounds. Peter sat beside him, rubbing Ben's back, and he looked at Abby as she lowered herself into a chair, raising his eyebrows questioningly. She shrugged and shook her head.

"Ben," she leaned forward and touched his knee. "What's wrong?"

"I'm such a screw-up." He spoke into his hands. It was difficult to hear his muffled voice. "I don't know how to tell you."

Peter spoke up. "The best way is to just get it out, Ben."

Ben sat back and sniffed loudly. "Right."

Hanna came through the door and handed him a box of tissues.

"Hanna," Abby started, but Ben interrupted.

"I don't care if she stays."

Hanna sat down on the armrest of Abby's chair, leaning in slightly. The light pressure against Abby's shoulder comforted her. Ben pulled a tissue from the box and blew his nose. He lowered his head and stared at his hands clenched together in his lap. Taking a deep breath, he began to talk.

"I never had a job at Starbucks. I lied about it because if you knew the truth, you wouldn't let me move to Toronto."

It was just as Abby suspected. She felt no satisfaction knowing she'd been right and hearing Ben say it shocked her nonetheless. She wondered how he'd paid his rent and was almost afraid to find out.

"I went to Toronto with Wes because we were both kicked out of school after we stopped going to class and flunked out. We played online poker instead."

"What?" The word shot out of Abby's mouth. Peter shook his head at her.

"I was really good at it, Mom." Ben briefly lifted his eyes to hers then lowered them again. "Wes and I both were. We played all the time. We won lots of money too. First it was just hundreds, and then I won, like, over a thousand dollars one night."

"A thousand dollars on a poker game? On the computer? Where on earth did you get the money to put up the ante?" Peter's raised voice shattered Ben's quiet narrative.

This time Abby caught Peter's eye and she shook her head at him. Peter lowered his voice. "Go on, Ben."

Ben still did not look up. "I got three different credit cards. They're easy to get when you're a student. They each had a credit limit of five hundred, but I managed to raise them to fifteen hundred dollars." He raised his head. "But that wasn't 'til later. After I moved to Toronto. Before that I just kept winning, so my poker account always had enough."

"Wow," Abby heard Hanna whisper to herself. Abby nudged her. She was beginning to feel a little sick.

"So what you're telling us," Peter said in a disbelieving tone, "is that you moved to Toronto intending to support yourself with your poker winnings?"

"Yeah. I mean, look at those guys on TV." Ben's eyes brightened. "They make millions. I could become a professional poker player if I wanted to."

"So what happened to this new career?" Abby could not keep the cynicism out of her response to Ben's statement. How could he believe he'd made a good choice?

The glimmer in Ben's eyes faded and he sat back, sighing loudly. "After we moved to Toronto, I started losing. Even though I played all the time, all day, all night. That's when I had to up the limits on my credit cards. I maxed them out. Borrowed money from my friends. I kept trying to win back what I lost, but I was losing more instead." A tear flowed out of one eye, trickling down his nose. He wiped it away. "I had to pay my rent. I had to buy food. I had no more money." His voice began to tremble. He took some deep breaths, trying to regain control.

Abby whispered to Hanna to get Ben a drink. Hanna snuck off to the kitchen, returning with a glass of water that she handed to Ben. He took it with a shaking hand.

"The guys in the house were great. They kept helping me out, lending me money. But then they stopped. I needed too much. Wes went home two weeks ago. He didn't want to get into any more debt. But I kept thinking I'd win and pay it all off and start making money again." He looked up at Peter. "It never happened, Dad. I totally messed up. I didn't even like playing any more and wasn't playing the cards or the people. I was just trying to win my money back." He looked back down at his hands. They were shredding the tissue. "I came home..." Ben stopped and inhaled deeply, his breath quivering. "I came home because I don't have enough money in my account to cover the debit charges that are coming off tomorrow. I need your help. Please?"

"Okay." Peter had his arm around Ben's shoulder. "Okay."

Abby was relieved that it was Peter sitting beside him. She was working hard to control her own emotions, and if she had to comfort Ben at this moment, she might break down herself.

"I'm so sorry," Ben's voice was muffled.

They all sat silent in the room, Ben's story hovering over them. Abby looked at Peter, her eyes holding his. She knew what he was thinking, because she had the same thoughts and questions. How should they respond? Yell? Sympathize? Lecture? Abby felt like strangling Ben. But she was also very sad. And disappointed. Betrayed. She plucked at her skirt. If they reacted the wrong way, would they push him away?

Hanna stood up. "It's amazing that you got so good at poker, Ben, but how could you think you would play it for a career?" Outrage flushed her cheeks. "And how could you lie to us? And go AWOL on us? Don't you know that you scared us?" She walked to an empty chair and threw herself down on it. "You acted like a shit."

Abby, frozen in her seat, stared at Hanna, speechless.

Peter brought the tissue box to Hanna. "You did scare us, Ben. We never heard from you. We didn't know what you were doing. You lost more than poker games and money in these months, Ben. You've lost the trust and respect of your family." Peter looked at Abby, as if for confirmation.

Abby nodded. How horrible to think she had lost respect for her son. "Dad's right. You betrayed us by living a lie and leading us to believe things about you that weren't true. You hurt us." Her voice was shaking. She swallowed the lump that was wedged in her throat. "You left us hanging. We felt like we lost you. We were worried sick."

"I know. And I'm sorry." He rubbed his chin on his shoulder. "Please, will you help me get out of this mess?"

"How much are you in debt for?" Peter asked, always the practical one.

"Six thousand, five hundred, and twenty-eight dollars." Ben said the numbers slowly. "And two months' rent. I don't remember the exact amount of interest on my credit cards." He sunk lower into the couch. "I had to beg for money on the street to buy the bus ticket to get here." He shook his head and said in a quieter voice, as if to himself, "I never want to do that again."

Abby was stunned, picturing him among the riffraff she'd seen on Queen Street near his house. "I think you have a bigger problem, Ben," she said. "A gambling problem. Do you realize that?" She knew money wouldn't fix the whole mess that Ben was in. "Will you agree to get help for that too?"

"I need help for everything."

Poor Ben. Beneath her anger and disappointment, Abby was relieved he was reaching out to them. "It took courage for you to come home and ask for help." She put her hand on Ben's knee.

"He had no choice," Hanna spoke angrily under her breath, but loud enough for them to hear. "Where else would he go?"

"That's true," Peter said, picking up Ben's glass and the tissue box. "But coming here can't have been easy for him. Dry your tears, Ben. Let's figure out a plan to help you get your life back on track."

Chapter Thirteen

I am a failure as a mother. This was the thought to which Abby awakened each morning since Ben had come home. Her son was a liar and a gambler. Somewhere in all those years of mothering him, of loving him, guiding him, teaching him, she'd slipped up, causing him to muddle his life. She tried to believe otherwise. She knew that children living away from home behaved in ways that had little to do with family, that they made decisions not necessarily influenced by their parents. Still, she must be to blame for Ben's lack of judgment.

She couldn't stop herself from searching through the memories of Ben's younger years to figure out what she should have done differently. Had she devoted too much time to herself, to her career? Had she not given enough attention to Ben as a baby? Or too much? Had she enrolled him in preschool too soon? Should she not have been so competitive when the family played euchre, not offered prizes for winning at bingo games? Did encouraging him to be creative contribute to his ability to lie? Should she have been more strict? Less strict? Had she not shown him enough what it meant to be a good citizen? Hadn't she taught him the right values? What, what, what would have made things different?

Peter was practical about it. "Ben did what he did," he said. "Let's close that chapter and move on. We need to focus on where Ben should go from here."

Abby didn't disagree, but she also couldn't let go of the betrayal she felt, the disappointment and feelings of failure that seemed to infiltrate her sense of herself. She didn't understand how Peter could be so blasé about it, so matter-of-fact. Didn't he feel any responsibility for Ben's failure?

She found it difficult to drag herself out of bed each morning with that mountain of despair on her shoulders. She'd lay awake, telling herself she should go walking with Diana. But she couldn't bring herself to face Diana's kind words of advice; words offered in comfort and support.

"You are a good mother, Abby," Diana had told her, contradicting Abby's self-recriminations. "You gave Ben a solid foundation. You taught him right from wrong. You loved him. What he did was his choice. It's not your fault." But these words, however kind, only brought on her tears. Abby simply needed to think her thoughts alone.

And so she lay in bed this morning, just like the past three mornings, watching the room get lighter. Peter getting out of bed prompted her to sit up and she tried to shake off her malaise. She looked at the clock, not registering the time. What day was it? Did she have to work today?

"Is everything set for us to leave tomorrow?" Peter's voice was a counterpoint to the running water. So it was Tuesday. She stood up and walked into the bathroom. He was covering his stubble with shaving cream.

"I guess so." She considered how Ben had complicated their plans. "Are you sure we should go this week? Leave Ben?"

"We've gone over this, Abby." He looked at her, shaving cream framing his lips. "He'll be fine. We have to take this trip to Richmond. Those meetings are set up for Friday to negotiate the final details of the offer."

She was amazed at how Peter jumped into high gear after Ben's revelations. She was relieved, too, that he'd taken charge, because her shock at Ben's admissions had made her ineffective. By Monday afternoon Peter had concocted a plan for rerouting Ben's life. Ben quietly agreed to everything Peter put in place for him.

He set up an appointment for Ben with a therapist who specialized in gambling and young adults. He arranged for an I.T. guy at work to install Web site blockers to gambling sites on all their computers. He set up job contacts for Ben, insisting that Ben follow through with calls. And he arranged friends to be available as backups so that he and Abby could drive to Richmond on Wednesday without any worries.

So why was she still worried?

"I know. It's just that..." She simply wanted to be home with Ben, even while she needed to be away from him. She wanted to hold him close. And she wanted to shake him.

"Abby," Peter put his hands on her shoulders, "as much as we want to fix his life, he really has to do it himself. Us being away this week might be a good test for him. He's going to have to be on his own when we move anyway." He kissed her nose and turned back to the mirror. "We have to direct our life forward as much as Ben does."

She caught Peter's gaze in the mirror. "I know you're right. It's just that the timing sucks."

Now she was talking like her kids. The aroma of shaving cream wafted into her nostrils and she stared at their comical reflection; Peter naked with a foamy beard, she in her nightie with hair tousled from the night, having a serious discussion by the bathroom sink. She wiped at the dab of shaving cream on her nose and looked at it cross-eyed, making a face for Peter. He smiled at her.

"Yeah, the timing sucks." Peter shook his head. "God, I hate that word." He held his razor under the running water. "But it'll be an adventure, Abs. Finding a new house, making a new life. Just the two of us. The kids will be fine, you know. Ben will right himself and Hanna's starting university. We all have to move on."

"I know it'll be exciting." Abby did believe that. "But it's also scary. How can we think about living so far away from the kids? They still need us so much."

"Well, they'll just have to assume responsibility for themselves sooner than they expected. You know if there was an alternative to moving, we'd jump at it."

"I know." She slipped her nightgown over her head and headed for the shower.

****

When Peter left for work and Hanna went to her job at the pool, Abby picked up the list she'd written the night before. Call Mom and Dad. Stock the fridge. Pack. Get American money. Passports. Gas in car. It was just past nine. She wondered how long Ben would sleep if she didn't wake him. On his first morning home, he'd gotten out of bed at noon. Sheepishly he had come downstairs and apologized, then the following two mornings he was showered and dressed by ten. She decided to leave him be and hoped he'd get up at a decent time on his own.

She picked up the phone and dialed her parent's number. It rang. And rang. After the sixth ring, just as she was about to return the receiver to its cradle, her mother answered.

"Hello?" Her voice was small and uncertain.

"Hi, Mom, it's Abby."

"Oh, hi." She perked up. "Are you coming today?"

"No, Mom, it's only Tuesday. I usually come on Thursdays, remember?"

"Oh, yes." She sounded defeated.

"But, Mom? I'm calling to tell you that I won't be coming this week. Peter and I have to go away for a few days and we won't be home until Sunday."

"Not coming? But it's been such a long time since you were here."

"That's not true, Mom." Abby had been noticing her mother's sense of time was becoming skewed. "I was just there on Thursday. Four days ago."

"That is a long time."

Abby sighed. Probably for her mom it was. "Well, I'm sorry, but I can't come this week. I will definitely come next week. On Tuesday instead of Thursday. That's a week from today. Okay?" If her mother was confused earlier, this switching of days would confuse her even more. Abby resigned herself to the idea it might be hopeless trying to help her keep things straight.

"I guess so."

"How's Dad?"

"The same. He's always the same."

Abby didn't really want to get into a discussion about her father, knowing the conversation would move into a downward spiral. "Well, you take care, Mom. I'll see you in a week. Love you."

"I love you too."

Shaking her head, Abby crossed the first item off her list. Phone calls with her mother always niggled uncomfortably at her conscience. She stood up. Time to get those errands done.

She walked upstairs and knocked on Ben's door, opening it.

"Ben? I'm going out to run errands. I'll be back in a couple of hours. You get started on stripping the wallpaper today, okay?"

Ben rolled over in bed and gazed at her through half-opened eyes. "Okay."

"And we need to keep Max in the basement, remember?" The cat was lying across Ben's pillow, just above his head.

Ben grunted.

She left his door open and went back downstairs. Redecorating the bathroom was a perfect project for Ben. It needed doing before they put the house up for sale. Hopefully he'd do a good job. She thought of him lying in bed, looking like a big bundle of guilt and defeat. Poor Ben.

****

Making dinner that evening Abby ran through the trip preparations in her mind. Her hands moved on autopilot, tossing the salad and dividing it among four bowls, grilling the chicken breasts and cutting them, placing a neat row of slices over each salad.

"I've put our passports in my purse and picked up two hundred American dollars from the bank today," she said as she handed Peter's salad to him. "And I'll end my ten-thirty class early so we should be able to get away by noon. I called my parents this morning to tell them I won't be coming this week. And I've almost finished packing. Just need to put toiletries into my suitcase." She handed Hanna and Ben their bowls and sat. "I went shopping today so there's lots of food in the fridge and freezer. Make sure you guys eat it."

"Abby, relax," Peter said. "Let's enjoy our dinner. Everything's under control."

"You've made good progress on the wallpaper stripping, Ben. You'll probably finish it tomorrow, right?"

"Yeah, I think so." He shoved a forkful of salad into his mouth.

"Don't forget that you have to wash the walls before you paint them, okay? To get residual paste off?"

"I know, Mom, you already told me." He formed his words around the crunching of vegetables as he chewed.

"I wrote up a list for you and stuck it on the fridge. Your appointment with Dr. Hanson is on Thursday at one thirty. Be sure you get there fifteen minutes early like they asked. And bring the check. Don't forget to mow the lawn on Saturday, and then you're going to dinner at the Newtons' that evening. You should get there around five."

"Mom." Hanna propelled the word in a short staccato. "Ben knows what he has to do. You've been telling him nonstop for days. Give him a break."

Abby looked from Ben to Hanna, then to Peter, who raised his eyebrows, then back to Ben. "Sorry, Ben. I just want to make sure that everything runs smoothly while we're gone."

"Just because I screwed up doesn't mean I won't be able to handle things here for a few days." Ben stabbed his fork into a piece of chicken. "I know what I have to do. You don't need to keep telling me."

"Okay." Abby mixed her salad with her fork. "Hanna, is everything organized for your camping trip? You've got Mrs. Newton's phone number in case of an emergency?"

"Yes, Mom." Hanna enunciated her words emphatically and rolled her eyes at Ben.

"And, Ben, remember to keep Max in the basement or outside if you're not spending time with him. He'll mess all over the house otherwise."

"Abby, why don't we let the kids show us how independent they can be." Peter picked up his water glass. "Let's just worry about getting ourselves packed and on our way tomorrow and trust in them to keep things running smoothly here."

"I'm not saying the kids aren't reliable," Abby blurted out, louder than she intended. "It's just the way I am. I worry about stuff. Ben's back home. We've got a long drive tomorrow." She leaned forward. "I have three days to decide whether I like Richmond or not." She shut her eyes tight and blinked a few times, regaining control of herself. Why did every stupid emotion make her cry? "I just don't know how it will all go."

"Mom." Ben put his hand on her arm. "Dad's right. Just relax. Hanna and I'll be fine."

"Yeah, Mom. It's a road trip with Dad, and you'll have fun." Hanna patted her mother's shoulder. "You're going to be leaving us anyway when you move to Richmond so we might as well get used to it now." She looked at Peter. "You're going to take that job in Richmond, aren't you?"

"I'm pretty sure I will." Peter leaned back in his chair, balancing it on the two rear legs. "Are you kids okay with that?"

Ben sat up straighter. "Actually, I'm not." He scraped back his chair and faced Peter. "What you're doing to this family sucks. Look at Mom. She's a mess."

Abby shook her head. "I'm not…"

Ben's voice got louder. "And my life is crap right now."

Peter's chair came forward with a bang. "Ben, I don't think…"

"And you're," Ben shook his head, "you're abandoning me. Hanna still needs you too. She told me she didn't like you moving so far away."

"I didn't mean…" Hanna put her fork down.

"You told me that, Hanna. I don't think it's okay," he spat out the word, "that you take a job and move Mom to fucking Richmond, Virginia, and leave us alone here."

Abby jerked her head up. "Ben, your language!" The tension around the table sent a wave of nausea through her.

Her words were drowned out by Peter's. "You have a right to feel angry, Ben, but watch your mouth," he said, his face reddening.

Abby held the edge of the table. "You know Dad isn't doing this because he wants to. He has no choice. We're making this decision together, for all of us."

"Mom," Ben leaned forward, "no offense, but you are not making this decision together. Dad is the one who's finding the job and you're just going along with it."

Abby had had the same thoughts. They were at the mercy of Peter's job. Wherever he was hired, they'd go. And yet she couldn't deny that a small part of her relished the chance to try something new, to feed her sense of adventure, to have this experience with just Peter and her. Did that mean she was betraying Hanna and Ben?

"What would you suggest as an alternative, Ben?" Peter said in a deliberate voice. "Me staying unemployed? How do you think we'd have gotten you out of your gambling debt if I didn't get another job?"

Abby was stunned that Peter would use Ben's transgressions as justification for moving to Richmond. "Peter." She tried to get his attention.

Ben looked as if he'd been slapped. "Dad, I didn't...."

"Everybody stop." Hanna's cheeks were wet with tears. "I don't want our family to fight. There's enough bad stuff happening to us already."

The color drained from Peter's face. "You're right, Hanna. We shouldn't be fighting. Especially about this." He reached his hand to Ben. "Son, I'm sorry you feel this way, but I have no alternative. I've looked for jobs close by and there aren't any. This one in Richmond is good and I think I should take it."

Ben's voice became quieter. "Why don't you start your own business or something? And stay here."

"It's not that easy. I looked into it but it isn't viable. We can make this work for all of us if we try."

"Yeah, sure." Ben sunk back in his chair. "It's just…my life sucks right now."

"I think it does for all of us," Peter said. "But we shouldn't take it out on each other."

"What Dad says is true." Abby clenched her hands in her lap. "We need to stick together, even if we won't be living together." She scanned their faces. The silence was thick and heavy. Almost in a whisper, she asked, "Anyone want fruit?"

Ben picked up his dishes. "No thanks. I'm outa here."

"Ben," Abby followed him to the sink and moved close to give him a hug. He shied away from her and left the kitchen. She started after him.

"Let him go, Abby." Peter's voice stopped her. He was right. Ben didn't want her right now. She watched him climb the stairs then turned back to the kitchen. She picked up the fruit bowl and brought it to the table and sat down.

Hanna pushed her last bits of salad around with her fork. "When do you think you'll start working in Richmond, Dad?"

"Probably in September." His voice was shaky, and its quietness matched Hanna's. "Hanna, are you as angry about this as Ben?"

"Kinda." She put her fork down. "No. Not really. But I do feel like everything is out of control. I mean, I don't have any say, do I?" She pushed her salad bowl away. "It's okay, I guess. I'll soon be busy at university anyway."

Abby knew Hanna was just saying that to appease Peter. She picked a pear out of the fruit bowl and began cutting it into quarters. "Life's going to change for us all, Hanna. It'll be a big adjustment. We don't have to pretend it's easy."

Peter polished an apple on his shirt. "That's true, Abby, but we have to make the best of this situation and focus on the positives."

"Like what?" Hanna's tone was challenging.

"We discussed them before, remember?" Peter started counting on his fingers as he ran through his list.

Abby felt a sudden irritation. Peter was always Mr. Positive. His name should be Pollyanna. She pressed her lips together as he continued.

"I found a job after losing the one I had. We'll get to experience life in a different country, in a different climate. We'll all have opportunities to travel more. Your mom will have time to pursue new interests. You and Ben will have a chance to be independent without your parents breathing down your neck." Peter took a bite. He started chewing, his cheek round with apple, and said, "And those are just off the top of my head."

Abby swallowed her comment about talking with a mouth full of food. Couldn't Peter let his optimist mantle slide once in a while?

"Okay, Dad. I get it." Hanna stacked her dishes and cutlery. "I'll keep my eye out for the silver lining." She picked up the dishes and stood. "Can I be excused? Jason's waiting for me to call."

Chapter Fourteen

In classes the next morning, Abby's lectures were disjointed and her responses to questions distracted. What preyed on her mind, instead of Alice Munro's techniques in *The View from Castle Rock* and P.D. James' use of conventions in *Lighthouse*, was the upcoming trip to Richmond. Earlier, at home, she set her suitcase by the door ready for Peter to put into the car and left for the university trying not to think about how this trip would impact her own life. Her thoughts kept jumping between Ben's struggles and Hanna's reluctant separation from the comfort of her familiar life.

But while standing at the lectern, sorting her pages of notes and watching students take their seats, the impact of the trip to Richmond hit Abby full force. Peter would take the job. She'd have to make new friends, get used to a new city, redefine her life. What would she do in Richmond? Without her children and without her job what kind of life would she have? She had to pull herself away from these thoughts to begin her lecture.

****

She arrived home well before eleven-thirty. Peter was packing the suitcases into the back of the van as she drove up. Hanna leaned against the wall of the garage, her arms crossed in front of her chest, right knee bent, foot flat against the wall.

"Hi, guys," Abby said, trying to sound cheerful. "How's the packing going?"

"Almost done."

"Did you put that blue canvas bag in the front? It's got my books and stuff to do on the drive."

"Of course. And the bag with the CDs. We just need to put the snacks into the cooler." Peter took her briefcase from her hand. "Do you want to take this too?"

"Nope. I'm leaving work behind on this trip." She put her arm around Hanna's shoulders. "How are you doing, sweetie? Do you wish you were coming with us?"

"Not at all." Hanna pushed herself forward and stood straight. "I can't wait for you guys to leave so we can party tonight." She grinned widely. "Just kidding."

As quickly as it appeared, her smile faded. "I would like to go and see what it's like, but I want to go camping more. Besides, I won't be moving there with you guys anyway."

"But, Hanna, it will be your new home. You know that, right?" Abby was reassuring herself as much as Hanna.

"Yeah."

Abby gave her a squeeze. "I'll go change and pack the cooler. Then we can get on our way." She looked at Peter. "How's Ben?"

"He seems all right. He was very civil this morning, even interested in the trip."

Abby was relieved. It would have been hard to leave him if he was still angry. "Is he working on the bathroom?"

"Yeah, just. He got up less than an hour ago."

"An hour..." Abby quelled her irritation and went to change her clothes. She put on the blue Capri pants and flowered t-shirt that she'd left out earlier, hung up her skirt and tossed her blouse in the laundry basket. She wanted to brush her hair but remembered she'd packed her hairbrush. Running her fingers through it instead, she went to check on Ben's progress. The bathroom door pushed against something, preventing her from opening it.

"Ben?"

"Just a sec." Ben's muffled voice came through the door. "The ladder's in the way." She heard the ladder grate on the floor. Hopefully not scratching it. Ben opened the door and smiled at her, small scraps of wallpaper stuck to his hair. "Hey. It's almost all off. I'm just scraping the pieces above the door."

"That's great. Be careful with the floor when you move the ladder, okay? We're not planning on replacing the tiles."

"Yes, Mother." Ben lost his smile. "I have drop cloths under it, see?"

"Oh, that's good."

"You know, I kind of like doing this. Maybe I can get a job with a painter or something."

"That would be a good thing to do while you're fig-uring things out." She reached up and ruffled his hair, shaking out the wallpaper bits. "I'm going to pack our snacks, and then Dad and I are off. Come down and say good-bye, okay?"

"In a minute."

In the kitchen, Peter and Hanna were making sand-wiches. The coffeemaker sputtered, emitting a tantalizing aroma. The table had been laid with place mats, glasses of water, and the fruit bowl. Abby was surprised. "We're eating first? I thought you wanted to get on the road as soon as possible."

"I do. But we might as well eat lunch before we go. Otherwise we'd have to stop in an hour or so anyway." Peter popped the end bit of a tomato in his mouth. "I thought it'd be nice to eat with the kids before we leave. It's the least we can do since Hanna took the morning off."

"What a nice thought." She kissed him and tasted tomato. "Can I help?"

Hanna put the sandwiches on the table. "Nope. We're all done. We packed the cooler too. And…" She waved her hand toward the coffeemaker. Two insulated mugs sat beside it. "Your travel mugs are waiting for the coffee to be done so you can take them in the car with you."

"Wow. I guess there's nothing left to do." Abby went to the cooler on the floor by the door and opened it. Bottles of water, grapes, trail mix, apples, and a package of red licorice. "Red licorice?"

Hanna came up behind her. "We always have red licorice on road trips. You can't sit in a car for eleven hours without red licorice. Also," she pulled a CD from behind her back, "I made you this for the road."

Abby took it and looked at the cover. There was a photograph of the four of them, taken last summer at MacGregor Park. Sprawled across the picture were large red letters spelling *Mom & Dad's Moving Music*.

Abby trailed her fingers over the picture. What were they thinking, leaving this sweet child? She blinked a few times and kissed Hanna's cheek. "That's so nice." She started to open the CD case. Hanna put her hand on it.

"No, don't open it yet. You can see what's on it when you're in the car. There's a printed list inside but keep it a surprise for now, okay?"

"Okay." Abby slid the CD beside the passports in her purse. "Thanks, Hanna."

"For what?" Ben came into the kitchen. "Oh lunch. Cool."

"Hanna made us a CD for the trip."

Peter pulled out his chair. "Let's start eating. Time's a-ticking."

Lunch felt rushed. The interaction seemed frantic as fragments of conversation circulated around the table. Hanna teased Ben about eating lunch an hour after breakfast. Ben countered with a retort about a working-man's appetite. Peter uttered one-word responses between bites. Then Hanna talked about her upcoming camping trip, and Ben told them about a friend who had formed a student painting company for the summer. Abby tried to stay focused on everyone's words but couldn't keep her eyes off Peter who was eating as if in a race. What was the matter with him? This meal was his idea. He finished first and had barely swallowed his last bite when he took his plate to the dishwasher and poured coffee into the mugs. Abby felt compelled to chew faster.

"This was nice," Peter said as he pressed the lids into the travel mugs. "Are you almost done, honey?"

"Think Dad wants to get going?" Abby popped the last bit of sandwich into her mouth.

"It's okay." Hanna peeled an orange. "We'll clean up the dishes, won't we Ben?"

Ben stopped mid-chew and nodded. He swallowed with a gulp. "Yeah, Hanna and I'll be okay. You go."

"Thanks, you two." Abby picked up an apple. "I'll eat this in the car."

In a jumble of activity they walked out to the garage; Peter picking up things and the kids trying to help, tossing out have-a-good-trip and let-us-know-what's-happening and drive-safe, everyone hugging. Abby stopped at the car door. Had she given Ben and Hanna enough instructions?

"Don't forget to go to your appointment tomorrow, Ben. And remember to give the paint a good stir before you use it. Hanna, be sure no one drinks and drives on the camping trip. And make sure everyone is sensible with the campfire. And...."

"Mom."

"Mother."

"Abby."

Three voices burst out with the words simultaneously. Abby stopped mid-sentence. "Sorry."

"Let's go, Abby. The kids will be fine."

Abby climbed in and shut the door. She looked at Peter. "Can you be more eager? Turn on the ignition so I can open the window." As the glass lowered, Hanna stuck her face in and kissed Abby's cheek.

"Bye, Mom. We love you."

"And I love you, sweetie." Abby looked at Ben. "Love you, too, Ben. Bye."

Hanna and Ben stepped away and Peter backed up the car. Abby stuck her arm out of the window and wiggled her fingers. The kids followed them out of the garage and waved as Peter pulled onto the street. Abby's heart swelled at seeing them there together, like two orphans. Would they be all right on their own?

Peter put the car into drive. "Look at those two," he said, turning the steering wheel. "They look so grown-up and mature, waving us off like that. Like the independent adults they're becoming."

His words lit a spark of insight in Abby's mind. Where she saw two helpless kids who still needed their parents, Peter saw two young adults ready to launch their lives. Why did they view them differently? Maybe Abby wanted them to need her. Was she preventing herself from regarding Ben and Hanna as adults? She sat back and pondered the idea. They'd tried to cut the cord with Ben; he'd ventured into a life of his own. And look what happened. He came crawling back, asking his parents to help him figure things out. What kind of an adult was that?

And Hanna wasn't even nineteen. Still a teenager. Although, Abby remembered, she herself had been pretty grown-up at eighteen and couldn't wait to move away from her parents. Maybe that was because Abby and her parents always seemed to be arguing, and Hanna's relationship with her and Peter was so different. Still, Hanna did seem to want to cling to her home life.

No, Ben and Hanna definitely weren't adults yet. Obviously Peter saw them as such; at least he wanted to. Maybe he had to in order to feel comfortable about moving away from them. She directed her gaze at Peter and shook these thoughts from her brain. She needed to focus on what was ahead of them on this trip.

As if he felt her eyes upon him, Peter smiled at her. He put his hand on her knee.

"How are you doing? Feeling okay about all of this?"

She rubbed her finger on the surface of Peter's hand, tracing the bones that led to his fingers.

"To tell you the truth, there's a part of me that is very excited."

"Really?" The surprise was evident in Peter's voice.

"Yes, but whenever that excitement bubbles up, I feel guilty."

"Why?"

"I don't know. It's like, well, you losing your job is a terrible thing. And us having to move away from the kids is a terrible thing. And abandoning my parents is a terrible thing. So with our moving away having all that impact, how dare I get excited about it?" She squeezed Peter's hand. "Illogical, I know. But it's what hits me every time I begin to anticipate positive things that might evolve from it."

She took a deep breath and exhaled through puffed cheeks. "It's as if I'm supposed to feel bad about it all, and sad, but a part of me doesn't. A part of me is excited about moving and about leaving all this," she waved her arm around the car, "and venturing out into new experiences." She wiped at her eyes. "I am feeling two such opposite emotions about it. Mostly I just want to jump around with anticipation but don't let myself."

"I'm glad you're having good feelings about this move. And it's probably natural for you to feel those opposite extremes." He patted her knee. "We both have all kinds of regret and sadness about it. It's shaking up our lives. But you do have an adventurous spirit. And we've often talked about buying a new house, maybe moving to a different city." He looked at her. "Now we get to do that. It's exciting and it's okay for you to feel that. So stop feeling guilty."

"On an intellectual level I know that." Abby looked out of the window. They were passing *Pioneer Sports World*, almost at the 401. "But my heart can't get past what it might do to everyone else's lives."

Peter reached over and squeezed her hand. "My dear, sensitive Abby. You need to give yourself a break. Think about how nice it might be to just move away from all those responsibilities and start fresh. Just you and me."

It was freeing to hear Peter verbalize the same thoughts she'd been holding back. How wonderful it might be to just escape everything. Leave the kids to their own devices without her constant intervention. Let her parents muddle along on their own in Chestnut Manor. Run away from her job, all of her obligations. Live the life together that just the two of them started so many years ago. She smiled.

"It has occurred to me that the guilt and sadness I feel about leaving everything can metamorphose into a sense of release and joy if I let it."

"Then let it."

"Hm." She shifted her feet around the canvas bag that was sitting on the floor in front of her and lifted it to her lap. She zipped it open and looked inside. Two novels, a Sudoku booklet, her embroidery project; she reached in and pulled out the coil bound road atlas that she'd bought for this trip. "What route are we taking?"

"We'll cross at the Peace Bridge into Buffalo and then take I-90, I-79, and I-70 I think, or 76, then I-95 through Washington and straight to Richmond. Can you find that route on the map?"

"Just a sec." She leafed through the atlas, looking for the different highways. "So we go through New York State, Pennsylvania," she turned some more pages, "Maryland, and Virginia. Four states. Cool."

An hour later they pulled behind a line of cars at the border. Abby opened her purse to take out their passports. Nestled alongside them was the CD that Hanna had given her before they left. She took it out too. Opening each passport to the page with the photograph, she handed them to Peter. "What will you say when they ask what the purpose of our visit is?"

"I'll tell them I have a job interview and that we're going to explore Richmond. It won't be a problem."

"I guess. For some reason border guards make me nervous." Abby shrugged. "Maybe some subconscious fear of authority?"

"Or men in uniforms?"

"They're not always men, Peter."

The customs officer in the booth they pulled up to was a man. A boy really. He looked to be about Ben's age. He was friendly and smiled at them, and when he asked Peter where they were going and how long they'd be there, he seemed only mildly interested in his answers. Peter handed him the passports; he took them and barely looked at them, punched in something on a keyboard in the booth and handed them back.

"Good luck," he said as he waved them off. "Have a good trip."

"That was easy." She was relieved. "I thought it would be more complicated."

"Abby," Peter said abruptly. "Help me figure out where to go. There's so much construction here. Do we need 90 or 190? We have to go south."

Abby looked through the confusion of cars changing lanes, large yellow machines rumbling, orange pylons, men in orange vests, a haze of dust, trying to find a sign that would tell them which way to go. Finally she saw one that had an arrow pointing to the left. I-190 S detour to I-90, it said.

"There." She pointed.

"Got it." Peter turned onto a road that took them into Buffalo. "What are we doing on this street?"

"It's a detour. There'll be more detour signs, I'm sure." She looked at the rundown storefronts. "Not the nicest part of town, huh?"

"Nope. I'm not comfortable driving around here. Oh, there we go."

Within minutes they were back on the highway. She pulled out a few ropes of licorice and handed one to Peter, then opened Hanna's CD and put it into the player. Andrea Bocelli's voice came through the speakers singing *Time to Say Good-Bye*.

"Gee, Hanna knows how to tug at my heart strings." She looked at the typed list in the CD case.

"Yeah. What else is on the CD?"

"I Will Remember You, In My Life, Wish You Were Here," She stared at him. "There's a definite theme here. She's trying to make us feel guilty about leaving."

"I don't think so. She's just put together a bunch of songs she thought we'd like."

"If you say so." Abby pulled out a pen and her Sudoku book, opening it to a blank puzzle. She wasn't so sure that Hanna wasn't trying to manipulate their feelings. Abby would have a talk with her when they got home, to try to help Hanna deal with all these changes in her life. She looked at Peter munching on his licorice. He was in his own zone, focused on his driving, thinking about who knew what.

"When you get tired of driving, I'll take over, okay?"

"Yeah, I want you to drive at some point anyway. I need to go over the material from Asset again, and I want to read through that book I bought. What's it called?" He thought a minute. "The Border Guide. It's about living and working in the U.S. as a Canadian, gives all sorts of advice on the financial aspects of relocating there and how to do it to the best advantage."

"Okay. Well, anytime you're ready to give up the wheel just let me know." She started to work on her puzzle. Through the speakers The Beatles were singing about places they remembered, places that have changed. Reaching over, she popped the CD out of the player. She had no desire for nostalgia or sadness now. She rooted through the bag of CDs that Peter had brought and picked out Supertramp's *Breakfast in America*. That seemed appropriate somehow. She put it in the player.

"How far do you think we'll go today?" she asked. "Do you think we should stop for the night somewhere?"

"I'm open to that. I'm also game to drive straight through, although we'd probably arrive around midnight. Let's see how we feel."

"Okay. But let's aim for going all the way."

"Yeah," he wiggled his eyebrows at her, "especially in the hotel tonight."

She punched his arm. He grabbed her hand and held it.

"You know, I'm pretty sure I'll sign the offer."

"I know. I can't believe that we're this close," she held up her hand and brought the thumb and index finger together, not quite touching, "to changing everything about our life."

"Not everything." He reached over and kissed her. The car swerved a little. He jerked up, straightening it. "I love you, Abs. I'm glad you're on this adventure with me. It's kind of scary for me too."

It was? Abby hadn't realized. She must be so focused on herself that she'd missed signals from Peter that might bespeak his anxieties. She put her hand on his knee and squeezed it gently. "We'll get through it and come out on top, sweetie. We're in this together."

Still, a thread of sadness wove itself around her because "together" didn't include Ben and Hanna.

****

It was after midnight when they pulled up to the *Embassy Suites* on Broad Street in Richmond. Abby had been fighting to keep her eyes open for the last hour, despite the surge of excitement she felt at seeing Richmond on a highway sign sixty-eight miles back. She opened the door and stepped out into the night. Her knees were stiff and her back was achy. The air was hot and heavy with humidity. It felt exotic, alluring. She reached and bent to touch her toes, then straightened, stretching her back with her hands at her hips. Peter put his arm around her shoulders.

"We're here." He kissed her cheek. "Isn't it amazing how hot and humid it is even this late at night?"

"Yeah. Is it like this all the time?" She gently shook his arm off.

"Apparently it is for most of August. Shall we go check in?"

Putting her hand in his, she walked with him to the entrance of the hotel. On the way she tried to distinguish the types of trees surrounding the parking lot, but they were only dark, interesting shadows. The atmosphere around her felt—she couldn't quite put a word to it— southern maybe? Foreign to be sure. Delight trickled through her. They were going to live here.

****

The next day they explored parts of the city. They drove the length of Broad Street from the dilapidated sections near VCU and heading west to Short Pump.

They explored residential areas: new developments geared to young families, old established areas with houses nestled in forests, downtown streets of beautiful row houses with splendid balconies and glorious trees. They ogled the magnificent homes, mansions really, on Three Chopt Road and River Road.

"What kind of a name is Three Chopt?" Abby asked.

"I have no idea. And what's with Short Pump?" So many of the names were strange, so different from what they were used to.

They walked on the cobbled stones of Main Street, had lunch in a quaint mid-eastern café, and then walked along the canal for a bit. They drove up Monument Avenue and admired the statues that kept watch on the traffic zipping past, tributes to past heroes. They ate dinner at Short Pump Mall and window-shopped, enjoying the open-air shopping center. Abby kept exclaiming over the stores they didn't have in Waterloo: Dillard's, Coldwater Creek, Crate and Barrel, Chico's.

"I'll have so much fun shopping here." She thought back to the limited shops she had to choose from in Waterloo. "We can buy anything."

It was odd, really. Shopping had never been important to her. But she was intoxicated with the newness of it all and energized by the fact that everything she was seeing would be a part of her new life.

Later, in the hotel room, they sat in bed with brochures, maps, and booklets strewn on the covers. Looking up from the real estate magazine she was holding, Abby stared at their reflection in the dark television screen. Leaning back on the pillows, Peter was engrossed in a binder from Asset Credit Union, his glasses low on his nose. His naked chest contrasted with her frilly yellow nightie. She smiled.

"You know, I really like Richmond. I think we can be happy here."

Peter gazed at her over his glasses. "Yeah? Me too. And the job…"

"I know. The job is good. And there are lots of nice places to live. I'm really getting excited. A new life. I can't wait for it all to happen." She pushed the brochures aside and turned to face him. She stroked his chest and then her hand went under the covers, caressing him. Taking off his glasses, he put them and the binder on the bedside table. He reached for her and held her tight, stroking her back, pressing his lips to hers. She nestled into him.

"Let's make love for the first time in our new hometown," she whispered.

****

The next morning she drove Peter to the Asset Credit Union building. As she pulled up to the front entrance, he picked up his briefcase. With his hand on the door handle he said, "Pick me up at this entrance around eleven, okay?" He was all business, tension radiating from him, his posture stiff. He smiled weakly. "I hope I know what I'm doing."

She reached for him and stroked his arm. "Relax, honey. You're making the right decision. I know you are. You know you are." She leaned over and kissed him. "Good luck. I'll be back here at eleven."

"I'll call you if I'm later or earlier." And with that he was out of the car. She watched him walk into the building. *I hope you know what you're doing too,* she thought. She turned the wheel and headed for the street. Where to go? She turned left. Spying a coffee shop on the other side of the traffic light, she headed toward it.

Choosing to drink her coffee outside, she picked a table that was near three women chatting animatedly. It was strange to be sitting alone while others were busily walking by, or participating in seemingly important conversations. She unfolded the map of Richmond and opened the realtor magazine they'd picked up the day before.

An hour later she had a list of houses that looked promising and the map marked up with X's. She looked at her watch. Ten-thirty. Too close to eleven to risk getting lost. She'd drive around staying close to Asset's office building.

In the car she slid Hanna's CD into the player. Driving aimlessly, not entirely sure of where she was but always keeping a sense of the direction of the office, she sang along to the music. She wondered how Peter was doing. She wondered how Ben's appointment with the counselor had gone. Whenever they'd tried to call the kids, the answering machine had picked up, so she hadn't had a chance to speak to either of them. Hanna would probably be packing for her camping trip. She hoped Ben had started painting.

"Can I sail through the changing tides," she sang along with Stevie Nicks. Struck by sudden realization, she listened to the rest of the words. This song was about her. Doubting whether she'd be able to cope with the changes that were assaulting her life. Wondering about leaving her children, whom she'd built her life around. Would she be able to maneuver herself through this change and come out of it intact? A horn blaring startled her out of her reverie and she realized she'd slowed the car to almost a standstill in the middle of the road. She pressed her foot on the gas pedal and sped ahead. It was almost eleven, time to head back to Peter's new office.

****

Peter jumped into the car, filling it with a current that revitalized the air.

"Well, it's done. I signed it. We're moving here."

Her stomach somersaulted. This was a good thing, she reminded herself. She leaned over and kissed him.

"Congratulations, honey. How are you feeling about it?"

"Kinda weird, actually. Excited. Happy. But scared. I keep wondering if we're doing the right thing. But we had to do something."

She put the car in gear. "Of course it's the right thing." She started to pull away from the building and then stopped. "Where to?"

"Oh, I have to go to this medical office on Broad Street to get drug tested."

"What?"

"Yeah, every new employee has to do that. The final signing off is conditional on it."

"Okay. Where is it?"

"Turn left. It's a few blocks east of here."

As she drove, she tried to think about all the positive aspects of Peter having taken the job. But unprovoked by any thoughts, her eyes filled with tears and she began to cry. She swallowed her sobs but the tears kept coming. Thankful she was wearing sunglasses, she tried to inconspicuously wipe them away. She needed to be happy for Peter. He just got a job. He had accomplished something good for their future. It paid well and would provide all kinds of new experiences for them. She did not want to dim this bright spot in his life with her tears. Please, she thought, don't let him know I'm crying.

"Abby, what's wrong? I thought you wanted me to sign."

"I do. I'm glad you did." She sniffed. "I'm sorry I'm crying." Her voice wavered and she had a difficult time getting the words out. "Just overwhelmed at what it means, I guess."

"It's okay. You don't have to apologize for your emotions." He rubbed her thigh. "When I held the pen to sign my name on the offer, I felt a wave of fear before I actually did it. It's scary."

She stared straight ahead at the car in front of her, trying to get control of her tears. "Where do I have to turn?"

"Um," he looked ahead. "There. Broad Street Medical Center. On the right."

She turned into the parking lot and switched off the ignition. "You go in. I'll wait here."

"Are you sure, honey?" He looked at her with a worried expression on his face.

She nodded. "You go."

He left the car and went through the door. She watched him and took out a tissue from her purse. Blowing her nose, she considered the last ten minutes. Why did she have to cry right then? She was excited about Peter taking the job. And she had begun to feel good about this move. She was happy that Peter had been able to secure a job so soon. She needed to be supportive of him. She took a deep breath and scrounged in the backseat for a bottle of water. Drinking in long gulps, she felt herself calming. She screwed the top back on the water bottle and followed Peter into the doctor's office.

Chapter Fifteen

It was all a matter of how she looked at it. She could either be depressed and think of it as the end or look ahead with anticipation and consider it a beginning. The trouble was, Abby couldn't always control her point of view. When she found herself dwelling on the life she would be leaving, she felt shadowed by a cloud of grief threatening to burst open with a torrent of tears. But at other times the prospect of her new life in Richmond seemed full of promise. Then anticipation would soar in her heart, cutting through that cloud and beaming rays of optimism about the new life that was in front of her.

The weeks after the trip to Richmond overtook her in a flurry of activity. There were so many issues to deal with that her to-do list, written up on the drive back to Waterloo, filled two long pages.

When they arrived home, Ben surprised them with the announcement that he had gotten a job and found a room to rent.

"Way to go, Ben." Peter clapped him on the back. "How did you manage that so fast?"

"You know the interview with that guy you set up? He hired me. I'm gonna be working full-time on the assembly line."

"Doing what?" Abby's emotions were battling between relief that Ben was actually moving forward and disappointment in the kind of job he'd acquired.

"Drilling holes in the backs of electronic units, I think. They're paying me eleven bucks an hour and it's full-time." He smiled. "Not bad, eh? I'll be able to start paying you back soon."

The room he'd found was one from a multitude of student housing available around the city. Abby had to go with him to co-sign the lease. The room was spacious and bright, not like the dark basement he'd had in Toronto. She thought back to that time not so long ago, remembering how anxious she had felt about Ben living there with his Starbucks job that didn't really exist. This time things were different. Ben really had a job and he seemed determined to set himself straight. She shook off the disquiet she felt, not really sure why it was there.

Standing on the threshold of Ben's future room, she eyed the piles of clothes, books, papers, and half-filled cardboard boxes covering the floor. Obviously there was a move in progress here. Stepping past the building manager, she explored the rest of the apartment. The common room was large, with a kitchen in one corner with a table and four chairs. There was a couch in the sitting area, and a coffee table and TV stand. Five doors led off the main room to four bedrooms and a bath-room. Two of the bedroom doors stood open and the room that wasn't Ben's looked to Abby as if a hurricane had blown through it.

"Do you know who your roommates will be?" she asked Ben.

"Nope." He followed her, as if her shadow.

"Those two rooms," the building manager waved her hand in the direction of the closed doors, "are being rented by two girls from Sweden. They're going to the university."

"Well, that will be interesting." Abby wasn't sure how she felt about Ben sharing an apartment with girls. Still, they'd be better for him than a bunch of poker players.

"Yeah. I might have to learn how to speak Swe-dish." Ben had a big grin on his face. No doubt he was envisioning two blonde beauties.

"And the other room," the building manager gri-maced as she waved her head at the hurricane fallout, "hasn't been rented out yet. But it will. These buildings always fill up by September." She looked at Abby. "And you can rest easy. The apartment will get a complete cleaning before your son moves in."

At the rental office Abby co-signed the lease that Ben carefully filled out. He seemed to be taking this step toward independence very seriously. Perhaps it was their impending departure that pushed him to assume respon-sibility for himself this way. Maybe their move was a good thing for Ben. Abby wrote a cheque for the first and last months' rent. Then a cheque to cover the rental fee for the common room furniture and appliances. And a check for Internet access. She felt a quiver of anxiety before signing her name to that one. What if his access to the Internet got him into trouble again? She squelched the thought. Ben himself didn't want to go down that path. She needed to believe in him. Besides, they'd installed those Web site blockers on his computer.

Ben's shoulders seemed to droop a little more with each cheque that she tore off and handed to the building manager. "I'm going to owe you guys so much money." His voice was quiet.

"That's true, Ben, but you're making a great start with your job. Just take it one step at a time." She was tempted to tell him that if he managed to get on his feet and figure his life out, they would probably forgive the debt he was accumulating with them. But Peter had said, and rightly so, that telling him would be counterproduc-tive to his progress. So she kept quiet.

When Abby started the car, Ben fiddled with the ra-dio and found a station playing noise. He stared out the window. Abby turned down the volume.

"Are you excited about starting your job next week?"

"I guess."

"How did your appointment with Dr. Hanson go? Did you make an appointment for another session?"

"Yeah, next Thursday."

"Good." She wondered how much she could ask. "What did you talk about?"

"Geez, Mom. Can't I have any privacy?" He turned to face her. "I don't have to tell you that."

"You're right, Ben. Sorry." But, oh, how she wanted to know. "Do you think Dr. Hanson will be helpful?"

"It's too soon to tell."

"Has he mentioned anything about going to a group?"

"You mean like AA, or what is it, gamblers anonymous? No. And I wouldn't go even if he did."

"Ben…"

"Mom. Let me be. I'll figure things out." He shifted in his seat. "I have to anyway, don't I. Since you and Dad are moving away." He turned up the volume on the radio and returned his gaze out the window.

Abby felt as if Ben had knocked her down. What had happened in these few minutes? He was so confident earlier, showing her the apartment, signing the lease. He'd been nothing but enthusiastic about his job. Now he seemed angry and resentful.

"Ben…" She didn't know what to say to him. He didn't respond. Probably hadn't heard over the radio. Best leave him be for now.

****

Walking up the path to Chestnut Manor, Abby rehearsed different ways of telling her parents about Peter's job and their impending move. Should she tell her mother before her father? Tell them together? In their room? Outside? Abby wondered if her father would even understand. Maybe inspiration would come to her in the moment. Distracted, she pushed open the door and walked past the waiters without greeting them in her usual way.

"Abby."

Abby stopped. Her mother was sitting in her wheelchair, fourth in a row of five white-haired ladies. She'd become one of the waiters. She had given in.

"Mom." Abby kissed her on the cheek. "You surprised me sitting here. Where's Dad?" She looked around.

"In the room. He doesn't go out."

"Shall we go see him?" She went around to the back of the chair and released the brakes.

"Not yet. I want tea."

"Okay." Abby pushed the wheelchair down the hall past the chapel and the library to the residents' café, a room set up with chairs and tables covered with red-checked tablecloths. On one side of the wall, a counter held coffee machines, a basket of tea bags, plates of cookies, cups and saucers. She parked her mother at a table overlooking the back courtyard and went to get their drinks.

Setting a cup of tea and a cookie in front of her mother she said, "They had these yummy looking chocolate chip cookies. I brought us each one."

"Thank you, Abby." Her mother moved the cup to one side. "It's good to see you. You haven't been here for a long time." She reached her hands toward Abby.

Abby took her mother's hands in her own, biting back the contradiction that she'd seen her only a week and a half ago. For her mother that was a long time.

"It's good to see you too. How are you?"

"The same. Always the same. I hurt." She pulled her hands back and touched her chest below her right breast. "Your father is so bad. I forget things." She picked up the spoon from the saucer and slowly stirred her tea. "And lonely. Nobody comes."

"Oh, Mom." And now Abby had to tell her that she and Peter would be moving even further away. "I'm sorry that life is so difficult right now."

"Yes, getting old is terrible. Nobody visits me."

Frustration surged through Abby. She sympathized with her mom but wished she would let it go for once. Wished she would just drop the guilt. Abby drank her coffee in an attempt to calm herself. "Ben has moved back to Waterloo."

"He did?"

"Yup. He's got a room in an apartment and a job in a factory. And Hanna is busy packing for her move to the university in a few weeks."

"It's nice to have your children near you."

"Well, Mom." It was the opening she needed. She clattered her empty coffee cup down on the saucer. "They won't actually be near us."

"What?"

"We had some bad news this summer, Mom. Peter lost his job. But he found a new one and..."

"No." Her mother banged the spoon down. Apprehension radiated from her eyes. "Don't tell me you're moving away."

Surprised her mother could deduce that so quickly, Abby became defensive. "Mom, we don't have a choice. Peter needs a job and there weren't any around Ontario. He had to look farther away." She heard how she sounded and took a deep breath.

Her mother's eyes filled with tears. "Where?"

"He just signed on with a company in Richmond, Virginia."

"Virginia? How far is that?"

"It's about a day's drive from here. But Mom..."

"You can't move so far. You have to stay here so you can visit me. Can't your man do something else?"

Your man? What an odd way to refer to Peter.

"No he can't. This was the best job Peter could find. And the closest."

"Can you stay and he go?" Tears rolled down her mother's cheeks.

How could her mother suggest that? "No, Mom. He's my husband and I have to go with him."

"But what about me? And your father? What about Hanna and Ben?" Those questions. Hearing her mother verbalize them broke through the walls of justification that Abby had built around her emotions since returning from Richmond. Resentment billowed within her.

"Why is it always about everyone else?" Abby exclaimed. Her face got hot and she struggled to tone down her voice. "I have to take care of everyone, but what about me? This isn't what I want either. You think I want to leave my kids? My job? My life? And be so far from you and Dad?" She bent down to reach into her purse, grateful to have a reason to be released from her mother's stricken gaze. She pulled out a packet of tissues and blew her nose. She straightened and handed one to her mother.

Picking up her empty coffee cup Abby carried it to the counter, the cup rattling in its saucer. She poured coffee into it, not really wanting more, and walked back to the table. What was she thinking, lashing out at her mother? She was a heartbreaking sight, so sad, so small and helpless, dabbing at her eyes with trembling hands. Abby set the coffee down and put her arms around her mother, hugging tightly.

"I'm sorry, Mom. I shouldn't have yelled at you." She kissed her mother's cheek and sat in her chair. "This isn't what we wanted to happen to our life either. It's been really hard for us."

"Yes, but not as hard as it is for me. I broke my hip and had to move here. And your father is bad, bad. And now you leave too. I wish I was dead."

"Oh, Mom." Abby sighed deeply. There was nothing to say. She picked up the cookie and took a bite. It was tasteless. She put it down. "Shall we go see Dad?"

"No. I'm drinking tea." Her mother picked up her cup and sipped. Swallowing, she said in a trembling voice, "When do you go?"

"In about a month. Peter starts his job in September. I have a lot to do before that, but you can visit us for a few days. See Ben and Hanna, and Peter."

"No. Not with this wheelchair. It's too much work to get in and out."

"Are you sure?" Guiltily, Abby felt relieved that her mother turned down the invitation. "It might be good for you to get out of here for a little while."

"I said no, Abby."

Abby looked out the window. A stooped, gray-haired man was walking along the paths struggling with his cane. Why was life so hard?

The clatter of cup on saucer made Abby turn to her mother, who was pushing her cup away. "Let's go to your father," her mother said, putting her hands on the wheels of her chair.

He was sitting in his brown recliner, not reclining but staring out the window.

"Hey, Dad." Abby kissed him on the cheek.

"Huh? Oh, hello." He pushed himself up. "Nice of you to come." His eyes were expressionless, not a spark of recognition passed through them. "Please splake down."

Splake? She put her hand on his arm. "Actually, I was thinking we could go for a walk in the garden. It's a beautiful day outside."

"Hmph." Her mother's voice pierced the room. She pointed to Abby's father. "Nick gets scared outside."

"Really? He was happy to go walking the last time I was here."

"Not now."

"Want to go outside, Dad? For a walk?"

His vacant stare became confused. "Huh?"

She pointed to the window. "Out there?"

"To the buckle? No." He sat back down in his chair, shaking his head. Abby wasn't sure what to do. Should she tell him she was going to move away? He didn't even know who she was. She looked over at her mother, raising her eyebrows, questioning.

Her mother worked her wheelchair over to her husband and positioned it between him and the window. Facing him, she held his face in her hands, forcing him to look at her. "Nick, your daughter Abby is here." She turned her head toward Abby and lowered her voice. "He doesn't get it." Speaking louder, she said, "She's moving away from us."

Abby's father said nothing. He gave his wife a weak smile, shook his head and turned to the window again. Her mother turned her chair toward Abby. "You see? He is bad, very bad."

"I see that." She moved closer to her mother and said quietly, "Are you still okay with having him in your room, Mom? Maybe he should be moved to the full-care floor."

"What? Leave me here alone? You don't know what you're saying, Abby."

"I was just thinking he might be getting to be too much trouble for you."

"He's no trouble. He stays here. He's my husband."

"You're right, Mom." Abby raised her hands in the air. "We have to stick with our husbands."

Her mother nodded, looking sad and sheepish.

Abby kissed the top of her father's head. "Good to see you, Dad." She turned to her mother. "Let's you and I go for a walk."

Out in the garden the sun dappled patterns on the walkway. Beds of red and white petunias, yellow and orange marigolds and purple phlox created islands of color in the green grass. Not for the first time, Abby sent a silent appreciation to the man who maintained the grounds.

"It is so beautiful out here, isn't it?" she said as she wheeled her mother toward the pond. "Those petunias are so lush and full, even this late in the summer."

"Ted puts Miracle-Gro on them." It was so like her mother to be on a first name basis with the gardener. No doubt she'd help him in the garden if not confined to a wheelchair.

Pushing the chair to a bench, Abby sat down. She looked at her mother and smiled tentatively. She touched her mother's knee.

"I'm sorry that we're moving, but it's going to happen whether we want it to or not." She leaned forward and held her mother's hands. "I'll miss you and miss being able to be here for you. But Richmond is only a day's drive away and I'll try to visit you as often as I can. Okay?"

"Not okay. But what can you do."

Abby knew she had to deal with another issue. Might as well just say it. "Mom, we need to decide what to do about your house."

"My house?"

"Yes. It's been sitting empty for months. You know Dad won't be able move back there any more. Probably you won't either."

"But…"

Abby held up her hand. "Let me finish. Even though you go to physiotherapy every day, you still can't move around without your wheelchair. How could you get through those narrow halls in the house?" Abby shook her head. This wasn't what she meant to focus on.

"You want to stay here with Dad because he can't leave anymore. And if something happens to Dad," she squeezed her mother's hand, "you'll probably stay here. The house is costing money just sitting empty. And Peter and I won't be able to take care of it when we've moved so it will get run down. It makes more sense to sell it."

"It's a good house," her mother said weakly.

"Yes it is, and we had great times in it, didn't we?" But Abby didn't want to get nostalgic now. "Maybe it's time to let some other young family have great times in it."

"Oh, Abby." Her mother's voice shook and she started sobbing. Abby waited her out, rubbing her mother's frail shoulders, trying to control her own tears. After a few minutes her mother took a deep breath, directing her gaze over Abby's shoulder. "I knew it. You put me here and you sell the house." There was no fire in her words, only resignation. "I don't want to."

"I know you wish things were different and you want to keep your house. But you can't. I think you know that."

Her mother nodded. "You do it. I'll sign the paper."

Abby had expected more resistance and was relieved that her mother had capitulated so quickly. And yet she missed her feisty mom who wouldn't have given in at all.

"Abby?" Her mother looked into Abby's face. "Why did Peter lose his job? Was he fired?"

"Oh, Mom, no. He wasn't fired." Abby leaned back on the bench and explained to her mother about the company needing to cut costs, and how in these times businesses let people go all the time. "We'll be all right, Mom. The job he got in Richmond pays well. And Peter's leaving Hearth Financial with no bad feelings."

"And you? What will you do?"

"I don't know yet, Mom. I guess I'll figure it out when we get there."

"It's bad that you have to go. Poor Ben and Hanna."

"Well, they're growing up too, Mom."

"I know."

They sat quietly for a few minutes. The sound of a lawnmower rumbled in the distance. A squirrel ran up a tree, chattering at them. Abby began a list in her mind of what she needed to do about selling her parents' house. She'd call a realtor and set it up before she left Woodstock this afternoon. And they'd need to figure out what to do with all of her parents' things. Maybe have a garage sale. That would mean spending a day or two in Woodstock....

"Abby?"

"Hm?"

"Will you visit me every month?"

Could she really promise that? "I'll come as often as I can, Mom. We'll see how the driving goes. But yes, I will try for every month. Okay?"

****

Abby awakened with the realization that her nest would become truly empty today. She opened her eyes and looked at the clock, sitting up with a start. How could she have slept so late on the day Hanna was moving to the university? Still, there wasn't any rush. They packed the van last night, ready for Hanna's move-in at eleven this morning. And Hanna was in charge of the last-minute things.

A knock sounded at the door.

"Mom? Can I come in?"

Hanna slowly pushed the door open. She was already dressed, wearing jeans and a red t-shirt, her hair pulled back in a ponytail. She held Max, who was squirming in her arm, hanging over it like a dishrag. "Dad said I could wake you. I brought you some tea."

"Oh thanks, sweetie, come on in." She patted Peter's side of the bed. "Come sit beside me."

Hanna handed her mother the tea and put Max on the bed. She sat down beside Abby, puffing Peter's pillow before leaning back on it, and brought her knees up, forming a triangular arch. Max walked through the arch, across Abby's stomach, and settled at the end of the bed beside the mounds that were her feet.

"Today's the day." Hanna put her arms around her knees. "I can't believe I'm moving out. I keep thinking there's more to do before I go, but everything's ready." She sighed. "I wish we could go sooner than eleven."

"Waiting is a drag, eh? But the school has to coordinate a lot of students moving in today." Abby remembered when they moved Ben to residence, a lifetime ago it seemed. A confusion of students, boxes, computers, trunks. "You are going to have such an exciting year."

"I know. I wonder what it'll be like." She leaned back. No doubt imagining campus life. Abby shifted her feet. Max pounced on them. She wiggled them, teasing him. Enjoy it while you can, she thought.

"I remember going off to university when I was your age," Abby said. "I felt so free, so independent, so grown-up."

"Yeah, but it's different for me. You still had your home to go back to if you wanted. I won't."

"You'll have a home, Hanna. It'll just be farther away." Abby wished Hanna's excitement about today didn't have to be dampened by their upcoming move to Richmond. "Besides, you'll be so busy making new friends, getting used to campus life, practicing," she poked Hanna, "and studying, that you won't even notice we're gone."

"Yes I will. I won't be able to come home to do laundry. And I won't have my room anymore. Just some other room in Richmond." Hanna scratched behind

Max's ear. "It won't be the same. My home will be gone."

Abby knew that to try to dissuade Hanna from this attitude right now would be pointless. "Have you heard from Jason?" Jason had departed for Windsor the day before. Hanna had gone to his house early in the morning to see him off and returned home sad and quiet.

"Yeah, he called last night. He likes his roommate and he says his whole floor is cool. He said they've got all kinds of lame frosh activities this week." Hanna looked at Abby. "They sound fun to me, but he thinks they're lame. We'll probably have the same kind of stuff."

"I think it's so great that Emily is your room-mate."

"Yeah, me too. Oh, I have to call her about those posters." Hanna jumped off the bed. "Get up soon, okay, Mom? We don't want to be late." She picked up Max, squeezing him to her chest. "You come with me, Max. This is the last day I can cuddle you too. Poor Max." The accusing look she shot her mother was fleeting, almost non-existent. She air-kissed in Abby's direction and left the room.

Abby would not let herself feel guilty about Max's appointment with death the next day. In fact, she was not going to think about Max at all today. She watched Hanna walk down the hall. Her baby. So grown-up.

She picked up her tea and sat back against her pillow. Wasn't life odd? You have these beautiful babies, you nurture them, you worry over them, you build your life around them, and suddenly they're grown-up and gone. What was it all for? Twenty years of emotional investment to end up without them. Abby thought about her mother, sitting in the nursing home feeling lonely for her daughter. Now it was Abby's turn. Ben was on his own. Hanna was going off today. Would Abby yearn for her kids the way her mother did for Abby? In the end, there didn't seem to be any point to it at all.

"Abby," Peter called from downstairs. "Do you want me to bring you breakfast up there?"

"No, I'll be down in a few minutes." She drank the last of her tea and headed for the shower.

****

The chaos was the same as she remembered from moving Ben to Nipissing. The only difference was the campus and the color of the volunteers' t-shirts. Purple and gold clad students guided their car to where they could unload Hanna's things and then showed Peter where to park. Now Abby stood amidst Hanna's boxes, feeling like a guard dog, waiting for Peter to return.

Hanna was talking to a volunteer, getting directions to her residence room. The area was a maze of boxes, trunks, suitcases, parents and freshmen unloading, people mingling, shaking hands, cars coming and going. Amazing how it all comes together, Abby thought.

"Abby."

She looked behind her and saw Diana helping to unload Emily's things.

Hanna brushed past Abby. "Emily's here." She ran to Emily and hugged her. The two girls jumped up and down, squealing. Abby walked over to them.

"Hi, Diana, Stan. Emily, I can tell that you're not excited at all."

"This is going to be so great." Hanna linked her arm in Emily's. "Let's go sign in and get our keys. I was waiting for you."

"How are you guys doing?" Abby took a box from the back of their van.

Diana put down the suitcase that was in her hand and stretched her back. "Oh, you know. Excited for Emily. Sad she's leaving home."

"And joyful," Stan interjected.

"That too. How about you?"

Abby looked in the direction the girls had gone. She couldn't see them. "The same. Won't it be strange to not have any kids at home?"

"Strange, wonderful, difficult, interesting. But I'm ready for it."

"I guess I am too. I have to be."

Stan pulled out a box with a picture of a computer monitor on it. "You'll be going through a move yourselves soon. Hopefully yours will be calmer than this." He chuckled. "Remember residence life? I loved it. Lucky girls." He put the box down and slammed the trunk door. "That was the last of it. I'm going to park the car."

Then suddenly Peter was in front of her. "Let's find the girls and get them settled into their new home," he said.

Hanna and Emily's room was brightly lit by a large window. On either side were mirror images of furniture groupings: bed, side table, desk, wardrobe. Abby opened a box and took out Hanna's alarm clock. "Are you going to have this bed, Hanna?"

"Um, I don't know." Hanna looked at Emily. "Do you care which bed you get?"

"They look the same to me."

Diana was unpacking a suitcase. "I'm putting your underwear in the top drawer, Emily."

"Mom." Emily closed the lid of the suitcase. "I'll put my stuff away."

"Yeah," Hanna said. "Why don't you guys go? Emily and I can set our room up. We want to do it."

"But there's so much." Abby wanted to make sure it was all organized so the girls could settle in quickly. "And we're here now so we can help you."

"But we don't want any help."

Peter climbed out from under a desk where he'd been hooking up wires to the computer. "You sure, Hanna?"

"Yes, go." She hugged her mother. "I love you, Mom. I'll call you this week."

The girls walked their parents to the door of the building. Hugs, kisses, words of advice, we'll calls, be goods echoed in the hall.

That was it? The good-bye? It felt so rushed Abby hardly felt the pangs of sadness she'd expected to feel while saying good-bye to Hanna. It all seemed too jovial.

Peter put his arm around Abby's waist. "Our little girl is off on her own. We're free."

"I know. Why aren't I sadder?"

He let go of her. "Geez, Abby, you don't always have to question your emotions. Just feel what you feel."

"You're right. Yippee." She didn't say it like a cheer.

"Abs," Peter stopped and held her shoulders. "It's okay to feel happy about having the kids grow up and move on. I'm sure there will be plenty of other times when you'll feel nostalgic and miss them like crazy. But let's enjoy this for what it is now. Okay?"

"Okay."

"Shall we go out for lunch?"

"Uh huh."

"And then we'll go home and peruse the realtor Web sites to see if we can find our new house."

Chapter Sixteen

The airport was bustling with travelers, but the room Abby and Peter were waiting in was quiet. The customs officer had taken their passports and sent them here to process their visas. Abby was a little anxious. What if the visa wasn't granted? Peter had explained to her that through NAFTA he should get a one-year visa just by showing his job offer and university degree. The process was supposed to be straightforward; show up at the border, hand them the documents, and they'd get their visas. Still, what if they hadn't brought the right documents? Before they left, Peter checked and re-checked the folder containing his letter of employment, his degree and certificates attesting to his professional designations. The only document Abby was required to bring was her passport.

"Are you sure?" she asked as they were gathering things together before leaving. "Don't I need anything else?"

"No, we're going because of my job." Peter sorted the documents into his briefcase. "You're just my spouse accompanying me. You'll get a different kind of visa and all you need is I.D. and proof of citizenship."

She felt a little insignificant in this process. Just a spouse? What exactly would her status be in this new life of theirs?

Now they sat in the U.S. customs and immigration office at Pearson Airport, like high school students waiting to be called to the principal. Peter squeezed Abby's hand and opened his briefcase, rifling through the papers in it.

She looked around at the other people sitting on the rows of plastic seats. A stylish couple sat in one corner. The woman, tall and thin, was wearing white Capri pants, a white sleeveless blouse, and white sandals with impossible looking heels. Her husband, at least Abby assumed it was her husband, was also completely in white, with his pleated white pants, white shirt, and white Dockers. He held a black briefcase, a stark contrast to their attire. Abby wondered why they would choose to wear white while traveling; surely they didn't expect to arrive clean wherever they were going. Sitting by the wall were a mother and father with two young children. The mother had on a bright pink sari, her dark hair hanging in a long braid down her back. She was rocking a baby bundled up in a sunny yellow blanket. The father wore a suit and tie, reading a picture book to his little son. "Big tuck," the boy kept exclaiming, pointing to the book. He was so cute, big brown eyes, dark hair, round cheeks, pudgy little fingers. Abby wanted to go over there and cuddle him.

A door at the far end opened and a uniformed woman, short and stocky with frizzy orange hair, came through it.

"Winston," she said to the room. The couple in white stood up and walked through the door. The orange-haired woman looked at the clipboard in her hand. "Settel," she announced.

Abby looked at Peter, who smiled at her as he stood up. "That's us."

She picked up her bag and followed Peter through the door. The woman directed them toward one of two wickets. The couple in white was nowhere to be seen. Abby stood beside Peter but had to lean in to see the woman who would help them. Peter took out his documents and laid them on the counter.

"What kind of job will you be doing for Asset Credit Union?" the woman asked him.

"I'll be in marketing and product development. We're still developing the job description."

"I see. And you, ma'am," the woman peered over her glasses. "Are you planning to work in Richmond?"

Abby was startled to be asked a question. "I don't have any immediate plans to, no."

"Well, with this TD visa you won't be allowed to work at all. So be sure you don't."

"Okay."

Peter's hand pressed on Abby's waist at the back, out of sight from the woman who was shuffling through Peter's documents. Abby touched it.

"Do we have everything you need?" he asked her.

"Oh yes. It's all in order." She got up and disappeared into the back. Peter gave Abby a quick kiss on her cheek, just in time it seemed, for the woman returned almost immediately. For the second time, Abby felt like a high school student, nervous in the face of authority.

"Okay, I've stapled your visas to your passports." The woman handed them through the wicket window.

Abby took them and looked at the card stapled in hers. Alien resident, it said. She felt a twinge of anticipation. The adventure was beginning.

Peter stuffed the papers back into his briefcase. "You keep the passports, Abby. We'll probably need them later." He looked at his watch. "It's a good thing we came to the airport early. We have to board in half an hour."

****

On the plane, finally, Abby had trouble focusing on her book. She nibbled on the pretzels the flight attendant had given her and sipped her cranberry juice. Peter was engrossed in his Border Guide book, headphones covering his ears. She leaned back and looked out the window, seeing nothing but sky. It was strange to be sitting doing nothing after the last weeks of what seemed like frenetic activity. Sorting what to take to Richmond now, what to take later. Listing their house with a realtor. Tying up loose ends at work. Farewell parties. Moving Ben. Moving Hanna. Taking Max to the vet for the last time. Selling her parents' house. A week after listing it, they'd received an offer that was three thousand dollars short of the asking price. Much discussion and cajoling with her mother ensued, but eventually she agreed and it was done. Abby hoped their own house would sell as easily. She laid her head back on the seat and stared at the video screen in front of her, wondering what her new life would be like.

Transition

"You can clutch the past so tightly to your chest that it leaves your arms too full to embrace the present."

~ Jan Glidewell

"One must lose one's life in order to find it."
~ Anne Morrow Lindbergh

"You change your life by changing your heart."

~ Max Lucado

Chapter Seventeen

Autumn
Richmond, Virginia

They stepped out of the elevator into the hotel lobby. "What does she look like?" Peter asked. He glanced around and stared at the front doors.

"I don't know." Abby directed her gaze toward the chairs. She spotted her immediately, a tall woman wearing a cream tailored suit with a bright red blouse, hair piled high on her head stiff like a helmet, and her lips bright red to match her nails.

The woman rose from her chair and approached them with her hand outstretched. "Hello, are you the Settels?" The scent of her perfume was strong and Abby sneezed.

"Yes, I'm Peter." He shook her hand. "And this is Abby."

"I'm Trixie," she said, shaking Abby's hand with a grip so firm it almost crushed Abby's fingers. Abby flexed her hand behind her purse to ease the pain.

"Now, what kind of home are y'all looking for," she asked in her soft, southern drawl after they sat down. "New? Old?"

Abby looked at Peter and replied, "New or old doesn't really matter. But we want something different from the regular family style home. It's just the two of us, so not too big, but with room enough for our two kids to stay when they visit."

"And low maintenance, if possible," Peter interjected, "so if it's old, it's got to be renovated."

Abby sat forward. "And I'd like to be in a location where I can walk to things, like the library and shops."

"And we'd love to find a house with lots of trees in the yard. They're so amazing around here."

Trixie looked from one to the other. "How about the older areas like the Fan or the museum district?"

"I wouldn't mind looking there." Abby glanced at Peter, who was shaking his head. "It would be great to be so close to everything."

"No, I don't want to park our cars on the street and deal with those big old house problems."

"How about Westhampton or Tuckahoe?"

Abby and Peter stared at each other.

"The West End? Southside?"

"We're not sure," Abby said. "Can you show us a mixture of places? We don't really know many of the areas."

"What price range are we looking at?"

"Um," Peter tugged at his ear lobe, "around three."

"Three hundred thousand?" Trixie sounded surprised.

"Well, between three and four, but we'd prefer to keep it lower rather than higher."

Abby knew he was being cautious because they hadn't sold their Waterloo house yet. But surely they could go higher.

Apparently Trixie thought likewise. "You can't go higher than four?"

Peter hesitated. "Why don't we first look at the three to four price range."

"Um," Abby opened the file folder she brought with her, "we've printed up some listings for houses we found on the Internet." She handed the pages to Trixie. "We're not really sure where they are. Can we see them?"

"Oh good. It'll give me some idea." Trixie took them from her, putting on glasses. The frames were multi-coloured with sparkly rhinestones. "Let's see." She leafed through the papers and flipped them over one by one. "Sold. Sold. Okay. Oh, you don't want that one." She briefly looked up, peering at Abby and Peter over her glasses. "Not a good neighborhood." She returned to the pages. "Sold. Nice. Sold. Not for my money," she said waving the last one, adding it to the discard pile. "There's been a lot of activity these past weeks. It's a seller's market."

She picked up the sheets she'd placed to one side. "I can call these two and print off other listings for you. We'll set up showings for tomorrow." Again she peered over her glasses. "Would that be all right?"

"That'd be great." Abby sat back. This was daunting. How could they decide what area to live in when they knew absolutely nothing about the city?

For the rest of the afternoon Trixie drove them around in her car, showing them different parts of Richmond. They saw new subdivisions with pretty houses built close together and few trees.

"We're not interested in places like these," Peter said right away. "Been there, done that."

Abby nodded in agreement.

Areas near downtown intrigued her, but Peter disliked the congestion. He was more interested in developments on the other side of the river, close to golf courses, like Stonehenge and Salisbury, with their charming houses, large lots, and abundant trees.

"But they're too big, Peter," Abby protested. "And wouldn't it take too long to drive to work from here?"

"This isn't going to be easy, is it?" Trixie said as she turned the steering wheel.

Abby agreed with her. It seemed that she and Peter wanted different things. Was her dream of a cute little love nest on a tree-lined street within walking distance to restaurants and shops going to be foiled by Peter's dream of land, trees, and golf?

****

Trixie had four listings to show them in addition to the two they'd asked about and they went into two open house showings. But none of the houses were quite what they were looking for, not that they really knew what that was. They were either too large, or in too much disrepair, or too far from the office, or with rooms too small, or had odd layouts. The asking price rose with each subsequent house Trixie showed them.

"I'll just have to keep looking to find what you want," Trixie said as she pulled into the hotel parking lot.

"I guess we're not quite sure ourselves." Peter sounded apologetic. "It's hard to know when the city is unfamiliar."

"And it's just the two of us, not our kids," Abby interjected, "so we're trying to figure out what will fit this new life of ours."

"I understand, hon. I'll keep looking. You want to get together again tomorrow?"

"I'm starting work, so not me." Peter turned to Abby. "Do you want to look at places with Trixie tomorrow?"

"I have to move our stuff into the apartment and settle in, so no. In fact, why don't we wait until I come back from Canada."

"You going back there again?" Trixie looked surprised.

"I fly back Wednesday. I'll be picking up my car and bringing back things we couldn't take on the plane. But I'll come back on the weekend. Let's look at more houses then. I'll call you."

After Trixie dropped them off, they drove around on their own looking for For Sale signs, trying to decide where they might want to live. All Abby wanted was a smallish house within walking distance to amenities. And Peter wanted something they could pay cash for. Would they find such a place in Richmond?

It was difficult not to feel discouraged as they settled down to bed.

"It's too bad that most of the ones we found on the Internet were sold already," she said, fluffing her pillow and opening her book. "One of them could've been the one."

"Yeah. It's the market. If we see something we like, we might have to jump on it quickly." He sounded distracted. He leafed through the Asset Credit Union binder.

"Are you nervous about starting work tomorrow?"

"A bit. I'll have to learn a whole new job. It'll be interesting, considering I've been doing the same thing for the last eighteen years. But kinda scary too."

"But the people there are nice, right?"

"Yeah, it'll be good." He put the booklet on the side table. "You okay with moving our stuff to the apartment alone?"

"It's only three suitcases, Peter. I think I can manage." She leaned over and kissed his cheek. "I'll have the place set up and dinner waiting when I pick you up to take you home." Home. An apartment with rented furniture. How strange that would be.

The next morning they packed their things into the car and checked out of the hotel. Abby dropped Peter off at work and drove to the Village at Willow Park. She smiled going through the gates of the apartment complex and walked into the office with a bounce in her step. She was moving in today. Her home in Richmond, phase one.

The woman in the office was very apologetic. "I'm sorry Mrs. Settel, but there's been a delay with the furniture rental company. They won't be moving in your things 'til ten and it'll take them a few hours. Then the relocation company has to do the final walkthrough. They're coming at three. You can move in around four, I would imagine."

"But I've already checked out of the hotel. I thought I'd be able to get settled this morning." Abby was not so much disappointed as panicked. Where should she go? What was she going to do until four?

"I know. And I'm sorry. You're welcome to use our facilities. You can sit in the community room here. Or in the business center and use the computer. Or you can go for a swim." The woman smiled helplessly at her.

"No, that's all right." Abby did not want to delve into her suitcase for a bathing suit. She wasn't sure she'd even packed one. "Can I at least get the key?"

"I'm sorry, you'll have to come and pick up the key when the relocation company drops it off."

Dejected, Abby walked to the car. She drove through the maze of apartment buildings until she found number forty-two and parked directly across from the entrance. She climbed the stairs to the third floor. It was a novelty to have the stairs exposed to the outdoors. She guessed that in this southern climate it was normal. At number nine she stopped. This was going to be her temporary home. She knocked. There was no sound from within. She tried the knob. The door was locked. How she wished she could have a look inside.

She started back down the stairs and sat on the bottom step. She looked around at the other buildings, at the trees surrounding the complex, at the parking lot. She gazed at the rental car. What an ugly thing. The Dodge 300 looked like a big white tank. At least the trunk held the three big suitcases with no problem. Soon they'd be able to replace it with Peter's company car. It would be nice to drive around in a brand new Acura. But she wished she had her Honda here.

She pulled out her cell phone to call Peter. Flipping it open, she realized she had no idea how to reach him. He was probably too busy to talk anyway. She punched in Diana's number instead and got her voice mail. The same for Hanna and Ben. About to call her parents, she snapped the phone shut. No need to burden her mom right now. She thought about her life back home and wondered who was teaching her courses. And how the new freshmen classes were going. She sighed. What should she do? No places to go. No people to see.

Her seat was getting cold on the concrete step and she stood up. Ruefully, she remembered the last time she had sat on concrete steps, at Ben's house in Toronto, wondering frantically where he was. Hopefully he was doing okay on his own in Waterloo.

She walked to the car. A whole day to fill and nothing with which to fill it.

Chapter Eighteen

Abby sawed at the tomato, squashing it under her fingers. This knife was too dull. She picked up the tomato and threw it and the knife down in frustration. Pulp and seeds scattered on the floor; the knife clattered and bounced away from her. Shocked by her actions, she stared at the mess, then tore off a length of paper towel. What was she doing in this apartment filled with things that weren't hers, preparing food with impossible utensils? She should have brought more of her own kitchen things. She couldn't believe she'd been excited about living in this place.

"It's so cute," she'd said to Peter when they ate their first meal here. "It'll be like playing house." Four weeks of playing house were enough for her. The bed was uncomfortable. The couch was hard. The walls and carpet were beige and bland. The dining table and chairs were flimsy on their metal legs. And the kitchen was under stocked. Dull knives, thin saucepans, not enough dishes. How she longed for home.

Her days were dull too. And lonely. She'd never spent so much time alone. Each morning when Peter left for work, she was faced with hours as blank as white sheets of paper. She'd stay in her nightgown most mornings, e-mailing friends, playing computer solitaire, surfing realtor Web sites, watching TV. Often she'd get dressed only to go to Blockbuster to rent DVDs.

Some days she would force herself to be more productive. She'd exercise in the fitness room, wander around the mall, or drive around exploring Richmond. Once she went to a support group for women who'd moved, but she'd run out and hadn't gone back. Other days she'd call Trixie, even though the woman annoyed her, just so she could talk to someone who knew her, and they would tour houses Abby didn't want to live in. But those days were infrequent. Mostly Abby stayed in the apartment, alone, wallowing in her life of nothing.

She hated herself for being like this. She knew that, compared with much of the world's population, she had it good. A husband and children who loved her, overabundance of food, shelter, good health. She'd even moved to a country that spoke the same language. She pointed these things out to herself, trying to talk herself out of her malaise, admonishing herself for being ungrateful. But plucking these strings of guilt didn't work. She continued in her despondency, inexplicably feeling powerless to change.

Today had begun like most. She climbed out of bed to walk Peter to the door and then went to the window to watch him drive away, waving him off to work. In the kitchen she put on a pot of coffee and made up her breakfast tray. Granola, yogurt, and fruit. Once again she was frustrated that she'd forgotten to buy vitamins. She took the tray to the living room and pulled out the DVD case for the current series she was watching, Sex and the City. She had only two episodes left, and a whole other disc with special features including three alternative endings. Maybe she'd finish by lunchtime.

When the final chapter ended, she stared at the pile of wet tissues on the coffee table and considered the show. Carrie Bradshaw had tried a new life in Paris, away from her friends, having left her job, her home. She wandered the streets of Paris alone, day after day, adrift. Abby knew exactly how she felt.

But Carrie returned to New York, back to the life she knew she was meant to live, back home. Abby wondered what life she was meant to live. This hollow one here in Richmond? Could she ever go back to her old life, the way Carrie had?

Abby knew her life didn't compare. She was here with Peter, who was her partner, her soul mate, had been for almost twenty-six years. Their love and commitment were enough for her to stay here, to make a life here.

Weren't they?

She blew her nose and rewound to watch the final scene again, munching on a cookie. The reunion of Carrie with her friends at one of their regular New York restaurants started Abby's tears afresh. They were so happy to be together again, confirming the bond that had held strong through many of life's hurdles. Abby felt a kinship with them, as if she knew them. She felt like she was part of their group. She wanted to be in that restaurant with them.

"These are the only friends I have in Richmond," she lamented aloud. "And they're not even real."

She was pitiful.

Enough!

She turned off the TV and put the discs into their case. She would not watch the special features disc. This was the end of her couch-potato life.

She gathered her breakfast dishes, coffee cup, Oreo cookie bag. The bag was empty, even though she'd just opened it this morning. Had she eaten them all? No more junk food either.

A new Abby would emerge today.

She put on sweats and went to the fitness room where she power walked for a half hour on the treadmill. She cleaned the apartment and did the laundry. She showered and dressed, returned the DVDs without picking up more, then shopped for groceries. She walked to Barnes and Noble and bought the Richmond Source-book, hoping it would give her ideas of things to do. Back at the apartment she made lasagna, one of Peter's favourite meals, and set the table with candles, was just now making a salad. She was proud of her productive afternoon.

But the squashed tomato undid her. She sank to the floor, leaning her back against the cabinets. How pathetic it was, to feel such pride in accomplishing these minor things that had been commonplace in her old life.

Pathetic indeed. It was as if she'd taken giant steps backward, back to being Mrs. Housewife, with no role except to keep the house—apartment—running smoothly. There was no point to this life. She wrung the paper towel in her hand, trying to swallow the lump that had wedged itself in her throat. She wiped her eyes with the twisted paper towel.

Staring at the knife and tomato pulp on the floor, she was startled by the phone ringing. She took a deep breath as she picked up the receiver.

"Hello?" She hoped her voice didn't sound like she'd been crying.

"Mom?"

"Hanna. Sweetie." The sound of her daughter's voice was like honey. She missed Hanna so much. It was hard being here without her kids. And now, here was Hanna, calling her. "How are you?" She tossed the paper towel on the counter.

"Oh, Mom, I bombed in master-class today. It was awful."

"What happened?"

"I don't know. I practiced the Allemande a lot, but when I played it in front of the class, I just blew it. My trills were a mess and I couldn't work the breathing right. Dr. Wallace didn't have anything good to say about my performance. I wanted to sink into the floor."

"I'm sorry, honey." Abby walked into the living room and sat down on the couch. The Richmond Sourcebook lay on the table and she rifled its pages.

"You'll do better next time, I'm sure. How's everything else?"

"Not great. Theory sucks and my history professor's a joke. I hate residence. It's so noisy; people are always getting drunk. Emily's hardly ever around. And Jason isn't calling me." Hanna's voice started quivering. "I just wanna come home."

So do I, Abby thought, so do I. "Hanna, you know we...."

"I know, Mom." Hanna sighed loudly through the receiver. "It's just hard. I miss you."

"I miss you too. We'll see you Friday for Thanksgiving when you come down here." Abby tried her best to comfort Hanna, to boost her spirits. But she didn't know how to drag herself out of despair enough to help Hanna.

When the phone call ended, when their voices stopped—hers, Hanna's—the silence in the apartment pressed in on her.

She punched in Ben's number. It rang and rang, finally his voice mail answered.

"Hey, it's Ben," his voice said cheerfully. "Leave a message."

"Hi, Ben, it's Mo..."

A digital voice interrupted. "The voice mail box is full."

Ben should be available to answer his cell phone. He would be finished work by now. That too familiar feeling of dread overcame Abby and she quashed it down. He was fine, she told herself.

Unwilling to relinquish the phone just yet, the contact with people, she dialed her parents' number. Listening to the ringing she stared at the picture on the wall above the TV. Shapes of black, gray, and brown, to blend in with the carpet she supposed, but what was it meant to represent?

"Hello?" Her mother's voice sounded hoarse.

"Hi, Mom, it's Abby. How are you doing?"

"Not so good. I have a cold. I sniffle and cough." She coughed into the receiver as if to prove it. "They give me medicine for it. Are you coming to visit soon?"

"No, Mom, I was just there a few weeks ago, remember? When I came to pick up my car and stuff?" Abby thought back to that hectic and emotional trip home and the long drive back to Richmond alone. She wasn't ready to take that on again so soon. "I was just thinking about you and called to see how things were going. How's Dad?"

"He has a cold too. But he's not so bad. I sniffle and cough more than him. They don't let us off the floor because everyone has a cold." She coughed again. "And nobody visits."

"Has Aunt Josie been lately?"

"Yes, she was here this morning. She brought me muffins."

"Oh, that was nice of her." As they spoke of trivial things, Abby realized her own life had been reduced to one not unlike her mother's. Neither of them did anything worth talking about. If only she still lived in Waterloo, she'd take her mother out, stimulate her more. Her dad too. She shouldn't be living here, so far away.

****

The sound of the door opening jerked Abby into wakefulness. She found herself curled in a fetal position on the couch and bounded upright. The phone clattered to the floor. Peter stood beside her.

"Abby? Are you all right?" He looked around the apartment and she remembered the tomato mess on the kitchen floor.

"Um, yeah." She ran her fingers through her hair. "I guess I fell asleep." Bending down to pick up the phone, she started to cry. She put the phone on the table and leaned her elbows on her knees, covering her face with her hands.

"Aw, Abs." He sat down beside her and held his arm around her shoulders. "You're not doing so well, are you?"

"Well I was earlier, but not now."

"Did you go out today? Make any new friends? Find something to join?"

She wiped at her eyes and sniffed, staring incredulously at him. "Why would you think that? Can't you see I'm a mess?" She shook off his arm and stood.

"I just meant…"

"It's easy for you. You go to work every day. You have an instant social life at the office. I have nowhere to go." She glared down at him. Self-pity gave way to anger and a fire flamed inside her.

He rose off the couch. "But you could…"

"Don't you get it?" She shook her head. "It's like I've been erased. Everything I was is gone. I'm not a mother here. I'm not a teacher here. I'm not a friend here. I'm a nobody here."

Peter sighed, shaking his head. "You know, your continuous self pity is getting a little stale. You…"

"Really? I have no status. I can't get a social security number. I can't arrange anything in my name. It took me weeks to get a damn library card. Our credit card is in your name. This rental lease is in your name. So's my cell phone. I couldn't even register our new Acura. It's a wonder I have a driver's license."

"Abby, you know that's temporary. Eventually…"

"Your new life is blossoming. My new life is nothing. Nothing! I hate you for bringing me here."

He grabbed her shoulders. "You know you don't mean that."

"Just leave me alone." She shook him off. Kicking aside his briefcase, she turned the knob on the door and stepped out. Briefly she looked back at him. "The lasagna in the oven will be ready soon. Eat it. I'm going out." The door slammed behind her and she ran down the three flights of stairs into the parking lot.

Now what? Standing on the asphalt, she heard their door open above her. Peter's voice echoed in the stairwell.

"Abby?"

His footsteps clattered on the stairs.

"Abby?"

No. She didn't want to talk to him right now. In a frenzy she looked for somewhere to hide. She could hear him getting closer; already he'd turned on the landing and was coming down the second flight. Running to a big van parked beside her Honda, she crouched behind it, peering round the side.

He stopped at the bottom of the stairs and looked around.

"Abby, where are you?"

He walked toward her car and looked from it to his. She shrank back, still hidden.

"You can't just run away." His head turned from left to right. "Where'd you go?"

She covered her mouth with her hand. Her frantic heart beat in her ears and she wondered if he could hear it, he was so close. Her knees started to ache but she didn't dare shift position.

He looked past the cars to the road. "Where'd she get to so fast?" he wondered aloud. Cupping his hands around his mouth he called out. "Abby, come on. We should talk about this."

He walked around the parking lot toward the swimming pool, his head swivelling as he scanned the area. She sat back on the asphalt and wrapped her arms around her knees. What was she doing, cowering behind this car as if she were afraid of her husband? She should just stand up and show herself. She strained to watch him.

Eventually he walked back to their building and slowly climbed the stairs up to the apartment, disappearing from view. He must wonder, she thought, he must think I evaporated. He must think I've gone mad.

She stood, her knees creaking. Stretching her back, she looked up at the apartment window. Should she go up and talk to him? Not yet. She wasn't ready to face the words that had spewed out of her.

The air was hot and humid although the sun was low in the sky. Closing her eyes, she inhaled deeply, absorbing the scent of the crape myrtles and the oily smells of the parking lot. Her heart was still beating fast. She felt overwhelmed by what had happened, by what she'd said. She didn't hate Peter. And she wasn't mad at him for moving here.

She walked. Past the parked cars. Past the swimming pool. Past the apartment office with its fitness room and business center. On the sidewalk toward the plaza. Cars drove by. People walked and talked. The sky became a fiery mixture of reds and pinks. She breathed deliberately, filling her lungs deeply and slowly expelling the air. Gradually she felt herself calming down.

The inside lights of stores she passed shone a welcoming glow in the fading light of dusk. Through the window of Patsy's Coffee Shop, she saw a group of women sitting together. They were knitting, talking, laughing. She stopped and stared longingly. Taking a deep breath, she walked inside.

"Are you a knitting group?" she asked the woman sitting closest to the door. The woman was young, with long brown hair and glasses, knitting something florescent pink.

"Yes. We meet here every Tuesday evening at six."

An older, blonde woman beside her looked up. "But it's very loose. Anyone can join us. Do you knit?" She was working on what appeared to be a black scarf.

Abby felt a swell of optimism. "Well, I used to. When my kids were babies. But I'd love to start a project again."

A plump, curly-haired woman across from them patted the empty chair beside her. "Sit down here. Join us. My name is Jane."

"I'm Abby. I just moved here. A month ago. From Canada."

"Canada." A woman whose hair was in a ponytail wearing a tight t-shirt with a low scoop neck put down the yellow yarn she was unraveling. "What part?"

"Do you know Ontario at all? Toronto?"

"No."

"Oh, I know Toronto." A gray-haired woman knitting a multi-coloured sweater turned to Abby. "I love Toronto."

Abby smiled at her. "Well, I lived in a city called Waterloo, about seventy miles west of Toronto."

The woman with the ponytail leaned toward Abby. "Can you tell me what a providence is?" Her southern drawl was very pronounced, reminding Abby where she was.

"A providence?"

"Yes, at school my son learned about that new part of Canada, what's it called, Nuva...Nuvanite?" She said the word very slowly. "They told him it's a providence and he asked me what that was and I didn't know."

"Oh, a province. You mean Nunavut. It's actually a territory. That's sort of like a province. And a province is like a state. You know like Virginia is a state of the U.S.? Ontario is a province of Canada."

"It's up north there, isn't it? That Ontario providence? And cold and snowy?"

Abby had thought that the American view of Canada as the "great white north" was a joke, a cliché. But this woman really thought that. She couldn't believe it. "Only in the winter. In the summer, where I'm from gets almost as hot as here."

"Really? But isn't it up north?"

Heat flared within Abby, as it had earlier with Peter. She stood. The words burst out of her, loud enough to be heard throughout the coffee shop. "You Americans. Do you think we walk around in parkas and snowshoes all the time? Live in igloos? We're not that different from you." She stopped. The women stared at her, their eyes wide, and their mouths open in disbelief. Abby's face flushed. What was she doing? This was no way to make friends. "Uh, sorry. I have to go now."

She left the coffee shop as fast as she could and did not look back. That was one group she would not be joining, one coffee shop she wouldn't be returning to. What was the matter with her? She ran away from the plaza. Crossing Broad Street, she strode toward the mall, cutting through the parking lot to the stores.

Darkness dissolved the dusk as the sun set. Streetlights cast eerie glows on the pavement. She knew she should go back to the apartment, but instead she veered toward the Barnes and Noble store.

She wandered among the aisles, browsing books without paying attention. Her stomach grumbled. She'd only nibbled on carrots and celery when she prepared the salad hours ago and had eaten nothing since. The sounds and aromas from the coffee shop in the store tantalized her, but she had no money with her. She thought longingly of the lasagna in the oven. She hoped Peter had taken it out and eaten it.

What would she say to him when she returned home? The apartment, she corrected herself. Not home. Home was in Waterloo. Home was where her family and beloved things were. Home was where people knew her and where she knew people. Where she knew herself.

Eventually she found a vacant chair in the opposite corner from the coffee shop, a cushy upholstered one, and sank into it, leafing through the books she'd picked up in her browsing. But the words on the pages didn't register. Her mind kept replaying that awful scene with Peter. She felt sick every time she heard herself shout I hate you for bringing me here. And she cringed when she pictured herself hiding behind that van.

It wasn't Peter's fault she was miserable. She was choosing to live her nothing life. She could decide to live differently, couldn't she? She was the one who needed to make her life happen. That's what she always told her kids.

This move had changed her. She didn't know herself any more. She had never before been content to sit and stare at the TV for hours at a time. She never would have allowed herself to wallow in self-pity day after day. What kind of person had she become?

She thought ruefully of the plans she'd shared with her friends for adjusting to her new life. I'm going to take a map of Richmond and divide it in sections, she told them, and every week I'll thoroughly explore one section. I'll join newcomer clubs, find a book club, volunteer. It'll be great. A brand new life. Why hadn't she done any of those things?

She remembered the Lost in Transition meeting she'd run out of last week. The knitting group she'd just insulted. No wonder she was lonely here. She wasn't trying to be a friend. She wasn't giving people a chance.

In e-mails to her friends in Waterloo, she wrote lies. Richmond's great. My life is great. There's so much to do. It was easy to write about something she'd driven past, describing it in detail as if she'd actually participated in something. Via the written word she could be in any mood she chose. There was no quivering voice, no watery eyes to give away how she was really feeling. If only they knew how the tears streaked down her cheeks while she typed at the keyboard.

Only Diana knew. Diana's phone calls were Abby's lifeline. If not for them, Abby could live days on end not speaking to anyone other than Peter. Diana would commiserate with her, comfort her. But then she'd encourage Abby to go out, sounding just like Peter. Take a class. Join a group. Volunteer. Abby would agree with her. Yes, she'd go out, dry her tears, make friends. But when she hung up the phone, she fell back into a pit of self-pity she couldn't crawl out of.

Sitting in the chair at the bookstore, Abby resolved to be different. She would stop being this person she didn't like. She would stop waiting for life to happen.

And then she thought again of Peter. He must be worried sick, wondering what happened to her. He might have gone out again to search for her, maybe called the police. No. He wouldn't have done that.

She didn't know how to face him, how to face the angry words she'd hurled at him. If only she could erase the evening as if it hadn't happened. If only she could go home to Peter and he would say nothing about it; they could carry on and she would try harder to build her life here.

She stayed until the staff began their store closing ritual, until the announcement over the loudspeakers told customers they'd be locking up in fifteen minutes. Reluctantly she got up, tired, hungry, anxious, and walked back to the apartment in the dark.

She dragged herself up the steps to the apartment, relieved to get out of the oppressing darkness and into the welcoming light of the stairwell, but dreading the encounter with Peter. A knot of anxiety was tight in her stomach. Maybe he'd be asleep so she wouldn't have to face him tonight.

She stood outside the door and hesitated. She couldn't hear a sound. Putting her hand on the door-knob, she was suddenly reminded of Ben, understanding how he must have felt when he came home to tell them of his transgressions, waiting at the door afraid to come in.

Quietly she turned the knob. The door was pulled from her hands and Peter stood in front of her. He wrapped his arms around her and held her tight.

"Oh, my God, Abby, you're all right. I was so worried."

"I'm sorry, Peter." Her words were muffled in his shoulder, tears dampening his shirt. "I didn't mean…"

"Shh." He rubbed her back. "I know, Abs. I'm sorry too. As long as you're okay."

He shut the door with his foot, his arms still holding her. They stood like that for a while, he caressing her back, she crying with her face in his shoulder. She held on to him as if to a life preserver, the only familiar person, the only one who knew her in this new life of hers.

Chapter Nineteen

Once again Abby stood in front of the door with the sign that read Welcome to Lost in Transition. She pushed it open and walked through the carpeted hall, ignoring the arrows taped to the walls because she knew the way. Arriving at the meeting room, she didn't allow herself to hesitate and strode right in. Ellen noticed her immediately.

"Abby. We're so glad you came back." It struck Abby that there were no longer only strangers in this room. This woman knew her name.

"Thanks. I decided…" Despite her resolve and purposeful entry, Abby was suddenly self-conscious. "I mean, I think I might need this group after all." She looked down at her sandals. Imagine sandals in October. She raised her head and smiled tentatively at Ellen.

"We'll help in any way we can." Ellen touched her arm. "You'll find it's nice to have people around who know you. That's why we're here. Would you like to fill in a registration card? And a name tag?"

Nodding, Abby followed her to a table. Amidst the pamphlets and newsletters was a stack of cards. She picked one up and looked at the spaces she needed to fill in. Name. Address. Phone number. If she did this, she'd be committed. They'd know how to find her. No running away again.

Ellen gave her a pen. "Just put it in this box when you're done and then have some coffee. Holly baked muffins for us this morning." She waved her arm in the direction of the refreshment table where women stood talking and then went to greet someone at the door.

Abby leaned over the table and began writing. Embarrassed to have forgotten the address of the apartment, she pulled out her driver's license and copied from it. At least she remembered her phone number. She printed Abby Settel on a nametag and peeled off the back, pressing it onto her sweater.

Glancing at the women drinking coffee, she straightened her shoulders and walked over. She picked up a Styrofoam cup and poured coffee into it, putting off the moment when she would have to break into a conversation. Stirring in cream and sugar, she turned and came face to face with the woman who had sat beside her the last time.

"Abby, isn't it?" she asked in her gravelly voice. "I'm Anne, Anne Carter. I remember you from a couple of weeks ago."

Abby's face grew hot. "Yes. I...I couldn't stay."

"Oh, I know it. It can get pretty intense sometimes." Anne sipped her coffee. "You'll be glad you came back, though. This is a good group."

"Have they helped you?" Abby recalled Anne saying she wanted to move back home.

"Kind of. I'm still here, aren't I?"

Another woman approached and gave Anne a quick hug.

"Hi, Anne," she said. "Good to see you."

Abby recognized the woman's highlighted hair and the laugh lines around her eyes, remembered her name was Holly. Happy Holly, she thought.

"Yeah, I'm here again." Anne pointed her coffee cup at Abby. "This is Abby. Who decided to give us another try."

Holly guided a strand of hair behind her ear and smiled at Abby. "I remember you. You're from Canada, right? Moved here without your kids? I did that too. We should get together sometime."

"I'd like that." Something lightened inside of Abby. "It's Holly, isn't it?"

"Yup. Holly from Chicago. I've got two kids, both in college. How about you?"

"I also have two. Hanna's in university. Just started in September. My son Ben's working, taking time off school. They're coming to visit this weekend."

"That's great," Holly said. "You must be excited."

"I am." Abby turned to Anne. "How many kids do you have?"

"I've got three." Anne's voice lost its enthusiasm. "Two teenagers and a ten year old."

"Are they doing any better?" Holly asked, her tone indicating she knew more about them than just their ages.

"The same." Anne looked at Abby. "They're so miserable here. It's been two months and they still hate their schools, still don't have friends. I don't know what to do."

"Oh," was all Abby could think of to say. Imagine Ben and Hanna moving here with them; had they been younger they would have. They might have been just as miserable as Abby was. No, she decided. She would work extra hard to make the adjustment easier for them.

So why wasn't she working harder to make the adjustment easier for herself?

She was now, she reminded herself. She was at this meeting, wasn't she?

"My husband is so uninvolved with it all, so wrapped up in his job." Anne continued her story. "He came here four months ahead of us to start work. I stayed back in San Jose to sell the house and let the kids finish out their year. I had to do everything for this move, drove the U-Haul cross-country with the kids." She shook her head. "And now we're here and Jeff has no time for us. He's such an a…such a jerk."

Abby reflected on Peter, how immersed he was in his job, working longer hours than he used to. But when he was home, he spent time with Abby. He tried hard to make things better for her, even though he didn't know how. She felt lucky.

"Hi, you guys. Good muffins, Holly." Chris, the woman who had cried so much when Abby was here before, joined the three of them. When she caught sight of Abby, she hugged her. "Hi. You're Abby, right? Welcome back. I'm Chris."

Startled by the display of affection from this woman she didn't know, Abby stepped back.

"Hi. Nice to meet you." It came out stiff, standoffish. Relax, she told herself, and held out her hand. Chris shook it then turned to Holly.

"These muffins are awesome. I love the bits of pineapple in them. Can I get the recipe?"

"Sure," Holly said. "You're happy today. What's up?"

"For a change, you mean?" Chris smiled wryly. "I am feeling good today, though. The painters are finished and our house looks great." She turned to Abby. "We just had the whole inside of the house painted. Four weeks of chaos." She laughed. "But not any more. We're all settled."

Abby liked it that Chris was so cheerful. It made her believe there was hope for her too. A woman behind her poured a cup of coffee and came up beside Abby.

"We're glad you came back," she said to Abby in a quiet voice. "Abby, right? I'm Patty, one of the group leaders."

"I remember," Abby said. "I remember your story. How's your baby?"

"Belle's great. I just left her laughing in the nursery." Then she spoke louder, addressing the group. "We're going to start in about five minutes, so get your coffee and muffins and come sit down." Smiling at Abby, she went to the circle of chairs.

"Hey," Holly said. "Do you guys want to go for lunch after the meeting? Do you have any plans, Abby?"

"Hmm, let's see. What's on my agenda? Sitting alone in my apartment." Abby joked, surprising herself. She laughed. "I think I can fit you in." She couldn't remember the last time she'd laughed. It felt good.

Around the circle they talked about how they needed to let go of their old lives in order to embrace their new ones.

"We have to learn to cherish the past and not cling to it," Ellen said. "It's hard to move forward if you don't let go of what you've left."

Patty nodded. "We need to keep our memories close to our hearts because they're important. But," she opened her arms wide, "we also have to let ourselves embrace new experiences, make new memories. Do any of you think you're still clinging?"

Abby considered how she wasn't letting her old life go. When she wasn't distracting herself with TV or the computer, she was thinking about what she was missing back in Waterloo. She mused about her classes at the university and who might be teaching them. She pictured Diana walking with someone else in the mornings. Worries about Ben and Hanna and her parents were always beneath the surface of her mind. And the main reason she hated the apartment so much was because it wasn't their familiar house.

"I remember talking to my best friend on the phone last week," Mandy said. Abby wondered where Mandy's baby was today. Josh, wasn't it? Maybe he was in the nursery with Belle. Mandy twirled a strand of hair. "She was telling me all about how she went to a movie with our friends and then out for dessert. I cried after that phone call." She wiped at her eyes. "All I could think about was how they were having so much fun without me, how everything was still the same back home, except I'm not there."

"I had that too." Chris offered Mandy the Kleenex box. It seemed to have taken residence on Chris's lap, since Chris had been crying almost from the beginning of the discussion. What had happened to her good mood? "I phone my friends all the time, but I'm always crying when I talk to them."

Mandy handed back the tissues and Chris pulled one out, blowing her nose with it. Abby was reminded of the phone call she'd received last Thursday from her book club. They phoned during their meeting, surprising Abby as she was washing dishes. Each of her friends got on the phone in turn, to say hello, to say how much they missed her. But in the background, behind the voice of the person speaking to her, Abby heard conversations continuing, laughter, camaraderie. And even while she was glad to be talking to her friends, she experienced the same feelings Mandy had described. Life back home went on without her. They didn't really need her.

She knew her friends had made that call to cheer her up, but it had the opposite effect. Abby hung up the phone depressed and went to bed right after, rolling herself into a tight ball and crying into her pillow. Peter's words of comfort did nothing to help her.

Abby lowered her head and closed her eyes. She didn't want to go back to those feelings. She didn't want to start crying again.

"I went through the same kind of thing," Holly said. Abby's head popped up. Happy Holly?

"But then Carl pointed out all the good things about being here. Like my new friends in the neighborhood, like you guys." Holly's eyes scanned the circle. "And I realized I was lucky to have friends here and in Chicago."

"That's a good point," Patty said. "By moving to a new place we enrich our lives and expand our circle of friends. We don't really lose our good friends, even if they live far away. And if we cherish them, instead of clinging to them, we open ourselves up to new friends."

"Yes," Ellen agreed. "If we try to live with one foot in our old place and the other in our new place, we're not really living anywhere, are we?"

She was right, Abby realized. She wasn't really living in Richmond, although it was her new home. And she certainly wasn't living in Waterloo anymore, even though everything familiar was there. She was living in a state of limbo. She needed to grab hold of her new life. She needed to stop clinging to her old one.

The trouble was, she didn't really want to let go.

Chapter Twenty

Puzzled, Abby pushed her shopping cart past the freezer aisles a second time. Why couldn't she find frozen pie shells? Kroger should carry them. Americans ate pie, didn't they? She still needed to figure out the layout of this grocery store. It wasn't all that different from Loblaws back home, though there were some things that struck her. They sold wine and beer for instance, something you wouldn't find in Loblaws, or any store in Ontario that wasn't the LCBO. Peter loved that he could pick up a good bottle of wine at the grocery store. And, oddly, pasta was in the international section. Pasta exotic?

She approached a green-shirted man at the ice cream freezer.

"Excuse me, sir?"

He turned, holding a carton of Dove Bars in his gloved hands. His round belly strained against the buttons of his shirt, spilling over his belt and mirroring the sphere of his bald head. Pinned to his shirt was a nametag that said Billy. He smiled at Abby.

"Yes, ma'am." She could almost hear the apostrophe as he pronounced the word in two syllables.

"I'm trying to find frozen pie shells, you know the unbaked ones? Do you have them?"

"Oh, right over here." He put down the Dove Bars and started to walk in the direction he was pointing. Raght ova heya.

"You don't have to take me there. If you just tell me, I'll find them."

"No, ma'am. Store policy. I have to show you 'xact-ly."

"Well, thanks." Abby followed him with her cart. At the end of the row, he opened a freezer door and pointed.

"You want big ones or little'ns? They're all here. What kind of pie you baking?"

"Pumpkin. It's for Thanksgiving dinner. My kids are coming." She smiled as she spoke those words.

"Thanksgivin'? That's not for a couple of months yet. Why you wanna bake your pumpkin pie so early?"

"Oh, it's for Canadian Thanksgiving. The second Monday of October. We just moved here from Canada. And my kids are coming to celebrate with us."

"Oh. Ah figured you might be Canadian." Abby looked at him surprised. He shrugged. "Your accent. Ah can always tell."

Abby didn't speak with an accent! And she was very careful not to say eh at the end of her sentences. She leaned in and took a box out of the freezer. It had a picture of a cherry pie on the front and inside was three frozen pie shells. She looked at the ingredients list.

"Do you have any with only one in a box?"

"Just what's there, ma'am."

"I've never used these pre-made ones before. I always make my own crust. With butter. But we're living in this little apartment and I don't have a rolling pin to make pie dough. We don't have much that I'm used to. Not even a big roasting pan for a turkey. I sure miss my own kitchen things. I miss a lot of things. And people."

"Is that right?" The man looked back at the cartons of ice cream stacked where he'd left them. "Is there anythin' else I can help you with, ma'am?"

"Um, no, I don't think so. Thanks very much." Abby blew out her breath and shook her head as the man walked back down the aisle. It was stupid to always tell strangers her life story. Why did she go on and on? They didn't care.

At the checkout, she placed her items on the conveyor. A frozen rolled turkey breast instead of a whole bird. Cranberry sauce in a can. Boxed stuffing. She wasn't happy with the selections. Everything was so...so pre-made, but she had no choice, considering her limited kitchen. At least she'd found those canned French sweet peas that Ben loved. And sweet potatoes to make her special casserole.

This year's Thanksgiving certainly wouldn't be like ones of the past. A house filled with family, three different kinds of pie cooling on the counter while people sipped hot mulled cider. There would be no Mom and Dad, no Aunt Josie, no Christina and Bill with their kids. No cozy fire crackling while Hanna and her cousin played duets on the piano. No shushing through the leaves during their annual Thanksgiving walk. The leaves here hadn't even started to fall yet.

It would just be the four of them in the little apartment, Ben and Hanna jostling for space as they sat crowded around the small table, eating prefab turkey and pumpkin pie made with a Pillsbury crust. Abby sighed. Her mood plummeted into a pit of nostalgia and self-pity.

"Well, hey Abby. How are you?"

What? Here she was at Kroger and someone knew her name? She turned and saw the woman from the apartment fitness room. They'd exercised at the same time the past three days.

"Hi, Angela. Nice to see you here." Abby smiled. "You look different without your gym clothes." It felt almost like being back home, where Abby wouldn't be ten minutes in the grocery store without bumping into someone she knew.

Angela held out a clear plastic box containing a salad. "I'm eating low-cal for lunch. When do your kids arrive?"

"Their flight comes in at seven."

"Well, have a good weekend with them. Maybe I'll see you on the treadmill next week."

There was a bounce to Abby's step as she carted her bags to the car.

****

She stared intensely down the long passageway as if she could conjure up Ben and Hanna just by looking for them. She knew it would take time for them to make an appearance since their plane had landed only a few minutes ago. Still, they might be the first ones off.

She looked back at Peter, sitting in the middle of a row of chairs working on a Sudoku puzzle. Why couldn't he stand here and wait with her? Always he was preoccupied with something rather than being in the moment with her. The kids were coming. Surely he could put away his puzzle and share the anticipation with her. She shook her head. Peter was like that, couldn't stand to just sit and do nothing, especially when waiting for things. Even important things like their kids. This was no different than a zillion other times. It shouldn't bother her so much now.

She thought back to that awful night when she'd run from the apartment, from him, and stayed away most of the evening. When she'd returned, Peter was so understanding he didn't even want to hear her apology. He commiserated with her, listened to her. For once he didn't advise her on what she should do and just heard her words. She couldn't have asked for a more sympathetic husband. Yet still she harped at him all the time, was constantly annoyed with him. Abby recoiled at the word that invaded her thoughts. Bitch. That's what she was.

He was still the fun-loving man she'd married. Right now he was wearing his favourite lime green shirt that the kids always teased him about. He probably put it on just for them. The cowlick at the right side of his head, now greying, was sticking up.

Maybe she was mad at him because his experiences with this move were better than hers. Because he was moving forward while she was staying still. Because he was finding good things about being here and she saw mostly bad. Because he was around people every day and she was usually alone. She was mad at him because she was jealous.

As if he felt her stare, Peter looked up. Catching her eye, he smiled and winked. She returned the smile and waved, then turned back to the corridor.

People appeared, walking purposefully in Abby's direction. Men carrying briefcases. Mothers carrying children. Children carrying teddy bears. And then she saw the two of them far back; she'd recognize Ben's loping gait anywhere.

"Peter, they're here." Abby hurried forward and waved her arms. Hanna saw her and waved back, a smile lighting her face. She ran to Abby, her knapsack bouncing on her back.

"Mom." She put her arms around Abby's neck and kissed her cheek. "It's so good to see you."

"You too, sweetie. You look good." Abby stood back and appraised her daughter. It was just over a month since she'd seen her, but she seemed different, more grown-up somehow. She turned to Ben and hugged him. "Hey, Ben. Great to see you."

"Hi, Mom. Dad here?"

"He's right over..."

"So, how are our two independent travelers?" Peter came up behind Abby, grabbed Ben's shoulder and put his arm around Hanna. "Welcome to Richmond."

****

In the car, Abby kept turning to the backseat. She'd probably end up with a crick in her neck, but she couldn't stop looking at her two kids, couldn't stop telling them things.

"We've got lots of places we want to show you. And our realtor is taking us to see houses tomorrow. The ones Dad and I've narrowed down from all the ones we've been to. We want your opinions on them." She squeezed Ben's knee behind her. "It's so great to have you two in Richmond. I've missed you."

"I know, Mom. We get that from your phone messages and e-mails." Ben's tone was indulgent. "It's good to see you guys too. It's weird not having you in Waterloo."

"No kidding." Hanna leaned toward her mother. "When I go to the house, it's so quiet. And empty. Even though the furniture is still there."

Peter seemed surprised. "You go to the house?"

Abby looked at him. "I told you the kids would be checking on the house, remember?" She sighed loudly and shook her head.

Ben shifted in his seat. "I went there once to do laundry, but I didn't stay long. There's no life there, you know?"

"Yeah, I know what you mean." Hanna sat back. "I keep expecting Max to meow around my legs. And then I remember and get all sad."

"Aw, sweetie." Abby reached back and patted Hanna's hand.

"But I still visit it a lot. I lie on my bed sometimes. You don't mind, right? I call Ruth every time I go, in case she's showing the house to someone." Ruth was their realtor in Waterloo.

"Not at all." Abby shook her head. "We're glad you two use the house. It's still ours after all."

"Hopefully not for long," Peter said quietly. Then louder, "But yeah, you guys keep going there as long as it's for sale. It'll make it look like people live there. Good for security."

"There was a pile of realtor cards on the table." Hanna said. "I brought them along. And a bunch of mail too."

"This is an awesome car, Dad." Ben was scanning the dashboard. "I'm glad you got an RDX."

"It's pretty cool. And it drives like a dream." Peter pointed out his side window. "There's the office where I work."

"Where?" Hanna leaned over Ben to look through the window. Peter started describing things about the office.

Abby inhaled deeply, as if to absorb the intimate kinship that surrounded them. The four of them talking in the car. It felt so ordinary, so familiar, the way things should be. Her previous weeks of loneliness and depression faded out of existence.

****

The little red brick house was Abby's favourite of the five houses they'd decided to show the kids. There were drawbacks, but it had charm and character, with a slate roof, screen porch, and brick pathway. And it was in a quaint neighbourhood with lots of trees and other picturesque houses.

"It looks small," Hanna said as she climbed out of the car.

"Too small," Ben added.

"Well, we don't need a big house." Abby slammed the car door shut.

"The last house we went through was big."

Peter took Hanna's hand. "Why don't we just go look at it."

Inside, seeing the rooms again through Hanna's and Ben's eyes, Abby had to agree with them. Damn it, it *was* small. A cramped kitchen that needed updating, tiny living room, small bedrooms.

"Isn't this just the most charming room?" Trixie asked as she followed Abby and Hanna into the dining room. "Look at that carved mantle above the fireplace, and the beautiful wainscoting."

"Hmph," Hanna raised her eyes to the ceiling. "Are those cracks up there?"

"Come and see the sunroom and screen porch, Hanna. You'll love them." Abby put her hand in the small of Hanna's back and propelled her forward. The sunroom leading to the screen porch was wonderfully airy and spacious. Abby could envision herself sitting in here with a book and a cup of tea.

"Isn't this lovely and bright?" Abby felt as if she was the one trying to sell the house.

"Yeah, it's nice and light. I like this room." Hanna glanced around, then pushed open the door and joined Ben and Peter on the screen porch.

Trixie looked at Abby and shrugged. "I don't think she likes this house, either."

"I don't think we could show her anything she'd like right now." Abby glanced in the direction of her family. "Thanks for taking us through all the houses again. It's good for the kids to see what we have to choose from."

"There's still the Sweetbriar Hollows one starting to show on Tuesday. Maybe that'll be the one for you."

"I hope so." Abby was discouraged about their house hunting. Nothing had jumped out at her, saying it was home. Panic was taking root, entwining itself within her discouragement. What if they never found a house that felt like home in Richmond? She followed Hanna to the porch and heard Ben's voice.

"There's not even a garage."

"That seems to be pretty common around here. I guess with the mild climate they don't need garages. I have to admit I'd miss having a garage." Peter looked up and smiled at Abby as she walked up to him. "Ready to go?"

"I guess so."

"You aren't going to buy any of the houses we saw today, are you?" Hanna asked as she opened the door to the backyard. "I don't like any of them."

"Well, that's obvious." Abby's voice resonated in the porch. "You've had nothing good to say about any of them."

Hanna held the screen door with one hand and turned toward Abby. "Well, I didn't see anything that was good." Her tone was defensive.

"That's for sure. The Loreine Lake house was too dark. The Salisbury one was too big. You hated the yard in Stratford Hills. No good bedrooms in Westham. This one is too small. What do you want?" Abby's heart pounded. Could they see it beating through her shirt? She placed her hand over it and took a deep breath. "We need to find a house in Richmond. And these are the ones we have to choose from. What are we supposed to do?" Adrenaline was shooting through her.

Peter put his hand on her arm. "Abby, calm down."

"Calm down?" She shook off his arm. "You uproot us, put our home up for sale, and now we can't find anything to replace it. And I'm supposed to calm down?"

"Okay, folks? I'm ready to lock..." Trixie's last words faded away as she came through the door. She looked uncomfortable. Abby knew her outburst had created tension, but she couldn't stop herself.

"Yes." Abby said. "You can lock up. We're going." She stepped outside, the screen door slamming shut behind her. As she turned the corner of the house, she heard Ben ask, "What's up with Mom?"

Abby strode to the car, not wanting to hear Peter's answer.

Chapter Twenty-One

"Mm, smells like Thanksgiving." Peter came through the door with Ben and Hanna, suddenly filling the apartment with an energy that Abby hadn't realized was missing. She closed the oven door on the sweet potatoes and turkey and walked over to them.

"The turkey does smell good."

"Here's the whipping cream," Peter handed her a bag. "I showed the kids around the city a bit more."

"I wondered why you were gone so long."

"We went to Carytown." Hanna slid off her shoes. "It's cool."

"And we drove around the universities, the downtown area again..." Peter walked into the living room and sat down in the chair.

"Yeah, those cobblestone streets in Shockoe Slip are so cool. Or is it Shockoe Bottom?" Hanna asked.

"I can never remember. And I don't know what Shockoe means." Abby turned to Ben, who had thrown himself on the couch. "Want some hot cider?"

"Sure. We drove past that other house again, Mom, in Sweetbriar Hollows? I really like it on the outside. Maybe it'll be just as good inside."

Finally a house the kids were positive about. Maybe they'd find one after all. "We're hoping so, Ben. I really want to be in a house for Christmas." Abby ladled steaming cider into mugs, handed two to Hanna and followed her to the living room with two more. She sat on the couch, squeezing herself between Ben and Hanna.

"Isn't this nice, just sitting here? We haven't had a chance to really talk yet." She sipped from her mug then rubbed shoulders, first with Hanna, then Ben. "How's your job going, Ben?"

"I hate it."

"What do you mean? I thought you were happy to have it?"

"Mom, it sucks the soul out of me, you know? Hour after hour sitting there, drilling hole after hole. It's mind numbing. Sometimes I feel like I'd rather be dead."

Her heart stopped and she couldn't swallow the cider she'd just sipped. Peter leaned forward.

"Ben. Do you mean that?"

"No. I'm not suicidal or anything. Don't worry about that. It's just...it's a horrible job."

Abby put down her mug. "So why don't you change it? Find a new job. You're the only one who can make your life better, you know." Why didn't she follow her own advice? "What does Dr. Hanson say? Do you talk to him about this?"

"I'm not seeing him any more. I," he curved two fingers on either side of his head, "graduated weeks ago."

"What?" Peter sat straighter. "What about the money we left in your account to pay for him? We transferred enough for at least eight more sessions."

"Oh yeah. I, um, lent some of it to a friend of mine, for textbooks and stuff. He's supposed to give it back to me next week."

"You need to return it to us, Ben," Peter's face was red, "if you're not using it for counseling.

"I will. I'll pay you back." Ben shifted his eyes. "Soon."

"You darn well better."

Abby didn't believe Ben, that he'd lent the money to a friend. She wanted to. But she knew, she just knew. "You're lying," she blurted out. "You can't just use our money for something without asking. What did you do with it?"

Ben looked up at her, surprise in his eyes.

"Mom, I'm not lying. Adam borrowed it for school stuff. I'll get it back."

"Over nine hundred dollars for school stuff? I don't believe you. I bet you gambled it away." She was shouting now. "What's the matter with you? Why don't you get your act together?"

"Abby, don't." Peter leaned forward and touched her knee. "Lower your voice."

She pushed his hand away and jumped up, feeling her face getting hot. Furious tears pricked her eyes.

"He can't take advantage of us like this. He can't keep messing up his life."

"Mom," Hanna pulled on Abby's hand. "Sit down."

"No." She yanked her hand away. "You kids. You think it's so easy? That you can just do whatever you want while your father works hard to earn money for you to fritter away?"

"I didn't do anything." Hanna pleaded. "What are you mad at me for?"

Abby stared down at Hanna. "Nothing." She strode to the bathroom and shut the door, locking it. Leaning on the counter she gazed at her face in the mirror, shocked by the person staring back at her. Turning on the tap, she splashed water on her face.

She needed to go back out there. She couldn't stay in this bathroom. But there was nowhere else to go in this stupid apartment. She inhaled deeply as she dried her face. Squaring her shoulders, she opened the door.

The three of them stood in the doorway facing her. Peter's hand was raised as if he were about to knock. She glared at them looking expectantly at her.

"Excuse me." She tried to push past them. Peter took hold of her shoulder, stopping her mid-stride.

"Abby, stop. Don't be like this. We love you. We're a family. It's Thanksgiving." He opened his arms wide.

"Come here." Reluctantly she walked into them. Peter pulled in Ben and Hanna as his arms encircled her. His voice continued over her head. "This is a tough time for all of us. We're all on edge. Let's just have a nice Thanksgiving." And his arms squeezed the four of them together.

Abby slid out of Peter's grasp. "I need to see to dinner."

"We'll talk about the money later, Ben," she heard Peter whisper in Ben's ear. Ben squirmed away and went back to the living room.

Abby sensed Hanna following her. Poor Hanna, innocent victim in the wake of her mother's explosion. Abby turned around and hugged her.

"I love you, Hanna."

"Yeah, me too."

Peter came into the kitchen. "Shall I set the table?"

"Okay. Hanna and I'll see to the food." She took Hanna's hand. "Okay?"

"I was thinking we could phone Grandma and Pops. Wish them a happy Thanksgiving?"

"That's a good idea." Why hadn't Abby thought about doing that? "You call while I check the food."

While Hanna punched in the number, Abby pricked the potatoes with a fork and opened the can of French peas. Peter clattered dishes as he set the table, making it impossible for Abby to hear Hanna's side of the conversation.

"Peter, sh," she hissed. He looked up and she pointed to Hanna. He began to lay the cutlery very gently. Abby turned to Hanna and saw her worried expression.

"Grandma's sick," Hanna said, handing her the phone.

"Hi, Mom, it's Abby. Happy Thanksgiving."

"Abby." Her mother's voice was hoarse. She cleared her throat. "Thank you. Same to you."

"Mom, how are you feeling? How's Dad?"

"I'm getting better." Her breathing was raspy. "I'm up in my wheelchair again. But your father is very bad. Worse." She coughed. "Are you coming today?"

"No, Mom, I can't. We're in Richmond, remember? The kids are here with us and we're phoning to wish you a happy Thanksgiving."

"Oh. Are you coming soon? I miss you so much." Her voice quivered. Combined with her noisy breathing she sounded miserable.

"We'll visit in November, Mom, over American Thanksgiving. I'll spend some time with you then, okay?"

"I suppose." She coughed again.

"Does it hurt to talk, Mom?"

"Not so much, no. My throat's getting better."

"Has the doctor been to see you?"

"Yes. We got medicine."

"That's good. Can I talk to Dad maybe?"

"Wait. I'll bring him the phone. He sleeps all the time, but I can wake him up."

"No, wait, Mom..." Abby heard a clack and then faint muttering. She closed her eyes and pictured her mother with the phone on her lap, wheeling her chair to the bed. Faintly her mother shouted, "Nick. Nick." Then hands clapping. "Here. It's Abby."

"Huh?" Her father's voice was unrecognizable.

"Hi, Dad? It's Abby."

"Okay." He coughed. "Huh?"

"How are you, Dad?"

"Uh, mah," he wheezed.

"Dad? I love you."

"Beh."

The phone clattered loudly, hurting Abby's ear. She felt a wave of alarm and called into the mouthpiece.

"Hello?"

Her mother muttered and breathed with exertion.

"Dad? Mom?"

"Sorry." Her mother was panting. "He dropped it. I had to pick it up."

Poor Mom, struggling with all of that. "Dad doesn't seem so good, Mom."

"He isn't, Abby. I worry about him."

"What does the doctor say?"

"She says he'll get better. Just like me."

"Well that's good to hear. Do you want to talk to Peter and Ben?"

"Yes, okay."

"Okay, Mom. You get better. Dad too. Love you." She handed the phone to Peter who took it to the living room, returning to hang it up minutes later.

An uneasiness settled in Abby. She saw Hanna watching her, worry and questions in her eyes.

"Is Pops as bad as Grandma?" Hanna asked. "She sounded bad."

"Actually, Grandma sounded better than she did on Monday."

"Will they be okay, Mom?"

"I think so. I'll call their doctor tomorrow and find out what's going on. All right?"

Peter put his arm around Hanna's shoulders. "I know we don't want to think about it, Hanna, but Grandma and Pops are in their eighties and it's hard to recover from being sick at that age. We should prepare ourselves that something could happen to them."

Abby bristled. "They're my parents, Peter. How are we supposed to prepare ourselves?"

"I didn't mean it won't affect us. Just that we could expect...."

"We know, Dad." Hanna twisted her sweater. "But it's so sad. And they're all alone there."

"It makes me sad too, Hanna." Abby turned back to the kitchen. She didn't want to think about anything happening to her parents while she was a thousand kilometers away.

She opened the oven door and the aroma of sweet potato, cinnamon, and turkey wafted out in the heat that blasted her face. She took out the casserole and set it on the stovetop, then lifted out the rolled turkey breast.

"Dinner should be ready in about ten minutes," she said, moving the turkey onto a cutting board, tenting foil over it. She opened a tin of cranberry sauce and scooped the red-gelled berries into a bowl, regretting again that she hadn't been able to find fresh ones. Hanna leaned on the counter peninsula.

"What can I do, Mom?"

"Wanna whip the cream for the pie?" Abby motioned toward the pumpkin pie on the counter. She was pleased with how it had turned out, despite the prefab crust. The taste would be the true test, but it looked and smelled just like her usual creamy pie.

"Okay." Hanna came around the counter and stood beside Abby, who was draining the potatoes. Steam rose from the sink and Hanna stepped back. "Whew. Where's the mixer?"

"No mixer here. Use the whisk." Abby began pounding the masher into the potatoes.

"I have to whip the cream by hand?"

"Welcome." Pound. "To my world." Pound. Abby added more cream to the potatoes. "This is the kitchen I have to work in." Pound. Pound. "It didn't come with a mixer." She pointed the masher at the whisk. "The whisk is a good one, though. I just bought it." Abby stopped mashing and plopped the white glop into a bowl. She bumped into Hanna as she reached for the carving knife.

"Sorry. Small space." She watched Hanna stirring the whisk weakly in the cream. "Come on, Hanna."

Annoyance bled into her words. "Put some muscle into it. We want the cream whipped before tomorrow."

"Geez, Mom. You don't have to be so grouchy." Hanna stirred the whisk faster. "Better?"

"No. Let me do it." Abby grabbed the bowl and whisk out of Hanna's hands. "Like this." She fiercely beat the whisk through the cream, splattering small white dots on the counter, on her apron, in her hair. "See? Getting thicker already."

Hanna shrugged and walked away from the kitchen, mumbling. Abby called after her. "What did you say?"

"Nothing."

"You said something."

Hanna stopped and stood silent, her shoulders tense. Turning to face Abby, she said. "You're right, I did. I said you're being such a bitch." Abby blanched, recalling she'd used the same word earlier to describe herself. Hanna's face flushed. "Ever since we came. I thought we were going to have a nice weekend, but you've been yelling at us all the time. And yelling at Dad too. We can't do anything right."

"I haven't been..." Abby's voice trailed off when she saw tears trailing down Hanna's cheeks. Peter called out from the living room.

"Everything okay there?"

"Yes." Abby put down the bowl and went over to Hanna, encircling her in a hug. "I'm so sorry, Hanna," she said. She raised her head over Hanna's and saw Peter and Ben staring at the two of them. "We're fine," she insisted.

Moving her hands to Hanna's shoulders, she looked into her eyes. "Life's hard right now. Everything is so different. I don't mean to grouch, especially at you." She wiped a tear that was running down Hanna's nose. "You know that, right?"

Hanna sniffed. "I guess." She shrugged out from under Abby's grip. "But it's not my fault, you know?"

"Of course it isn't. I'm just having a bad day."

"More like a bad weekend."

"Right, a bad weekend. I'm sorry. I'll try to stop." Abby kissed Hanna and smiled half-heartedly before calling out, "Dinner in five." She watched Hanna walk away not looking at all appeased and picked up the bowl and whisk.

She was slicing the last bit of turkey when Peter approached her.

"What was that all about with Hanna?"

"Nothing. Everything's fine."

He stared and seemed about to say something. Then he shrugged his shoulders. "Dinner looks great, Abs." He picked a piece of turkey from the plate and popped it into his mouth.

"Yes, it all turned out okay. Load up your plates here at the counter, guys, 'cause there's no room on the table for serving dishes."

It almost felt cozy, everyone jostling each other for the food, reaching for one dish or another. But there was something in the room Abby couldn't quite put her finger on, something that interfered with the usual Thanksgiving ambience.

Ben examined a slice of meat. "The turkey looks good, even though it's not a real bird."

"It is real turkey meat." Abby took her plate to the table. Peter was the last to sit, and when he did, he raised his wine glass.

"A toast. To our first Thanksgiving in Richmond."

Abby's stomach tumbled. "To Thanksgiving." She clinked her glass to Ben's, then Hanna's and Peter's, and looked around at her family. It felt so odd, the four of them sitting around this little table for a big dinner as if it were home.

Peter sipped his wine and put down his glass. "Life's pretty different for us these days, huh? It's kind of weird having Thanksgiving dinner in this little apartment. Hopefully by Christmas we'll be in a house."

"Hear, hear." Abby said.

"You know," Peter held a forkful of stuffing in mid-air. "Even though we're not home, we can still carry on our family tradition. Why don't we all say what we're thankful for. Wanna go first, Ben?"

Ben stopped mid-chew, his cheek distended from the food in his mouth. He resumed chewing quickly and swallowed, then put his fork down. "Are you deliberately being obtuse, Dad?"

"What do you mean?" Peter's cheeks reddened and his jaw tightened.

"Look around you." Ben swung his right arm in a semicircle. "We're having our Thanksgiving dinner in a rented apartment. Hanna and I have to sleep in a guest unit because there's no room for us here." He shook his head. "Mom thinks I gambled away your money," he looked pointedly at Abby, "which I didn't. I have nothing to be thankful for. Life sucks."

"Ben's right." Hanna put her fork down. "We should all say what we're not thankful for."

Peter looked at Abby. She raised her eyebrows but kept silent. He said, "But that's not construct…"

"Dad, stop pretending." Ben pushed his chair back. "None of us are having a good time here. This family…" He stood. "Oh forget it. I'm outa here."

Before Abby could react, Ben had left the apartment, slamming the door. She stood to follow him then sat back down.

Peter turned to Hanna and took her hand. "Hanna…."

Hanna pulled her hand back. "Dad, you really don't get it, do you. We all feel like shit and don't want to play happy family right now." She pushed her plate away. "I've lost my appetite." She looked at Abby. "Sorry." And she too walked to the door and went out, closing it quietly behind her.

Abby leaned on her elbows, closing her eyes and took deep breaths. In through the nose, out through the mouth. In. Out.

"Dammit, Abby, you ruined our Thanksgiving." Peter's voice penetrated the quiet. "What's the matter with you?"

"Don't, Peter." She looked at him, his fork still in his hand. "Just leave me alone for a while." She pushed back her chair and walked to the bedroom, leaving Peter sitting at the table with the dinner spread out in front of him like the rubble after a bomb had exploded.

Chapter Twenty-Two

Abby's gaze followed Ben, then Hanna as they walked through the security checkpoints at the airport. A uniformed man took Ben off to a corner while Hanna stood at the end of the table waiting, knapsack in hand. She looked in Abby's direction and waved tentatively. Abby waved back and turned back to Ben, whose arms were stretched wide while the man ran his hands all over him. Why did they have to pick Ben to search? She hoped he didn't have anything questionable among his things.

The man emptied Ben's knapsack and sorted through its contents. Abby fought the urge to march over there, past the other security people, to demand an explanation. She berated herself. They weren't little children. She didn't need to keep protecting them.

She looked at Hanna again. Even from this distance she could see Hanna was scared. Tears blurred Abby's view of them. When she wiped them away, she saw Ben shoulder his knapsack and walk toward Hanna. He said something to her, and the two of them turned toward Abby and waved. Abby waved back and watched until she could see them no more.

Driving away from the airport, regret about the weekend washed over her. She'd so looked forward to spending time with the kids but for some reason was constantly annoyed or frustrated with them, always nattering at them for one thing or another.

She'd wanted to probe Ben on his life but was only able to scratch the surface. And that was mostly her fault. Whenever he said anything, she just blew up at him.

And Hanna needed support and encouragement but Abby had been unable to give her those things, snapping at her for no reason.

She had to admit it. She was a selfish mother, so tangled up in how miserable she was that she couldn't be there for her children.

The thing was, it felt good to blow off steam. It was liberating to say exactly what she was feeling, instead of weighing every word, filtering every emotion. Unfortunately, the people she loved most were the ones who suffered the onslaught of her outbursts.

But that's what it meant to be part of a family didn't it? That's why kids rebelled and yelled at their parents because they knew they were loved no matter what. That must be what she was doing. Rebelling.

When she closed the door to the apartment she noticed the message light on the phone flashing. Four messages. She pushed the button.

"Hi, Abby and Peter." Trixie's voice came through the receiver. "I wanted to let you know we're all set to go through the Sweetbriar house tomorrow evening at seven. I'll pick you up at six thirty. See you then."

Abby felt excited. This could be their house. She knew it was priced higher than they wanted to spend but they could afford it. They might even be moved in time for Christmas. Please, she prayed, let this be the one.

"Hey, Abs, did the kids get off okay?" It was Peter. "I tried to call your cell but got the voice mail. Is it on?" Abby glanced at her cell phone lying on the kitchen counter, charging.

"Abby and Peter, it's Ruth." Abby perked up. "I've got some out-of-town clients who are very interested in your house. They've been to see it three times and I think they're getting close to making an offer. They have a couple of questions for you. Can you call me?"

The final message almost made Abby's heart stop.

"Mrs. Settel," Abby didn't recognize the woman's voice, "this is Sandra White. I'm a nurse at Chestnut Manor. Please call us immediately. It's about your mother. My number is…"

Abby scrambled for something to write with. Her hands shook and her breath came in short gasps. When she finally found a pen, she'd forgotten the number and had to work her way through Trixie's cheery voice, then Peter's solicitous one, and then Ruth's optimism in order to listen to Sandra White's again. Surely the nurse meant her father, not her mother. It was her dad who wasn't doing well. Her mom was getting better, wasn't she?

****

An hour after calling Sandra White back, Abby was driving north on I-95. Her mother had suffered a stroke and was in critical condition in intensive care at the hospital. The nursing home staff couldn't wake her that morning and she'd not yet regained consciousness. The doctor at the hospital strongly suggested that Abby come as soon as possible.

She'd tried to get on a flight, but the soonest one that had seats available wouldn't leave for hours yet. It didn't make sense to fly when she would arrive at the same time as driving. And she needed to be doing something, anything, even if it meant sitting behind a steering wheel rather than in an airport for hours.

Peter agreed she needed to go. Agreed she should drive up there. He offered to take time off work and go with her, but Abby wanted to do this alone, although she couldn't explain why, not even to herself.

It felt strange to be driving to Canada alone in her car. She'd been back only once since they moved to Richmond, just days after they'd left, to pick up her car and other things they couldn't do without. Then, despite her sadness about moving, she'd been filled with anticipation and excitement about her new life. This time she was simply filled with dread. She wondered if her mother would ever wake up, if she would recover from her stroke. Abby needed her to; she had to tell her things. To tell her that she loved her.

It was ironic to think that Ben and Hanna, unaware, were sitting in an airplane flying north at the same time that Abby was driving there. They would probably arrive in Waterloo around three. She'd call them then; no need to distress them as they made their way home from the Toronto airport. Or maybe she should wait until she knew her mother's condition firsthand. The kids might want to see their grandma. But if she stopped to pick them up, it would add close to an hour onto her trip. She wasn't sure she wanted to delay getting to her mom's bedside.

The trees were a blur of green through the windows, becoming colorful palettes the farther north she drove. Glancing periodically at the outside temperature indicator on her dash, she saw the numbers dropping. Like her heart into the pit of her stomach. Music from the CD player filled the car with tunes and rhythms that belied her anxiety. She was tempted to turn it off, especially when the fourth cycle of the same three CDs was about to begin, but driving in silence with only her worries to entertain her was too daunting a prospect. She should have brought more music.

It was close to seven when Abby arrived at the Peace Bridge in Buffalo. Less than two hours and she'd see her mom. The sky was already dark and the bridge was lit up by lights along its sides. Their reflections glimmered in the murky water of the Niagara River. Driving across the center of the bridge, passing first the American flag, then the red and white Canadian one, she felt an unexpected sense of relief, of comfort. She was in Canada. Home.

Pulling up in the shortest line at the border kiosks, she turned off the music. The silence settled in her ears. She sighed deeply and lowered her window. Cold air blasted her face, refreshing and repelling her at the same time.

The car ahead of her pulled up to the booth. She rooted in her purse for her passport and opened it to the page with her picture. It was such a bad photo. Her hair was too short and her skin looked sallow. Holding the page with her thumb, she drummed her fingers on the wheel. The customs officer leaned into the driver's window of the car in front. He was taking a long time.

Her phone ringing startled her and she dropped the passport. Damn. Maybe it was the hospital. Her cousin Christina had called a few hours ago reporting that her mother was stable. Still, things could change quickly. As she groped for the passport on the floor beneath the steering wheel, she looked at the call display. Hanna. She flipped open the phone and just then found the passport. Clutching it tight, she maneuvered her arm out from under the steering column and brought the phone to her ear.

"Hanna? Can I call …."

"Mom? Where are you?" Hanna sounded like she was crying.

"Actually I'm in…."

"Mom, I can't bear it."

How did she know? Had Peter called her?

"Oh Hanna, I know it's hard but…."

"You knew Jason was breaking up with me?" Hanna sounded incredulous. She sniffed.

"He what?"

"He did the turkey dump on me, Mom. He was…"

A horn blared. Abby looked ahead and saw that the car in front of her was gone and the customs officer was waving at her to move forward.

"Hanna, I'll call you back in a few minutes." She snapped the phone shut and drove ahead.

As soon as she was past the border, she called Hanna, who answered the phone before the first ring was finished.

"How could you hang up on me, Mom?" she berated. "I was in the middle of telling you my awful news."

Her anger quickly subsided when Abby explained she was in Canada on her way to the hospital to see Grandma. That she was just at the border when Hanna had called. At first Hanna wanted Abby to come to Waterloo to pick her up on the way so she could see her grandmother, but then she changed her mind. Probably afraid of what she might have to face, Abby thought.

"You go first, Mom, by yourself. I can see her when she's better." Abby didn't say out loud the horrible possibility that Grandma might not get better. And it seemed that Hanna didn't want to think about it either.

"Tell me about Jason, Sweetie."

"Oh, Mom, it was so awful. He was at the airport, to pick Ben and me up. He'd cancelled the airport bus. I was so happy he did such a nice thing. And the whole drive to Waterloo he was great, asking about school, about Richmond, about Ben's life. It was awesome to be with him. Then he dropped Ben off at his place. I asked him to come to my dorm so he could see my room, but he didn't want to. That's when I first knew something was up."

Hanna sobbed and sniffled, then blew her nose. Abby wished she could hold her daughter and comfort her.

"He took me to Williams for coffee and told me there were so many people at Windsor U. that he wanted to get to know. Obviously he meant girls. He said he didn't want to be tied down to anybody right now. And that I should meet new people too. I begged him not to break up, Mom. I was a mess, blubbering right in the middle of Williams. And Jason kept looking around, like he was embarrassed or something. He said he still loved me, but more like a sister now, like a friend. Hmph."

Hanna's disdain jumped through the phone. "And then, all of a sudden, he just stood up and said he'd drive me home. But I said no. I told him to get my bag out of the car, that I'd walk to the dorm myself." An element of satisfaction crept into Hanna's voice. "How could I sit in the car with him after that?"

"That would be hard, Hanna."

"I was so hurt. But I was mad too. Remember how I told you he hardly called me since school started? He must have been planning to do this all that time. Why didn't he tell me before?"

"I don't know, Hanna."

"Oh, Mom." She started crying again. "I'm going to miss him so much. I love him."

Poor Hanna. Abby did her best to console her. She assured Hanna that when she arrived at the house in Waterloo, she'd call her, no matter how late it might be. And Hanna promised to call Ben to tell him about Grandma.

When she shut her phone, Abby was surprised at how close she was, only a couple of miles from the exit, and then twenty minutes to the hospital. She pressed harder on the gas pedal.

Driving on the 401 again reminded Abby of the last time her mother was in the hospital, when she'd fallen down the basement stairs. Then, too, Abby had dropped what she was doing and rushed to Woodstock Hospital, afraid of what she'd find. It had been in the afternoon, with the sunlight pouring into the car. This time it was night, just after nine, dark when she pulled into the hospital parking lot. Walking toward the building, the darkness pressed down on her, giving her a sense of ominous foreboding. She shook it off and entered into bright light and busy bustling.

Stepping out of the elevator on the second floor, Abby saw a sign on the wall indicating the intensive care unit to the left. Her footsteps echoed in muted taps and the smell of sickness and chemicals assaulted her nostrils. Muffled sounds of ventilators and voices hung in the air. She stopped when she reached a closed set of doors with a sign reading ICU. Her mother was behind them. Abby took a deep breath and pushed one open.

Disoriented, she turned her head from one side to the other, finally focusing on the nurse's desk. It was shaped like a semi-circle, overlooking the surrounding rooms. Every room had a large window in the wall beside its door, allowing staff from behind the desk to see in.

Abby stood where she was and looked through each window. She could see people lying on beds, hooked up to machines that were beeping, pumping, whooshing. Which one was her mother? One of the windows had its curtains closed and Abby couldn't see into it. Please, no.

She walked toward the desk where the nurse looked up as Abby approached.

"Hi," Abby began. "I'm…"

"Abby." A voice from behind interrupted. Abby turned around and saw her cousin.

"Christina." She walked towards her. "Where's Mom?"

"Oh, Abby. I wanted to stay until you arrived." Christina put her hand on Abby's arm. "Your mom didn't make it."

"No." Abby gasped, feeling like the air was sucked out of her. "I need to see her." Frantically she looked around at the windows. "Where is she?"

Christina put her arms around Abby's shoulders and hugged her. "I'm so sorry, Abby." She pulled back as the nurse from the desk approached them.

"Abby is it?"

Abby nodded. She wiped her eyes with a shaking hand.

"I'm Susan. I'll take you to her. Come with me."

The nurse led Abby to the room that had its curtains closed and stopped at the door.

"Your mother never regained consciousness from the time she arrived here. She was peaceful the whole time. I'm certain she experienced no pain." She touched Abby's arm. "Would you like to go in there alone?" At Abby's nod she added, "We'll be right out here." And she moved away from the door to stand beside Christina, who squeezed Abby's shoulders.

"I'm here for you," she whispered.

Abby pushed open the door. There on the bed, in this silent, dimly lit room lay her mother, her tiny body nestled under a white sheet, her head resting on a pillow. Abby stepped closer and gazed down at her face. The nurse was right. She looked like she had no pain. She looked like she was sleeping, like she was calm, like all her worries had disappeared. Her fluffy white hair surrounded her head like a halo, her eyes were closed, her little mouth was shaped almost into a smile.

"Oh, Mom, why couldn't you wait?" Abby cried. "I still have so much to say to you."

Chapter Twenty-Three

She stayed the night at Christina's. After seeing her mom, after dealing with the hospital, she couldn't face the drive to Waterloo. Ben understood, but Hanna's sobbing over the phone made Abby want to climb right back into the car.

"I need you, Mom. First I lose Jason, now Grandma."

Abby did her best to calm her, explaining that she wanted to see Pops before coming to Waterloo. Reluctantly Hanna agreed.

"Okay, you stay. I'll just be sad alone tonight."

It hurt Abby that Hanna could be so self-centered. Yes, Hanna was having a hard time. But couldn't she understand that Abby was too?

Tossing and turning on Christina's sofa bed, Abby obsessed over the fact that her mother had died at eight thirty-three, a half hour before she'd arrived at the hospital. If she hadn't stopped along the way for a coffee, she might have seen her mom alive. Or if she'd left Richmond sooner, not stopping at Peter's office to get the road atlas. If she'd paid more attention at the border so she could have gotten through sooner. If she'd never moved to Richmond.

If, if, if.

The next morning she went to see her father. She found him in the dining room, eating porridge, dribbling it on the bib he was wearing. Surprisingly, his cold was better although his breathing was still raspy. Two other women were at the table with him, smiling and nodding at Abby, and the chair beside him was glaringly empty.

Her father barely acknowledged her and seemed to have no understanding of what happened to her mom, hardly noticed she wasn't there. Feeling as if she'd lost both of her parents, she decided to visit Aunt Josie.

"Aw, Abby," Aunt Josie greeted her upon opening the door. Abby broke into tears right on the front stoop and Aunt Josie wrapped her arms around her. Abby snuggled into the softness of her aunt.

"Come in, my dear, have a cup of tea," Aunt Josie said through her own tears. "And some banana loaf."

Aunt Josie gave her exactly what she needed, the feeling that someone was looking after her. She accompanied Abby to Bircher Funeral Home to make arrangements for the funeral, cooked her lunch, and then wrapped up the rest of the banana bread to take back for Ben and Hanna.

Feeling replenished, Abby stopped in to see her dad on her way out of town. At the sight of her mother's bed in the room she stopped and took a breath. She looked away. Soon she'd have to clear away her mother's things. Her father would have to move to a smaller room, maybe on a different floor, one with more care. She sighed and looked at him in his recliner staring out the window.

"Hi, Dad."

He didn't turn. She moved close and bent toward him, kissing his cheek. He looked up at her.

"Huh?" His voice sounded hoarse.

"Dad, it's me. Abby." Would he recognize her this time?

"Okay." He turned back to the window.

"Dad, Mom died." She wiped at her tears. "Do you miss her?" she whispered.

He coughed, then started humming tunelessly, stroking his hands on his pant legs. He looked up at her again, smiling this time.

"Hi. Nice to see you."

Oh, Dad. Was he talking to Abby, his daughter? Or to a woman he didn't know? Abby wished she could see some sign of recognition. She hugged him.

"I'll sit with you a while, okay?" She brought a chair over and put it beside his, sitting down. He stood up.

"No, you go." He pushed at her shoulders until she was on her feet. "You go." And he forced her to the door.

"But, Dad…"

"Bye." He gave her a final shove and walked back to the chairs. He pushed away the one Abby had brought over and sat back in his recliner.

****

She drove the roads to Waterloo on autopilot, hardly aware of the route. She kept the radio off. Somehow it didn't seem right to listen to music or hear commentary on regular life. Turning onto their old street, she pulled out the garage door remote and pressed the button. She stopped the car, watched the door roll up and drove in. It felt familiar, yet strange.

She'd barely turned off the ignition when Ben and Hanna threw open the door to the house. Her heart somersaulted when she saw them and she went to them, wrapping her arms around both of them. Ben quickly pulled away from her embrace.

In the house things were awkward; Hanna unable to control her crying, Ben silent as if not knowing what to say, Abby trying to be strong. She pulled out Aunt Josie's banana bread and in the bustle of cutting it, getting plates, making tea, the awkwardness fell away. Abby commented on how odd it was to be sitting at their old kitchen table together when only yesterday they'd eaten breakfast at the table in the apartment in Richmond. But it felt good, too. Normal.

Peter called to tell them about a flight he'd booked so he could be at the funeral, and Hanna took over the phone and told him her story about Jason. While she was talking, Abby pulled out photo albums, and she and Ben turned pages together, remembering happier times. Abby hadn't felt so close to her son in a long time. Later she ordered pizza for dinner and they reminisced about Grandma.

"Remember the time she built that Lego town with us?" Ben chuckled. "We wheeled my little cars through the streets and she made all those funny noises. We had it set up in the dining room for weeks."

Hanna nodded. "And the time we cut out all those paper people. Remember the funny faces she drew on hers?"

Ben rubbed his eyes. "She was awesome when we were little."

"And she baked all the time. The best lemon tarts. No one ever made them like she did." Hanna looked at Abby. "Not even you, Mom."

"I know. Even though I use her recipe, I can't make them the same."

"Remember all those little animals she used to knit? Bunnies, bears, ducks. She once made us a whole zoo, Hanna, remember?"

Hanna nodded.

Abby squeezed her hand. "And the sweaters? You were always the best dressed kids in the winter." Abby was glad they were remembering the good things. And not the times her mother interfered, in her controlling way, or shouted at her when she really needed to shout at Abby's father. But those were woven into her memories, not Hanna's and Ben's.

"And hats. And mittens." Ben held up his hands.

"And socks." Hanna stuck out her foot, enclosed in a colourful striped sock. "I put them on when you called.

It's like she's keeping my feet warm." She sagged into her chair, caving in on herself. "I miss her."

"We all do."

Hanna shook her head. "It was so sad that she had to move to Chestnut Manor. That she was hurt and had to be in a wheelchair."

"Yeah. We kinda lost her then." Ben sighed. "She wasn't the same Grandma after that."

Abby didn't realize Ben had even noticed; he'd been so wrapped up with his gambling life during that time. They sat silent, staring at the empty pizza box, grease staining the cardboard.

"Poor Pops." Hanna said.

Abruptly Ben pushed back his chair. "I'm going home. I'll see you tomorrow, okay? When Dad gets here."

He insisted on walking, and for that Abby was glad. She didn't feel like getting into the car again. When she closed the door behind him, she turned to Hanna.

"Want to stay here for the night?"

"Of course. In my own bed. I can't deal with residence right now."

After putting out the sheets and duvets, Abby lay with Hanna on her bed. They talked a little, mostly cried, sat quietly holding each other, then suddenly Hanna fell asleep. Just like that. If only it were so easy for Abby to escape into oblivion.

She gently closed the door to Hanna's room and wandered around the house, peering through doors, opening closets, closing curtains.

Home.

And yet, somehow it didn't feel like home anymore. It was familiar, but the house seemed to have lost its soul.

She walked into the kitchen and opened the fridge. It was empty. She should go to the grocery store to pick up food, but the thought of leaving the house was overwhelming. Still, she wanted something to fill her hollowness.

In the basement she looked in the wine fridge. Three bottles of red, one white, and a six-pack of Smirnoff Ice hidden in the back. Pushing wine bottles aside, she pulled out the carton of Smirnoff and took it upstairs. In the family room she opened a bottle and sat on the couch, staring at the darkness through the window, at the filmy reflection of the room. She downed two of the bottles quickly. The tart effervescence buoyed her spirits, quenching more than her thirst. She unscrewed the cap of the third bottle and sipped, startling when her cell phone rang. On the call display she saw the name of their Waterloo realtor and she flipped it open.

"Hi, Abby. Ruth Johnson here. Peter told me about your mother. I'm so sorry." She cleared her throat. "I know this isn't a good time, but these clients who are interested in your house want to go through it one last time before they submit their offer. They're only in town for two more days and I know I can lock up the deal before they leave. Could I bring them over for a short while tonight?"

Abby shook her head. "Can they come tomorrow? I'm exhausted and Hanna just fell asleep upstairs." She took a sip from the bottle.

"Tomorrow might work but it would have to be early, like say, nine?"

"Sure. Okay. We'll get out of your way then."

"Great, Abby. We might get this deal sealed up before you head back to Richmond. It's fortunate that you and Peter will be in town this week. Oh…" It seemed that suddenly she realized what she had said. "Again, I'm so sorry about your mother."

"Thanks."

"I'll call you tomorrow afternoon, probably with an offer."

Abby put the phone down and cried. Life was relentless. Could it not just stop for a while? She tipped up the bottle in her hand and drank the last of its contents, then opened another one.

Savouring the feeling of otherworldliness that comes after a few drinks, she laid back her head and closed her eyes. She was lightheaded and woozy. She should stop drinking this stuff and get a glass of water. Maybe some food.

The doorbell rang. Her head popped up, causing the wall to sway. Surely Ruth wasn't bringing those people after all.

Whoever it was rang the doorbell again. Then knocked. A muffled voice came from behind the door.

"Abby? It's Diana." Knocking again.

Diana? Unsteadily, Abby stood. Carefully she put one foot in front of the other and made her way to the door, using the wall for support as she walked into the hall. The floor swayed with each step. She tried to turn the lock but it wouldn't budge. Leaning in, she eyed it closely. Oh right, it turned the other way. She slid the bolt and opened the door.

"Diana." She almost fell into her.

"Whoa, Abby. Let me get this stuff inside." Diana was holding a plastic grocery bag in each hand. She gently pushed Abby upright and guided her back. Abby stood watching as Diana shut the door behind her, put the bags down, and slipped off her coat.

"Peter called and told me about your mom. I figured you'd need a friend. And some food, so I brought you a few things. And a bottle of wine," she looked closely at Abby, "but maybe we'll hold off opening that." She picked up the bags.

"I'm so glad you're here." Abby draped her arm around Diana's shoulders and steered her into the kitchen. It was nice to have the support as she walked. "Thanks for coming. And for the food." She opened one of the bags and took out a tub of yogurt. It slid out of her hands and fell to the counter, splitting open. White gloop spread across the counter. "Oh no."

"Hey, let me." Diana guided her to a chair. "I'll put this stuff away. You sit." She cleaned up the yogurt and began emptying the bags.

"Diana?" Abby's eyes filled with tears. "My mother died." Abby started sobbing, leaning her face in her hands.

"Aw, honey, I know." She felt Diana's arms around her, heard her quiet voice in her ear. "I know."

****

"Peter's flight arrives at eleven tomorrow morning." Abby put a piece of cheese in her mouth. They were sitting in the family room after Diana put away the food she'd brought and made up a plate of snacks. Abby leaned toward Diana and said quietly, "I'm not sure I want him here."

"Why on earth not?" Diana poured tea into Abby's mug. Abby didn't know what Diana had done with the two remaining Smirnoff bottles, but it didn't matter. She was still feeling the effects of what she'd drunk earlier, enough to feel not completely herself, which was exactly what she wanted.

"I don't think I like him very much right now."

"What do you mean? He's your husband. You need his support through this. You've always leaned on each other. You guys have a great marriage."

"Yeah, until we moved." She picked up the mug and sipped.

"That's just adjustment stuff. You'll get through it."

"He doesn't understand. I'm so miserable. And he's so...so happy about everything." Abby waved her hand in the air, sloshing tea out of the mug. "Oops." She carefully put the tea down and wiped at the sofa. "He's changed, Diana."

Diana peered over her mug at Abby. "Maybe you're the one who's changed."

"You're right." Abby's voice rose and she stood. "I have changed." She spread her arms wide, as if she were about to fly. "I've been transformed. I," she lightly pounded her chest, "am a depressed nobody," she spread her palms out, "who does nada in a nothing life."

"But it doesn't have to be that way, does it? You know you can do something about it."

"Yeah, but somehow can't I." Wait, did that make sense? "I mean, I can't. I think."

"You can, Abby. You're a strong person. You've just been through a lot. Give yourself a chance. I know you'll turn things around."

"Maybe I should leave Peter." When the words escaped from her mouth Abby covered it with her hand. She walked to the window and spoke to the drapes as she pulled them closed. "Maybe I should leave Richmond and come back here. I want to be here. With my friends. My kids. Then I could help Hanna get over Jason. Help Ben with," she spun herself into the drapery, wrapping it around her like a cocoon, stopping when she faced Diana, "with whatever he needs help with." She sank to the floor and started sobbing. "But I don't know how to do that any more. I can't even help my kids."

"Abby," Diana went to her and guided her back to the couch. "Your kids are going to figure their lives out. All kids have hurdles to cross and they need to cross most of them without us. Ben and Hanna will be fine." She sat beside Abby and held onto both of her hands.

"You love Peter. I know it. You know it too, and you don't mean what you're saying. Not deep down."

"But I could. I could leave him." She shook off Diana and stood again. "I could just walk out on him, leave him happy in Richmond at his wonderful job and come back here to live on my own." She turned toward the door and stared right at Hanna standing at the threshold.

"Mom," Hanna's eyes glistened, "what are you saying?"

"Hanna!" Abby hiccupped. "You shouldn't have heard that. I didn't mean it." She stumbled over to her and hugged her. "I've just had too much to drink."

Chapter Twenty-Four

Abby stared out the front windshield, hardly seeing the cars on the road in front of them. Streaking by them along the sides of the highway, the naked limbs on the trees were interwoven with a palette of gold and brown; every so often a splash of fiery red burst through. They were past Buffalo on I-90 and the way stretched endlessly. She had no desire to read, listen to music, talk. In fact, during the hours since she and Peter left Waterloo, they barely said a word to each other. Peter probably considered it a companionable silence; she felt desolate sorrow.

She looked at his profile as he drove. There were more crinkles around his eyes and the greyness that used to be just at his temples was now sprinkled through most of his hair. It somehow made him more handsome. His profile was so familiar. She loved him. She did. Would she really consider leaving him? That idea, once voiced aloud, had stayed at the edge of her mind like a splinter she couldn't ignore. Yet her unhappiness stemmed from the move, not Peter. Didn't it? Then why did she feel so angry with him? She breathed in deeply to still her negative thoughts.

As if he felt her gaze, Peter turned his head toward her and put his hand on her knee. "You doing okay?"

"Hm."

"A rough week, huh? But you were so strong. At the funeral. With the kids. Your dad. I don't know how you did it, holding yourself together like that. You're amazing."

She blinked. "Thanks."

"And you were so great with Hanna. Poor kid." He shook his head. "She'll get over Jason soon enough."

"It's hard on her, though."

"Yeah, but she's tough." He looked back at the road. "Like you. Did I tell you Ben gave me fifty bucks before we left? First installment, he said." The corners of his mouth edged up in a half smile, bringing out the dimple in his cheek. "That kid. You never know what to expect."

"True." She still wondered what Ben had done with their money.

"And in the middle of everything we sold our house. How bizarre is that."

Annoyance chafed the edge of the calm Abby was trying to maintain. "Yeah, bizarre." The house had sold quickly, too quickly for her.

"We've got an appointment with Trixie tomorrow at ten so we can see that house in Sweetbriar Hollows. I'm thinking we should put in an offer, even though it's a bit high." He glanced at her. "If you like it, of course. But I know you will. You'll love the layout. The kitchen's beautiful and it has a screen porch. I know you want that."

She thought of the pictures Peter had shown her when he'd arrived in Waterloo. The house did look wonderful and very close to what they'd hoped to find. And they could afford it. But right this minute she didn't want to think about buying a new house, or selling the one in Waterloo. Right now she didn't want to think about her new life at all. She wasn't ready to let go of her old one. She wanted to wallow in the loss of it all, her mother, her kids, her home, everything. Why wouldn't he just let her wallow?

"Peter…"

"Abs, I know your life hasn't been easy in Richmond. But it'll get better. I think you…we…need to be in our own home, not some rented apartment with rented furniture. I think it'll make a difference."

"Maybe." Her chest tightened.

"And once we're part of a neighbourhood you can meet people, get involved with things. That'll make your life better too."

"Uh huh." The car felt stifling.

"Richmond's a good place to live, even you've said so. We'll have a nice life there."

Suddenly the air closed in around her. "Stop the car."

"What?"

"Stop the car, Peter. Stop the car!"

"Here? It's the middle of nowhere."

"Stop the car, stop the car, stop the car!"

He swerved and pulled to the side onto the gravelled shoulder. It crunched on the stones as it slowed, sounding like something breaking. Abby flung open her door and ran out. She tore down the small embankment, almost sliding down, and when she reached the bottom, she bent over, hands on her knees, panting wildly. Peter came behind her, put his hand on her back.

"Are you sick?"

"Sick? No." She shook off his hand and straightened, moved away from him.

"Then what? Why are you out here? It's cold."

She faced him. He folded his arms across his chest, hugging his warmth close. The chill settled on her face, cold air in her lungs. Both of them were breathing out small clouds of vapour.

"I needed to get away."

"What does that mean?"

"I couldn't stand being beside you, listening to you."

"What?" His voice faltered.

"Your upbeat, positive..." she clenched her fists, "Pollyanna attitude is too much for me. I can't take it."

"We can't only focus on negatives, Abby."

She stepped up close to him, shouting into his face. "Well, you shouldn't just focus on positives." She pushed at his chest, causing him to stumble backwards. He grabbed her wrists and held her hands in front of her.

"Stop it! Are you crazy?"

"Agh!" She pulled out of his grip and moved further from him.

"Abby, losing your mother is hard; God knows I know that. And your life isn't great right now. I know that too. But you've got to stop feeling sorry for yourself all the time."

She put her hands over her ears. It didn't help; she could still hear his voice.

"You know what I mean."

"You're unbelievable." She glared at him.

He rubbed his hands on his arms. "Look, can we talk about this in the car? I'm freezing."

She felt the cold but for some reason wasn't affected by it, as if her pent up anger was stoking a flame deep inside of her, warming her.

"No. It's too...suffocating." She looked past him at the car still running, exhaust billowing out the back. "You go."

"Not with us like this." He walked toward her, his arms reaching out. "Come on, Abs."

"Don't."

He stopped mid-stride. "You can't stay out here," he fanned his arm in the direction of the car, "in the middle of the highway."

"I can't go back in the car right now. You go. Leave me alone."

He shrugged and turned, stepping up the embankment. She watched as he opened the rear door of the car and pulled out his coat, putting it on. He leaned back inside and when he straightened, he was clutching hers. He walked back to her and held it out.

"If you're going to stand out here, you might as well stay warm."

She crossed her arms in front of her chest. "I don't want it."

"Fine. Let me know when you do." He went back to the car, turned it off without getting in, and leaned against the fender. He faced her with her coat hanging over his arms, dangling it like a carrot, his right leg bent casually. Was he just going to stand there looking at her?

She turned her back to him and stared at the gray, bare trees in front of her. She puffed out her breath, watching the little clouds dissipate in the air. It was foolish of her to stay out here in the cold. What exactly did she hope to accomplish? An image flashed across her mind, of herself crouching behind the car hiding from Peter, and her cheeks grew warm with embarrassment.

She glanced back at him waiting by the side of the car. He blew into his hands and rubbed them together, then called out.

"Come on, Abby. Let's get on our way."

She looked away and ran into the trees. Stopping by a thick trunk, she kicked it. Damn him. Damn her life. Damn everything.

She leaned against the tree and squeezed her eyes shut to stop the tears, and started to feel calmer. It was tranquil here despite the highway noises, and a relief to be away from Peter's incessant optimism. Here she could breathe. How ironic that when she was alone in the apartment all day she couldn't wait for him to come home. Now she had him beside her for hours in the car and couldn't wait to get away from him.

Something chattered above her. Looking up she saw a black squirrel, its bushy tail quivering. It looked odd to her and she suddenly realized she'd not seen black squirrels in Richmond, only gray ones. Why was that? What other things there were different that she hadn't noticed?

An unbidden memory glanced across her mind, of years ago when they had a squirrel that would come to their patio door. Every morning Ben and Hanna argued over who'd feed it a slice of bread. They named it Gertrude. For weeks they fed it, and then one day it stopped coming. Ridiculously, she was suddenly overcome with such despair at the loss of Gertrude that she bent over and moaned.

The squirrel screeched and ran off. She felt very alone. Shivering, she put her hands in her armpits to try to warm them and peered around the tree to look up at Peter. He held her coat out. She looked down the highway. Cars rushed by, disappearing over the horizon, like so much of her life. Her mother. Her home.

Her marriage?

Sighing deeply, she left the trees and climbed up the embankment.

Slipping on the incline, she stopped her fall with her hands. The icy stones pressed into them, intensifying the pain as she pushed herself up. When she reached the road, Peter straightened and held her door open. Saying nothing, she maneuvered into her seat and pulled the door shut. He climbed in behind the wheel, placed her coat on her lap, and faced her without starting the ignition.

"We need to talk. We can't drive for another nine hours with this tension between us."

She twisted and put her coat on, wrapping it tightly around her. She stuck her hands in the pockets and stared straight ahead.

"Abby."

"I don't want to talk right now. Just drive."

He made no move to start the car and sighed loudly. "It's a long drive with no talking."

She was silent.

"We're two adults, Abby. Something's eating at you; just tell me."

She shifted in her seat and faced him. "You're so..." Her voice stopped and she shook her head.

"I'm so what?"

She took a deep breath. "I've been very unhappy these past months..." Seeing him nodding she turned to face the window. "And you're so damn happy about everything."

"Well, not exactly..."

"Please don't interrupt me."

He stared at her, open-mouthed. "Okay."

"In the car today, I was feeling really sad. Mom died, Peter, and our home is sold. And you act like, 'okay, let's move to the next phase.' I can't do it just like that. And I don't understand how you can. I need time to say good-bye."

"But I just..."

She shot him a look that silenced him.

"You make me so mad. For not feeling what I feel. Don't you miss our old life? Don't you miss the kids? Don't you feel displaced in that apartment?"

"Of course I do. I..."

"For God's sake, let me talk."

"But you asked..." He sighed. "Okay. Talk."

"We've abandoned our kids. We're living hundreds of kilometers away in that little apartment and they're by themselves. We took away the kids' home, took away their anchor. And my parents," Abby swallowed, "Mom died without me there." She sobbed. "I didn't...I didn't..."

Peter reached in the backseat and handed her a box of tissues. Pulling one out she wept into it, keeping her eyes covered until her breathing calmed. She blew her nose and faced him. His forehead was furrowed and there were dark shadows under his eyes. Why hadn't she noticed before? He stroked her leg. She pushed his hand away and exhaled loudly.

"Every day in that apartment I get up and think about doing something with my life and I can't. Losing my old life, the kids, it's paralyzed me, Peter. I can't seem to get my act together." She shook her head. "I told you this before."

"Yeah, after you ran away."

She pursed her lips.

"Well, you did run away from me that night."

"Just forget it, okay?"

"Fine. Go on."

"You told me you understood. But you're still so happy and oblivious to the fact that I'm not. It's infuriating."

"God, Abby. This move hasn't been easy for me either. It's been tough getting used to the job, to the people I work with. And I'm missing our old life too and the kids. I'm not thrilled with this situation, but it's the way things are so I try to make the best of it. I don't want us to be miserable all the time." He shook his head. "And I'm not oblivious to the fact that you aren't happy. I know you're having a hard time. But I didn't want to burden you. I thought if you saw I was happy, you'd have less to worry about, more incentive to feel good about things." He leaned back in his seat. "Guess that was a bad idea."

"A really bad idea. I thought we were always honest with each other."

"Yes, but…"

"Why couldn't you tell me what you were feeling? Why pretend? Don't you realize how that makes me feel? How it hurts me?"

"I just thought..."

"Geez, no wonder I thought about leaving you."

He backed up in his seat. "Leaving? You mean...leave? Why?"

She shredded the tissue in her hands. "I want to go back and you don't."

"We can't go back, Abby."

She glared at him. "Even if we could, it wouldn't be the same. It's too late"

They sat quiet, Abby not knowing what to say next, not knowing where this conversation would lead.

He chuckled joylessly. "We both wanted this adventure. Remember?"

"Yeah. Careful what you wish for."

"Look, I'm sorry for not being honest with you. And I'm sorry you're so unhappy." He moved closer to her and said in a shaky voice, "You can't be serious about leaving? Our marriage? You don't mean it, do you?"

Did she? "I don't know. It's all tangled up with everything else." She looked at him but quickly averted her eyes from his hurt expression. "I want..." she sighed, "I'm not sure what I want right now."

He sat back in his seat and stared in front of him. "Well, let me know when you do."

Silence filled the car. She gazed at the fogged windshield, the scenery through it as muddled as her emotions. Cars whizzed past, rushing like her heart, infusing the tense stillness with whooshing sounds. She was cold, but she didn't dare ask Peter to start the engine. She shivered and put her hands under her thighs but that didn't warm them. She shifted her eyes to look at him without turning her head. He stared straight ahead, rubbing his temples.

Suddenly he banged his hands on the steering wheel, startling Abby.

"I had no idea this move would threaten our marriage." His voice shook. "I knew it'd be hard, but I thought we were solid. How could I be so blind?" He shook his head. "Did you feel this way before I lost my job?"

Had she? She couldn't remember. "I don't think so."

"So it's only your unhappiness about the move that's making you hate me."

"I don't hate you, Peter."

"But you're mad at me for losing my job?"

"I don't know."

He started the car and turned the heat to high. Cool air blasted in her face and she angled the vents away, shivering until the blowing air warmed.

"Abby, I love you."

She spoke quietly to the windshield. "Let's just go."

"Have you stopped loving me?"

She sat rigid, staring straight ahead, huddling into her coat. "Just go."

Chapter Twenty-Five

She floated on the surface of early morning sleep, drowsing in a suspended state of half-dreams. She sensed Peter standing beside the bed but resisted the pull of full awakening.

"Abby."

Dragging herself to consciousness, she opened her eyes. He loomed above her, exuding the fresh scent of soap, his hair wet and combed, wearing jeans and a shirt. She felt, and then saw, his eyes boring into her.

"Shall I cancel the viewing?"

"What?" She ran her fingers through her hair as she sat up and yawned.

"We have an appointment with Trixie to see that house at ten. Shall I call her and cancel?"

"Why?" She glanced at the clock. Not quite eight. She pulled the bed sheet taut over her legs and tried to gather her jumbled thoughts.

"Well, considering the precarious state of our marriage, I think we'd be foolish to buy a house."

His words brought back all the intensity of yesterday's drive and her stomach roiled. She threw back the covers and ran to the bathroom, retching into the toilet. Omygod. What had she done? Never had she intended to precipitate the unraveling of their relationship.

"You all right?" He stood by the door.

"Please." She didn't know whether she meant please help or please go. He backed out and disappeared from sight. Her nausea faded and she sat back, crouching, surrendering to convulsive weeping until the storm unleashed by her fear and doubt abated, until her breathing calmed. She bent over, hands covering her eyes, and tried to think what to do, how to mend what she'd broken. Or whether she wanted to. Nothing came. Her mind was as blank as the darkness behind her eyelids, even as it was filled with turmoil.

"Here." His hand was on her shoulder and she looked up. He held out a steaming mug.

"I made you some tea. Careful, it's hot."

He helped her up, as if she were a fragile invalid. She closed the toilet lid and sat down, clutching the mug in both hands. He lowered himself to the edge of the bathtub and leaned forward, putting his hands on her knees. She watched him over the rim of the cup.

"Abby, I love you. I don't want us to be apart." He took a deep breath. "I know you feel differently, want something different." He faltered and swallowed. "I'll do anything to make you want to stay."

She nodded, blew steam from her tea.

He pushed himself to his feet and shrugged. "Anyway, I wanted you to know that." He walked to the door, his head lowered.

"Peter?"

He turned quickly. "Yes?"

"Don't cancel the house tour."

****

In the shower the stream of water beat down on her, washing the gritty feeling from her eyes but not from her conscience. She scrubbed, wanting to scour away that horrible yesterday, the words she'd flung at him, the pain she'd inflicted. She couldn't now understand the fury that had driven her, the impetus that propelled her to jeopardize her marriage this way.

Massaging shampoo into her hair she stared at the misted shower door, recalling the endless minutes she'd gazed at the fogged windshield in the car, the long hours she'd stared at her book without reading a page, not speaking, not looking at him. And he'd reciprocated in kind. It was as if they each sat under a glass dome, like her mother's brass anniversary clock whose workings were protected in the shelter of its transparent covering. They protected themselves with their silence, driven by their emotional pendulums.

Remembering how chilled she'd felt last night not sleeping, lying alone beside him, a wide chasm between them, she shuddered despite the heat of the shower. Rinsing the foam from her body, she stood under the torrent of water until it began to cool. She dressed and lingered in the bedroom. Uncertain what outcome to wish for, she was hesitant to confront him. Finally she went to the kitchen, smelling toast and coffee. He sat at the table reading the paper, but when she came in, he folded it and put it down. That unsettled her; at the same time it encouraged her. His attention was not easily drawn from the news.

"Feel up to eating?" He pointed to a plate with buttered toast. "More tea?"

"Rather coffee."

"Are you sure? With your upset stomach?"

"It wasn't my stomach that upset me." She could see from his face he thought she was referring to him, but he said nothing and went to the coffeepot. She didn't know what to say that might heal the gash she'd inflicted on their relationship, didn't know how to heal it without tearing it further, or whether she should try.

She lowered herself into a chair, picked up a warm slice. He brought two coffees to the table and sat, eating and watching her, smiling tentatively whenever he caught her eye. Together they sat, crunching toast, sipping coffee. It felt...not tense. Merely awkward. She sighed in relief.

She knew she should say something; they needed to talk about what had happened. But she didn't know yet what she wanted to say. And she suspected Peter needed her to speak first. He'd said what he wanted in the bathroom.

Abruptly, he picked up the plates and carried them to the sink. She got up and brought the mugs. In the tiny kitchen they suddenly stood facing each other. He looked from her face to his watch.

"Time to meet Trixie," he said, adding in an exaggerated southern drawl, "Well, mornin', y'all."

She couldn't help herself. She smiled. He hugged her then, tightly, held on for a long time. She returned his embrace. They parted without speaking, put on their shoes, and left the apartment. In the car he glanced her way.

"Okay?"

"Uh huh."

He was handling her with care, she realized, treating her as if she were a delicate object, like one of her grandmother's antique teacups. She remembered how cautiously he'd surrounded those teacups in bubble wrap when they packed up her parents' house so many months ago. He held each one so carefully, knowing how much they meant to her although he didn't like them himself. The memory grazed a tender spot in her heart.

Neither of them spoke. She probed this absence of conversation, the way she might poke a skewer into a baking cake to see if it tested done. But this didn't feel like the tense silence that existed yesterday. That had been like another passenger sitting between them. This morning it was simply an uncertain quiet.

And as they drove, she began to notice the surroundings. Closer to the house Peter pointed things out: Ukrops, Krogers, dry cleaners, coffee shop, the Y. When they turned into the neighbourhood, she saw it looked nice, friendly. Well-kept gardens. Colourful flags hanging from the mailboxes. A man walking a dog. Two women chatting on a driveway, holding mugs. Then suddenly she saw the house, looking better than she remembered, and he pulled to the curb. She stepped out of the car and saw Trixie coming out of hers.

"Well, mornin', y'all," she called, sounding just like Peter had earlier. Abby caught his eye over the car roof and they smiled at each other. Trixie slammed her door and approached them.

"Abby, I was so sorry to hear about your mother."

Abby nodded, her throat suddenly constricting. Peter walked over.

"Thanks, Trixie," he said, putting his arm around Abby's shoulder. "Shall we go in?"

They turned to look at the house.

"It looks great, doesn't it?" Enthusiasm edged Peter's words. "Look at all the trees. Hardly any lawn to mow. And it has a nice big garage at the back."

She liked the garden. Flower beds with still blooming impatiens among azalea bushes and other plants she didn't know the names of. It was still so green for October. Not like the autumn browns they left behind in Ontario. The yard was full of tall trees, with moss at their bases, patches of periwinkle and pachysandra growing beneath them. It was like a forest. She looked up at the house. Buttery yellow siding, a swing on the front porch, a dark wooden front door with a stained glass window above it. Despite herself, she felt a stirring of hope. Peter reached his hand out to her and she found herself taking it as they followed Trixie up the stairs.

"Now, when you get inside," Trixie fumbled with the lock box hanging from the door handle, "you'll notice how bright it is with all the windows and the tall ceilings. Be sure to look for the lovely stained glass panels like this one above the upstairs doors."

Then they stepped into the hall. Abby instantly experienced a sense of peace, of light. She let go of Peter's hand and walked into the living room. Sunlight poured in through large windows that overlooked a treed backyard. The fireplace had an intricately carved mantle with shelves built around it and the wood floors shone. Home. This could be home.

She walked through a wainscoted dining room into the kitchen. White cabinets lined the blue walls, large windows let light in all across the back, and there was a breakfast bar with stools. To the side, a glass paneled door led into a sunroom.

Trixie came in behind her. "The owners renovated this just last year and then the poor things were relocated." She ran her hands along the blue granite counter. "Isn't it gorgeous? She must love to cook."

"Like you, Abs." Peter pulled open the door of the wall oven and looked inside. "Can't you see yourself doing all your Christmas baking in here?"

She could. "How soon could we move in?"

Trixie sat down on one of the stools. "As far as I know, the owners are gone. I don't know when they'll move their stuff out, but it's listed for immediate occupancy."

"So why hasn't it sold yet?" Peter crossed his arms. "I expected when I left for Canada that it'd be gone before we got back."

"Not sure, really." Trixie looked over her glasses at him. "Maybe because it only has three bedrooms. Maybe because the master bath needs updating. I've been through it pretty thoroughly and can't see anything else wrong with it. Anyway, it's your luck that it's still on the market. Maybe it's just meant to be your house." She handed a listing sheet to Abby and pulled out her cell phone. "I think it's a great buy. Y'all take as long as you like to look around. I'll be here if you have any questions."

Abby walked into the bright sunroom and saw a door to one side leading out to a screen porch. She stepped through it and stood for a moment listening to the birds outside. She slowly spun around, breathing in the airiness of the space. She'd always wanted a screen porch.

"What do you think?" Peter's question stopped her mid-spin and she faced him. She searched his eyes, knew what he was asking.

"I think it's a serious possibility," she said softly.

Chapter Twenty-Six

Abby ran into the room. Everyone was already sitting in their chairs, and they watched her as she plunked herself into the seat beside Anne.

"Sorry I'm late," she said. "There was a line-up at the dry cleaners."

"That's all right," Patty said. "We're glad you could come. We're only just starting."

Anne leaned toward her and whispered, "I've missed you the past couple of weeks."

Abby smiled at her. It felt good to be back in this room. With these women. The atmosphere was friendly. Familiar. Like she belonged.

And warmer than the chilliness she felt in the apartment with Peter. The hurt she'd inflicted on him was taking time to heal. She still found it awkward to talk to him and she supposed he sensed that, and he'd become aloof. Or maybe he was just giving her space. Anyway, she was trying to make things better. It was just harder than she expected.

Ellen spoke up. "We've already gone around the circle and introduced ourselves, Abby. I want to say how sorry we are about your mother. We all prayed for you."

"Oh." Abby was taken aback. She'd told Ellen about her mother, in confidence she thought, when Ellen phoned her the other day wondering why Abby hadn't been to the group and to see if she was all right. Now Ellen's mention of her mother stirred up the anguish Abby had worked so hard to stow away in a corner of her heart.

Irritated that Ellen exposed her to the group, Abby glared at her, wondering how to respond. But when Anne touched her arm and smiled encouragingly, Abby realized Ellen only meant well. And she realized it was a good feeling to know these women cared about her.

"Thank you," she said, lowering her eyes.

Patty shuffled her notes. "Today we're going to talk about all the emotional baggage we bring with us when we move. Feelings that we carry around with us all the time. Like anger, or fear, or disappointment. Or a sense that we've lost our identity in this place. Maybe you're constantly comparing your new home with your old one and it doesn't come out favourably. Or you're grieving everything you've lost by having moved here. Or feeling overwhelmed by depression."

Abby nodded. Yes to all of those. It was validating somehow, to hear that what she'd been going through was not because of a failing within herself, but because it was what people went through when they moved.

Patty scanned the faces in the circle. "I see lots of people nodding. Ellen has a stack of cards with different feelings written on them. We'll pass them around. Hold up the one you think you carry around the most and tell us about it. Then we can talk about how to let it go, because we have to overcome these emotions if we're going to move forward."

"Or at least we have to deal with them," Ellen said. She held up a card on which was printed Grief. "The first months I was here I spent most of my time grieving for my friends in England, my house in England, my garden in England, just about everything I had to leave behind. I would sit home and cry, not go out exploring, not bother trying to make new friends. Because I couldn't get over the fact that I had to leave England. It wasn't until I met Patty and started volunteering at the hospital, that I realized all my grieving had been getting in the way of my life. Now I think back to England with affection, but I don't let my memories of it stop me from making memories here." She passed the cards to Chris, who sat beside her.

Abby knew that grief was preventing her from moving forward too. But she was not going to pick that card. If she did, she might end up talking about her mother and the funeral and then she'd start bawling. And she didn't want to cry at this meeting. As comfortable as these women made her feel, Abby still didn't like exposing too much emotion to them.

Chris was shuffling through the cards, obviously finding it difficult to choose one. The Kleenex box was passed from hand to hand toward Chris. It seemed that everyone here expected she might break down and cry. Finally she held up two cards. One said Disappointment the other Depression.

"I picked two. Hope that's okay." She smiled weakly. "I was really disappointed when I moved here because it was so expensive to buy a house that we got one that's really small. We had to get rid of a lot of our nice things. And my husband's not so happy in his job, either. Things just didn't turn out the way we expected." Chris's voice quivered and she sniffed. Holly, who sat beside her, held out the tissues. Chris shook her head. "And I'm depressed most of the time. I don't feel like doing anything except crying. Even after the house was painted. I was happy about that, but the day after it was done, I just..." She dissolved into tears and passed the cards to Holly, taking the Kleenex box onto her lap.

Abby worried. Chris didn't seem to be moving forward at all. And she'd been here a lot longer than Abby. Would she end up being like Chris for months to come? She hoped not.

"Chris," Ellen patted her knee. "I think your house is real pretty. And you've got a wonderful garden too."

Chris nodded. "I know. I just want to stop being so depressed all the time."

"How do you think you can do that?"

"I don't know."

"She could get involved in something." Holly said definitively. "Volunteer. Or take a class or join a club." Abby wondered if that's what Holly had done. There was no doubt she was moving forward.

Patty agreed. "Holly makes a good point. Sometimes we spend so much time focusing on ourselves, on how unhappy we are, on how hard the move is, that we forget there's a whole world of things to do out there. When we get involved, we distract ourselves from those feelings that paralyze us, and that helps us to cope."

Abby felt ashamed listening to Patty. She knew all this. And she didn't act on that knowledge. When she first came to Richmond, she'd planned to do all of those things—volunteer, take a class, join clubs—because she knew it would enrich her life. But she'd done nothing except sit home and wallow in self-pity. Just like Chris.

Holly held up a card that said Anxiety. "When I first moved, I was anxious about finding a doctor I liked, and a dentist. Even a hairdresser. So I just kept putting things off. Then one day, I really needed a haircut." She shook her hair. "So I finally sat down with the yellow pages and made appointments all over the place. And then I wasn't anxious any more." She grinned.

Doctor and dentist? Abby hadn't even thought about finding those yet. The whole health insurance issue made her nervous. She was used to their automatic coverage in Ontario, supplemented by a plan from Peter's work. But the American system was different. Peter talked about co-pays. And the kids' dental wasn't even covered by Peter's work health plan because they didn't live in the U.S. Maybe she should pick the anxious card too.

Li-Juan held the stack of cards together. "Not sure," she said, shaking her head. "I just sad. Miss my mother." She lowered her head and sat quiet. Abby wondered if she was weeping, but then Li-Juan looked up. "But chi'dren happy at school. Is good." She nodded, "Yes?" and passed the cards to Anne.

"Well, Li-Juan," said Patty. "You're doing great. It sounds like you're trying hard to move on. And your English is getting so much better too. Isn't it?" she asked the group. Ellen started clapping and soon everyone joined in.

Li-Juan smiled shyly. "Tenk you," she said.

Anne held up the Angry card. "I can't seem to get over being mad at my husband. Not for moving us here, although there is that. But because he's such a jackass all the time. Excuse my French. I don't know that I can move forward if I stay married to him. But then if I leave him and go back to San Jose, am I going backwards?" Anne shook her head and for the first time seemed sad rather than angry.

Abby's stomach tightened. Anne's anger reminded her of the huge fight she'd had with Peter on the drive back to Richmond from Canada. And how, although they'd arrived at some sort of truce since buying the house, she still hadn't been completely able to cast away her feelings of anger. She was scared to think that it might lead her to where Anne was.

"Anne, it sounds like you need to work some things out with your husband." Ellen said carefully.

"Yeah, but it's this move that's destroying our marriage. Destroyed our marriage, I should say. I just have to figure out if it's worth staying here. With or without him."

Anne handed the cards to Abby and sat back, exhaling loudly. Abby smiled at her, to offer some support, but Anne didn't see.

Abby looked down at the cards. The one on top said Loss of Identity. Perfect. Abby held it up.

"I really feel like I've lost myself since we moved. I don't know who I am anymore. People don't know me as a mother, because my kids didn't move with us. They don't know me as a professor because I'm not allowed to work here. Nobody knows me in Richmond so I feel like a nobody." Emotions she'd been trying to quash surfaced and her voice began to quiver. She cleared her throat. "I haven't been able to figure out how to overcome that feeling."

"But you've got friends here, Abby," Patty said. "We know you."

"Yeah."

"That's right."

"We're your friends."

Everyone spoke simultaneously. They were all trying to make her feel better. Their warmth spread through her, tingling along her spine and inside her heart. She smiled.

"Thank you," she said, "for knowing me."

They all nodded, returning her smile.

"And," said Ellen, "think of the opportunity you have here. You can reinvent your life any way you want. Redefine yourself. It's kind of exciting when you look at it that way."

Abby nodded. She simply needed to ascertain how.

****

She stirred the foam into her cappuccino. She'd had a delicious lunch, a salad with goat cheese and pomegranate seeds. And the camaraderie around the table fed her spirit. It felt so good to be having lunch with friends. In Richmond.

"And when Danny came home upset, and Jeff just told him to get over it and be a man, that was the last effing straw." Anne twiddled her unlit cigarette between her fingers. She was an unlikely friend, Abby thought. Gruff, coarse, a smoker. Although, Abby had to admit, she only smoked outside, blowing the smoke away from her friends. And she was kind, too, and empathetic.

Chris put her hand on Anne's, stopping the fidgeting. "You and Jeff have to work things out. It's not good for your kids to see their parents fighting all the time."

"Yes, and it sure doesn't help them adjust to living here." Holly took the tea bag out of her mug. "All their associations with Richmond have to do with the strife between you and Jeff."

Abby agreed with Holly. Kids shouldn't see their parents fight. She and Peter never fought in front of Ben and Hanna. They never fought. Until they moved here, anyway. Heat prickled her neck as she remembered the shouting at the Thanksgiving table a few weeks ago. Ben and Hanna were witnesses to her anger then.

"I think Anne needs to decide in her heart what she wants to do about Jeff," Abby said. "She has to figure out if her marriage is worth all this...this anguish. The move drove a wedge between them and that just doesn't go away like that." She snapped her fingers. Abby was voicing thoughts about her own marriage, she knew. Substitute her and Peter's names and she could be talking about herself.

"But there has to be to a weakness in the relationship to begin with. A move in itself can't destroy a marriage," Holly said.

"Oh yes it can!" Abby said, while at the same time Anne interjected, "It can so!"

"Whoa," Chris sat back. "Are you having trouble with your hubby too, Abby?"

Abby's face got hot. "Well, I'm having some issues, yes. But..." Voicing it out in the open would make it more real somehow, more immediate. Did she want to do that? "It's not like Anne and Jeff. Peter's been supportive and loving through all of this."

"Then what's the problem?" Anne's gravelly voice demanded.

What was the problem? Abby tried to come up with the answer. "I'm not sure. I guess it's me. All me. I've been unhappy and blamed him. When it's not his fault."

"Honey, he made you come here, didn't he?" Anne prodded Abby's uncertainties.

"Yes, but...no...it wasn't his fault. He lost his job and we had to come." Abby felt like she was betraying Peter by discussing him with these women. "Anyway, we've just bought a house we both like. And we're moving into it in a month. Then things will be fine. I'm sure of it."

But she wasn't really sure of anything.

Chapter Twenty-Seven

November
Waterloo, Ontario

Abby shivered in the doorway as she watched the "relocation foreman" secure the back door of the long transporter truck, their possessions disappearing behind the dented metal. Peter and Ben stood with him, talking and laughing. She shut the front door of the house, finally. It had been open for most of the day while the movers continuously went in and out. She walked through the empty chill, pausing at the kitchen doorframe that Ben had painted months ago. Though the markings were no longer visible, she touched the place where they'd been, a record of Ben and Hanna's growth over the years. Caressing the wood, she thought about what they were leaving behind in this house: family dinners, games of hide-and-seek, Ben and Hanna's childhood, a lifetime of marriage.

She stared at the backyard through the patio door. The deck, the garden, everything familiar was covered with a blanket of snow, the way their furniture in the truck was shrouded in padded gray moving blankets. Her life in a cocoon, ready to emerge in Richmond. Emerge as what, she wondered. A brilliant butterfly fluttering among the flowers? Or a dull moth bashing itself aimlessly against a burning light?

Dismissing the foolish metaphors with a shake of her head, she wandered around the kitchen. Running her hands over the counter, she thought about all the meals she'd cooked here, all the cakes she'd baked, and suddenly remembered a time when the kids were little, helping her bake cookies. Ben, three years old, apron tied under his arms, stood on a chair beside her. Hanna, a toddler, sat on the counter next to the bowl as they tossed raisins into the dough. The phone had rung, and while she carried on a long conversation with Diana, keeping them in sight but not really watching them, the two of them had eaten half of the unbaked cookies. She smiled at the memory of their buttery chins, their doughy fingers, and Ben's guilty, but oh-so-cute expression.

She sighed. She would miss this place, her home, her comfort. So much of her life, their life, had happened here, so many memories were contained in these walls. She brushed at her cheek and told herself not to cry. They were moving to a good house. Peter's job was working out. She was making friends in Richmond. The kids were healthy.

It seemed incredible to be back in Canada again, having left her mother's funeral a month ago. They closed on the Sweetbriar house last week and were ready to move into it. Their new home. So here they were, moving out of their old one, truly and finally leaving. Yet another occasion to say good-bye in this continuing pain of leave-taking. At each departure she felt as if another piece of her heart were sliced away. Might it all have been easier if they'd simply stayed away once they'd left?

"The truck's gone." Peter leaned his hands on the counter, interrupting her thoughts. "They expect to arrive at the house around eight on Wednesday."

"AM or PM?"

"Morning, of course. One day in, one day unpacking, and they're out."

"Great." Another first day of the rest of her life.

"It's weird to be saying good-bye to this place." He glanced around at the emptiness, finally resting his blue eyes on her. "But it'll feel good to be settled in the new house, eh?"

"Uh huh." She walked past him and stared out the window above the sink. Late afternoon darkening showed off the room's reflection in the glass. And Peter behind her, a translucent reflection of the man she loved. She hated that he looked so tired and stressed. The circles under his eyes had sunk into dark purple and the lines on his forehead had deepened. She'd done that to him, with her distance, her uncertain feelings. He tiptoed around her, so solicitous, so gentle. As if he were scared to say or do anything that might make her run.

She wanted to tell him not to worry, to erase those creases from his brow, but she couldn't. Everything in her heart was so unsettled that she was all off kilter. True, she had begun to feel better once she became busy with the new house. There was so much to do and she had no time for self-pity. The movers to arrange. Phone, Internet, and cable to organize. Decorating. The bathroom renovation to oversee. But it was all temporary. Once the newness had passed, what would her life really be like? She was afraid that once the boxes were unpacked she'd regress back into the empty life she lived in the apartment.

So she wasn't able to assure him that their marriage would hold, that things would be fine between them. She hoped it would; she wanted them to be. But how could she commit to the belief that they would survive before she knew how she'd survive?

And he hadn't asked again. Once they'd seen the house, they clung to it in conversation like a lifesaver. In the weeks that followed, they simply lived day by day, Peter going to work, Abby doing what the house needed. She'd often find herself wondering how two people who loved one another could live together in this cold, distant manner. They treated each other like polite acquaintances. She'd never understood those frozen relationships in the books she read, the films she saw. She'd believed in the strength of love. Now she wasn't so sure.

She pondered her reflection in the window, imagining it was her ghost staying in this house. Two ghosts, she and Peter; their reflections juxtaposed, together the way they used to be. Their eyes met in the window and she felt his need for her. It reached through the silence that filled the empty kitchen. He stepped toward her.

"Should I put this in the van?" Ben's voice caused him to turn away. Abby was unprepared for the disappointment she felt. In the doorway, Ben pointed to the broom leaning against the refrigerator.

"No," she reached for it. "I still need to sweep the floor."

"I'll do it." Peter grasped the handle, his fingers enclosing hers. She pulled the broom toward her.

"No, I want to."

Ben coughed. "So we're done here?"

"Yes." Peter let go then, put his hand on Ben's shoulder. "Thanks for your help today. It was great you could get the afternoon off work."

"Actually," Ben drew out the word. "I didn't really have the day off. I sorta don't work there anymore."

The broom fell out of Abby's hand, clattering to the floor. "What do you mean? Did you get another job?"

"No-o-o." Ben took in a deep breath. "Well, kind of. Me and Adam started an Internet company and it's making money. So I quit."

Peter crossed his arms. "What kind of company?"

"It's an online distribution thing. For gamers. Hard to explain. But it's doing great. Here," he reached into his back pocket and pulled out his wallet, "I can pay back more money."

"How exactly are you earning it?"

"Does it involve gambling?" Abby narrowed her eyes.

"Look, you guys don't have to worry. It's all cool." He raised his hands and shrugged. "I can take care of myself."

"But you're only twenty…"

"He's right, Abby."

She glared at Peter. "But we're his parents." She turned to Ben. "We still want to look out for you, Ben, to make sure you're on a good path."

"I am. Stop worrying, Mom. Your job's done."

Abby wasn't so sure. What exactly was this "online distribution thing?" Would it spiral him downward the way the gambling had? Could Ben really support himself with it? Build a life all by himself? Without a proper education? Without credentials?

Peter pulled keys out of his pocket. "Why don't we take your stuff to your place and you can show me the Web site."

"Yeah, uh, it's not really up right now. We disabled it for maintenance."

"We still have to take those boxes there. Want to drive?" He held out the key, the rental tag swinging as it dangled.

Ben reluctantly took it.

She touched his arm. "See you when you get back. You can tell us more about it then."

"Yeah." He glanced around the room. "Bye, house."

As Peter followed Ben out, he glanced at Abby and raised his eyebrows. I'll check it out, he mouthed. She trailed them to the open door, rubbing her arms in the cold, and watched them get into the van and drive off. Snow was still falling, big snowflakes dancing to the ground the way they had much of the day. When the kids were young she used to love this kind of snow; they'd lie on the ground flapping their arms to make snow angels. Throw snowballs. Good snow.

But not great for moving. The movers had left wet footprints through the house. The boxes and furniture got damp as they were carried to the truck. The cold settled in the house and penetrated her clothes. At least they wouldn't have snow when they unpacked in Richmond. She thought about a milder, snowless winter and felt an unexpected nugget of anticipation.

She closed the door and began sweeping. Starting in the hall, she made her way to the kitchen. Her footsteps echoed. The house felt hollow. How strange that the house they bought in Richmond, which was not really home yet, made her feel tranquil, while this one, where they'd lived so much of their life, left her emotions in disarray. She swept the dirt into a pile, gathering it together like the memories that engulfed her.

"Hello?" The door slammed and Hanna appeared in front of her, rosy cheeked.

Her energy abruptly permeating the stark house lightened Abby's mood and she smiled. "Hey."

Hanna looked around. "It's so empty. It almost echoes."

"Yeah, kinda sad, huh?"

"Really sad. Dad here?"

"He's taking stuff to Ben's. You coming with us for dinner at the Newtons'?"

Hanna nodded. "You and Dad going to sleep there tonight?"

"Yes."

"I wish you didn't have to go."

"I know, Sweetie, but our flight leaves at eleven tomorrow."

"This is really the end, isn't it?" Hanna zipped and unzipped her jacket. "Anyway, I thought of something." She pulled a marker out of her pocket. "Come to the basement with me, okay?"

Abby left the dirt pile and followed her down the steps into Peter's old workshop.

"What are we doing?"

Hanna crawled under the stairs. "This is the only home I've known. I want us to leave our mark here." Taking a flashlight out of her pocket, she shone it on the surface behind one of the steps and began to write with the marker. "The new people won't know it's here but we'll know. We'll always be here." She stepped out and handed Abby the flashlight. "Look."

Abby crawled to where Hanna had been and aimed the light. There on the unfinished wood, in red letters, she read:

The Settel family
1991-2011
Peter, Abby
Ben, Hanna
Max

She touched her hand to the words.

"Knowing that's there makes it easier to leave." She climbed out and hugged Hanna. "Great idea."

"Mom?" Hanna pulled away from her and sat on the stairs. "Can I ask you something?"

Abby lowered herself on the step beside her. "Sure."

"Well, you know when you were here last time? You, uh…" Hanna took a deep breath. "Since Jason broke up with me, I kind of know about relationships…" Her voice faltered.

Abby put her arm around Hanna's shoulders. "What is it, sweetie?"

Hanna blurted out, "You said you might leave Dad. Are you?"

"What?" Abby's arm dropped. She stood.

"I heard you tell Mrs. Newton." Hanna's voice wavered. She stood, too, and held the banister with one hand, as if poised to flee. "You said you'd live here on your own. Leave Dad in Richmond. You're not, are you?"

Abby stood with her mouth open. The recollection of that night and her alcohol-induced proclamation forced a wave of shame through her. She couldn't move, couldn't speak. She should just tell Hanna no. No, we're fine. I'm not leaving Dad. What was stopping her?

Hanna's leg was jiggling. "Mom? I tried to forget it. You were drunk. You said you didn't mean it. So I didn't say anything after and I figured it wasn't true." She paused and took a deep breath, her shoulders rising. "But when I see you with Dad now, you're so...you're just not...you talk to him like..." She blew her breath out, her confidence deflating. "Things just don't seem right."

Abby wrapped her arms around her daughter. "Shh, Hanna. Don't worry. I'm not leaving."

Rubbing her hand along Hanna's back, she realized the implication of what she was saying. She'd better follow through. But what if she couldn't? "Life's so hard lately, you know? And I'm kind of taking it out on Dad. It'll work itself out. Please don't worry about it. You've got enough to deal with."

Hanna pulled away and sniffed loudly. "Really?"

Abby swallowed. "Really."

"You still love him and everything?"

Abby nodded.

"Cuz..."

"Hanna, next week Dad and I move into our new house together. Once I get my life going there, we'll be fine." She steered Hanna up the stairs. "We'll be fine."

Hanna looked back at Abby as she started climbing the steps. "I've been worried all week. I mean, it would be cool if you moved back but awful if you came without Dad, you know?"

Abby could hear relief in Hanna's words. Surely the reassurances were worth her daughter's peace of mind. She could make things work for that, couldn't she?

"And if you left Dad, where would that leave Ben and me? Even though you're in Virginia, I want the family to be together. I don't want my parents to be divorce..." She stopped suddenly. Peter stood at the top of the stairs, Ben peering over his shoulder behind him. Peter's face was drained of color.

"You're discussing this with Hanna? My God, Abby, how can you involve her? What are you thinking?"

Abby shut her eyes and shook her head. She lifted one foot to the step above her and ascended the stairs, an effort that felt like climbing a mountain. At the top she brushed past her family.

"No, that's not how it was." She felt weak, like she needed to sit down but there was no place to do that. When she faced them, she flinched from Peter's accusing gaze, Ben's stricken one.

"I didn't discuss things with Hanna. I was answering her question. She overheard me talking to Diana." She looked at Hanna, as if for corroboration. "Ages ago. I had a lot of wine and I was upset and depressed. And I was wondering out loud if I'd be happier back here in Waterloo. That was it. I didn't mean it. It just came out." She leaned her back against the wall, staring at a spot on the ceiling behind them. She moved her eyes down, glancing from Hanna to Ben, then to Peter, forcing herself to hold his gaze. "I just need to get through this move. To get control of things. This family is too important to me." And she slid down the wall, the weight of her words pressing her down. She put her elbows on bent knees and covered her eyes.

Chapter Twenty-Eight

December
Richmond, Virginia

She stood in front of the open cupboard, staring at its crowded contents. The mugs wouldn't fit. She'd have to reorganize again, find a different part of the kitchen to put the cups and glasses. Frustration crept through her tiredness and she took a deep breath.

"You're not keeping up, ma'am." Ed, the mover, smiled as he unwrapped a mug and set it on the counter beside the others. He was a speed demon in emptying boxes and unwrapping. The counter was so filled with dishes there was hardly room for anything else.

"Why don't you stop with those. I'll do the rest myself when I figure out where to put it all."

"It ain't easy, is it? A different kitchen from what you're used to."

Abby nodded.

"You know, most ladies just put everything in the cupboards and then figure it out later. I betcha they switch 'em around a few times, too, before they get it right."

"But I know how I want it to be. It just isn't working." Abby squeezed her eyes shut and shook her head.

"But it's sure a better kitchen than the one you left."

"Yes," she gazed at the cupboards, the wall oven, and the vast counter surface. She did love this kitchen and couldn't wait to cook in it. "Yes it is."

He nodded toward the living room. "Shall I do those boxes of books in there? I've still got a couple of hours left to help you."

"I think..." She stared at the disarray around them. Afternoon sun shone through the windows on flattened boxes, trash bags overflowed with crumpled paper, bowls and pots covered the tabletop. She looked beyond to the sunroom, where rays of light settled on more boxes, as yet unopened. That's where she wanted to be, sitting in that quiet, airy room, away from the chaos, calming herself with a cup of tea. They should fill it with wicker furniture, white wicker with soft flowery cushions. And plants. A big tropical palm or something.

"Mrs. Settel, ma'am? Should I unpack the books?"

She pulled her mind back to the kitchen. "You know what, Ed? I'll do the rest. Most of the big stuff is done and I really need to figure out where to put everything. So I think you can go. Thanks for all your help."

"Are you sure? Cuz it's only three and I'm on the clock 'til five."

"I'm sure." She nodded.

"Okay then. Thanks. I'll just take these empty boxes and trash outa here."

****

Standing in the doorway, she watched the truck drive down the street, its rumbles fading as it disappeared from sight. Breathing in the fresh air, she turned her face to the lowering sun. Not a cloud in the sky. Here it was December and she stood outside wearing a sweatshirt. The lawns were lush; there were leaves on the azalea bushes and some of the trees. She thought back to the Ontario winter they'd left just last week. All grey and white and dull. Here it was bright and green and...were those flowers?

She walked over to the bush and pulled down a branch. Yes, they were, dark red petals with a yellow center. A tree blooming in December! She wondered what it was and decided she needed to buy a book on gardening in the south.

"That's such a pretty color for a camellia. I love that tree."

A woman came up the driveway with a dog on a leash. She carried a flat casserole dish covered in foil. In jeans and a thick blue jacket, she wore a knitted hat on her head. Abby wondered why when the temperature was so mild. The dog, a fluffy little black thing, pulled on the leash around the woman's wrist, straining to sniff Abby's feet.

"Is that what it is? A camellia?"

"Uh huh. A sasanqua camellia. Yours is a single bloom. I've got a double in my backyard; it's pink, though. You should come over and see it sometime. Should be in full bloom by Christmas, like a shrub full of roses." The woman smiled and held out her hand, the leash looped around her wrist.

"I'm Pamela, Pam. I live across the street." She pointed to a red brick house with a yellow door. Her words had a faint hint of southern accent. "Welcome to the neighbourhood."

Abby shook her hand. "Thank you. I'm Abby." The dog was jumping on her leg and she stepped back.

"Rufus, no!" Pam yanked on the leash and the dog sat down. "Sorry, we're still in training."

"Rufus? He's awfully cute." Rufus perked his ears, cocked his head and looked at Abby, his tail quivering on the ground. Abby bent down to pet him.

"He is. Too cute for his own good. I just saw your moving truck leave. You're probably in a big mess with boxes and all and haven't given a thought to dinner."

"You're right about that."

"I've made a lasagna for you so you don't have to worry about cooking tonight." Pam held out the dish she was carrying.

"That's really nice of you. In fact, it's wonderful." Abby put the dish on the steps. "Thank you."

"My pleasure. Listen, if you need any help with unpacking or anything just let me know. Tonight my girls have dance, but I'm free tomorrow." Pam glanced toward Abby's open front door. "Do you have kids?"

"Yes. Um, no. Well, I've got two but they didn't move with us. One's just started university and the other's working so they stayed in Canada."

"Canada? Wow. It must be hard to move so far away from them."

Abby simply nodded, afraid of caving into the sadness she felt about setting up house without Ben and Hanna.

"You don't look old enough to have grown-up kids."

Abby managed a smile. "Believe me, I'm that old."

"At least you've survived the teen years. I have twin girls who are almost thirteen." She grimaced. "Can't wait. I'll be relying on your expertise, I'm sure." She laughed. "And listen, you can come over any time you need a dose of kids."

"Thanks. Maybe we can have coffee tomorrow. In my chaos. I know I've unpacked the coffeemaker."

"At least you've got your priorities straight. I'll come by later in the morning, after the gym and help you unpack. I know how crazy moving can be. We just moved here last year. From the Southside." Pam looked over at her house, then back at Abby. "I should get back. Time to be the homework police." She gave the leash a gentle tug. "Come on, Rufus."

Abby couldn't help smiling as she watched Pam walk to her house, Rufus prancing beside her. For a dog in training, he seemed pretty well behaved.

Things were looking up. A new friend. Nice weather in December. Flowers in the garden. Maybe life would be okay here in Richmond. She picked up the lasagna and walked into the house.

In the dining room she saw that Ed had unpacked all the good china and arranged it on the table. She could organize this room, clear off the table and set it for a nice dinner with Pam's lasagna. Make their first meal in the house special.

As she moved the items into the cabinet, the memories flooded in with the dishes. Place settings, white with small blue forget-me-nots around the edges, from her grandmother. The tea set inherited from Peter's mom, beautiful Royal Doulton that Abby had never used. The crystal pitcher given to her by Peter's dad a year before he died.

She realized that Ed had unpacked the boxes from her parent's house too. Her mom's collection of teacups stood carefully stacked, two by two, side by side, and next to them the set of crystal glasses, goblets, and dessert cups. And there was the anniversary clock, its workings bubble-wrapped under the glass dome. She guessed Ed hadn't wanted to risk fiddling with it. She sat down and pulled it toward her. Lifting the dome she unwound the plastic, fleetingly thinking about how Hanna and Ben might argue over who'd get to pop the bubbles.

Her mother had been given the clock by Abby's father for their twentieth anniversary, when Abby was fifteen. Usually her parents celebrated their anniversary by going out for dinner, the only time they did other than Mother's Day, but this time her dad had said he wanted to eat in. Her mom had cooked a roast beef dinner with Yorkshire pudding and roast potatoes. Abby remembered helping her get ready, setting the table with the forget-me-not dishes, the good silverware, wine glasses, and tall white candles, which was really special, because candles usually came out only at Christmas. Her dad brought home a bottle of sparkling wine, André's Baby Duck. She felt very grown-up to be allowed a half glass of it. Years later she bought a bottle for Peter when they were dating, but they had both spewed out their first sip. It was plonk, but then, on that anniversary day, it was special.

She closed her eyes, remembering that evening. While they ate, her parents reminisced about how they met, their wedding day, and how special it was when Abby was born because they'd wanted a baby for so long. At least, her mom reminisced; her dad mostly nodded and smiled. Abby cleared the table so her mom wouldn't have to, and after she'd placed a crystal dessert cup containing lemon mousse at each of their places, he brought out a box from under his chair and ceremoniously handed it to her mother. It was wrapped in pink flowered paper with a big white bow on it. Inside was the anniversary clock. She remembered her mother's face when she saw it, tears making her eyes shine. And her father gently winding the key, setting the time. And the way they'd looked at each other, for hours it seemed to Abby, who was eager to get her spoon into the lemon mousse.

She wound the key now and set the pendulum turning. This clock had been so precious to her mother, a symbol of a relationship Abby could never quite figure out. Her father had been a quiet husband, but strong-willed and controlling. Her mother could be controlling too, especially with Abby, but she always acquiesced to her husband. And in their later years she became obsequious and tread cautiously around him.

She wondered what had happened in their relationship for it to have evolved that way. Why did her father become the silent ruler and her mother his timid servant? Was her mother afraid of losing her husband? Was that why she handled him with care?

Abby stiffened. That was what Peter was doing too, wasn't it. Handling Abby with care in case she left him?

She shook her head. No. They were not like her parents. She and Peter communicated, even if it was through fighting. She couldn't remember her parents ever doing that. Her images of them together were always of her mother busy and chattering, her father silent and nodding.

Abby rubbed at her eyes with the heels of her hands and checked her watch so she could position the little brass hands to the right time. Now her mother was silent, never to say another word to Abby or to her husband. And her father, still silent in his dementia, might as well be gone too.

Replacing the glass dome over the brass workings she sat back in her chair, staring at the little balls on the pendulum go round and round, back and forth. She couldn't keep living like this, dwelling on all the sad things in her life. She needed to move on. Isn't that what she'd learned at the Lost in Transition meetings?

She had too much empty time, too much time alone. She needed to start filling it. And she needed to nurture things in her life that would make her happy.

Resolutely she stood. She would not let her marriage become like her parents', not have Peter always feel the need to tiptoe around her. Last week she told Hanna she'd stay; now Abby realized how much she wanted to. Not sure where its final home would be, she moved the clock to the middle of the table, an odd centerpiece for their first dinner in their new home but a reminder to Abby of her resolve, and got back to work.

****

As she wiped the last fingerprint from the cabinet door, she surveyed the dining room with pride. The boxes were empty and flattened, taken to the garage. The china and crystal were installed in the cabinet and the furniture polished. The room looked moved in. Inhaling the aroma of the lasagna from the oven, she actually felt like she was home. She smiled at the table she'd set, tablecloth unfolded and laid out so it covered just enough for two people, the rest of the surface stretching out empty. Except for the clock, which she'd left in the centre. Linen napkins, crystal glasses, candles. No wine, but no matter. She and Peter would have a cozy dinner at their little corner.

She leaned over to light the candles.

"It smells good in here. You cooked." Peter's voice startled her and she almost knocked one of the candles over. Righting it, she turned. He was standing in the doorway holding a large potted palm taller than he was, his face hidden behind its fronds, and he seemed to be struggling with its weight. She rushed over to him.

"Let me help you."

"It's okay. I'll take it to the sunroom and put it down. It's more awkward than heavy."

She followed, marvelling at the coincidence of Peter bringing home a palm tree just hours after she'd thought about wanting one. He pushed boxes aside with his foot and set the pot in the corner, windows surrounding it.

"There. Looks good here, eh?"

"It totally suits the room. Just today I was thinking we should get one. Thanks."

She put her arms around his neck and kissed him. He seemed taken aback, then responded, holding her tight and pressing his lips to hers. Had she been so distant that he no longer expected her affection? She leaned in closer, as if apologizing. It felt good to be in his arms.

"I love you," she whispered.

"I love you too." He drew away slowly and stared at her, his eyes penetrating as if trying to determine her motives. She found it difficult to pull away from his gaze.

"Uh, I think the lasagna's ready. We should eat." She took his hand and led the way to the kitchen.

They sat at their end of the table, eating, discussing what room to unpack next, her new friend Pam, Peter's office politics, the Lost in Transition group. When conversation turned to their suspicions about Ben's Web site and how Hanna was coping at university, Abby's mood plummeted. Worries about her kids were a constant weight on her heart. And she missed them being a part of her life. She suddenly saw the empty spaces on the other end of the table as a sad reminder that she and Peter were alone, that Ben and Hanna weren't living in the house with them. She swallowed and turned her gaze away from the blank, shiny wood.

"It's a big table for just us," she said.

"But this is so cozy and romantic. I love how you put us together at this end." He placed his hand on hers. "Thank you for doing this. For making our first dinner here special."

Then he chuckled, not entirely with joy. "This house will be our little love nest."

She understood his cynicism, intended or not. Love nest indeed. They hadn't made love for, well, she couldn't remember the last time.

She smiled at him. "Yup, our little love nest." Life could be nice with just the two of them. And really, Ben and Hanna wouldn't be living with them even if they'd stayed in Waterloo. She moved her hand away and picked up her glass, holding it as if to toast. "Too bad we don't have any wine to christen it."

"Yeah, too bad. Next time." He picked up his water and clinked her glass. "To our new home."

"Our new home." She took a sip and put her glass down.

"Abs," he touched her arm, "look at me."

She faced him and was pulled into his insistent blue eyes. He stroked her cheek.

"I haven't seen you like this for a long time. You seem happier. Like a cloud's been lifted or something. It's nice."

She nodded. "Uh huh. I decided I was tired of being sad all the time. I miss being happy. Unpacking all the family stuff made me think about what's really important in life. So I realized I need to stop feeling sorry for myself and start taking charge of how I live. Make choices, you know? Make it what I want."

A look of something, she wasn't sure what, flitted across his eyes. Fear? "And do you know what that is?"

"Some of it." She shrugged. "The rest I'll figure out."

"And me? Am I a part of what you want?" He looked at her with an intensity that caused her to grow hot.

"Yes." She grabbed his hand. "Yes. I know I've hurt you and I'm so sorry. You've been very patient with me." She shook her head. "I'm amazed you put up with it all."

He shrugged. "I love you. You're my life." He continued to stare at her, his expression questioning, expectant. She leaned forward, closing the distance between them.

"I want our marriage to survive. I want to stay. For you and me, not just the kids. I want us to be partners again."

His eyes brightened and he straightened his shoulders. "Oh, Abs, you can't imagine how much I've been wanting to hear that."

He stood, scraping his chair. He pulled her up and turned her to face him, kissing her forehead, her eyes, her cheeks, her lips. His hands roved round her back, caressing her shoulders and moving down to the small of her back, then to her buttocks.

She felt her body responding, her heart beating faster. Tracing her hands down his spine she kissed his face and when their lips met, pushed her tongue into his mouth.

He slid his hands under her bottom, lifting her up. She wrapped her legs around him. He sat her down on the empty side of the table.

"Let's christen the dining room this way," he whispered as he reached under her sweatshirt.

"On the table?" She giggled.

"Yes." His breath in her ear made it tingle and she hummed in agreement, unbuttoning his shirt then pulling down the zipper of his pants.

Moving her seat back from the edge of the table, she struggled with her own jeans, pushing them down with her feet. Peter pulled off her shirt then pressed against her. She leaned back, welcoming him. How she had missed this. How she had missed him. Lying on the smooth surface of the table, she stretched her arms up, revelling in the sensations she hadn't experienced for so long. Her hand hit something hard and she heard a crash. Their movements stopped, as if in a freeze frame.

"What was that?" Peter pulled back and looked around. She slid off the table and stared at its center.

"I think I knocked the clock off."

He crouched down and looked under the table at the floor on the other side. She crouched down beside him. The clock lay on its side, its dome shattered, pieces of glass scattered around the floor.

"Your mother's clock," he said with dismay, putting his arm around her shoulders. "I'm sorry."

She shook her head. "It's okay." She touched his hand that hung just above her breast and gazed at the glass shards. "It doesn't matter. It's just a clock."

"Maybe we can get a new dome for it."

"Maybe."

Their heads turned at the same time and they stared at each other. The sight of him crouching on the floor half naked, knees up, pants bunched around his ankles and shirt unbuttoned was too much for her and she started to laugh.

He laughed too, and together they helped each other to stand. He wrapped his arms around her and rocked her in his embrace, whispering in her ear.

"Welcome back, my Abby. Welcome back."

She nestled into the familiarity of his arms, the warmth of his welcome. Her heart pounded. Her mind darted. Yes, she thought. This was love. This was home. This was where she wanted to be.

Wasn't it?

Settled

"My heart today smiles at its past night of tears
like a wet tree glistening in the sun
after the rain is over."
~ Rabinfranath Tagore, "Fireflies"

"Burdens shared are easier to bear."
~ Jesse Jackson

Chapter Twenty-Nine

May (Six months later)
Richmond, Virginia

The table was filled with an abundance of treats. Muffins, cheese and crackers, veggies and dip, devilled eggs, cake. Abby added her plate of cookies to the array.

"Hi, Abby, what'd you bring?" Patty put a quiche onto the table.

"Cookies. Oatmeal-cranberry." Her father's favourite. Probably not anymore, though. He wouldn't have a favourite anything, sitting in his chair staring at nothing, not knowing who he was.

She inhaled the collage of smells. The aromas blended together to create a complementary mixture. Like this group, she thought, looking around the room. Women who came from all over, seeking each other out, leaning on one another. It was hard to believe she'd been so hesitant about joining them all those months ago. She couldn't imagine her life in Richmond without them.

Juan-Li placed a silver platter covered in foil on the table. She smiled at Abby.

"I bring spring roll," she said. "My chi'dren like. I tink you like too."

"I know I will, Juan-Li. I love spring rolls."

Holly, putting down a bowl of fruit salad, joined them. "Hey, Abby. How was your trip to Canada?"

"It was okay. Hanna's concert was great. I can't believe she's finished her first year of university." She shook her head.

"Has she got a job for the summer?"

Abby grimaced. "No, she's traveling cross-country in a band with her new boyfriend. She says she'll make a pile of money because they have gigs lined up everywhere."

"Wow. Do you like the boyfriend?"

"He's got a motorcycle," Abby said, as if that would explain her uneasiness about Derek. When Abby first saw him, she almost grabbed Hanna and ran. Tall, muscular, a dark beard hiding half of his face, hair down to his shoulders, leather jacket. He looked to be twenty-five, even though he was only nineteen. He played the guitar, was in the same program as Hanna at WLU. Which was supposed to be a classical music program. How do you go from playing classical guitar to playing gigs around the country in a band?

She'd so hoped Hanna would come to Richmond for the summer. She and Peter had even accepted that she wouldn't earn any money, since she wasn't allowed to work here. But no, Hanna made her own plans. She was head over heels for Derek. She was insistent that playing in the band would be a stepping-stone to her career.

And, Abby had to admit, aside from the fact that Derek looked like a bad boy, he was a nice kid. Polite. Well-spoken. Smart. And most importantly, he was kind to Hanna. Peter had checked up on the band and their travel plans. He was satisfied. They even had a manager.

They couldn't stop Hanna anyway.

"Poor Abby." Holly bit into a cookie. "You lose control over your kids when they leave home, huh? I worry about my kids now more than I ever did."

"Yeah, me too." Abby considered Ben. Worrying about him was an undercurrent to all of her other thoughts. He answered his phone infrequently. He still didn't have a regular job and they wondered what exactly he was up to.

"Okay, everyone." Ellen called over the din of people's conversations. "Welcome to our graduation celebration and brunch. We don't have a formal program today, but we thought it would be a good idea to each share something we've learned during these months." She smiled. "So take a few minutes to fill your plate with all those goodies on the table and then take a seat so we can get started."

Balancing her plate on her knees, Abby put her coffee on the floor under her chair. She smiled at Chris sitting beside her and thought sadly of Anne. She missed Anne's contributions to the discussions, missed her friendship. Anne hadn't even said good-bye before she left.

"Oh, she went home," Ellen told her at the meeting after Christmas. "And not just for Christmas. Two weeks ago she called to tell me she decided to leave Jeff. Packed the kids up, rented a U-Haul, and drove back to San Jose."

This unsettled Abby. She'd been gauging her and Peter's situation with Anne and Jeff's, hoping she and Anne would both figure out how to resolve their conflicted emotions. Things had gotten better for Abby. She'd thought Anne was going in that direction too.

But Anne had given up. Abby was disappointed. And a little scared.

"Did she give you a number so we can call her?" Abby asked. "An e-mail address?" She needed to talk to Anne, find out what the catalyst was that finally propelled her to make the decision.

"Nope." Ellen shook her head. "I think she just wants to forget about Richmond. Close it as a bad chapter in her life."

"But," Abby felt abandoned, "we were friends."

"I know." Ellen shrugged. "Clearly she has stuff she needs to work out that doesn't include us."

Chris's soft-spoken voice brought Abby back to the present.

"I'd like to go first, if that's okay." At Ellen's nod Chris continued. "I've learned that I need to be content where I am. And to not only think about myself. When I started volunteering at the shelter, I realized there were people worse off than me. And I could help them." She smiled sheepishly. "I really like my house now and I'm embarrassed at how upset I was about it. I'm happy in my life here."

"That's great, Chris." Patty gave her a long-stemmed carnation. "You've come a long way."

"I know," Chris said. "I was a mess, wasn't I?"

"I was too," Abby said. "I didn't know I had it in me to be so pathetic. I spent months being depressed and angry." She looked around at everyone listening. "I was too busy feeling sorry for myself to figure out how to live my life here. When I finally decided to take control, things got better. I made friends." She smiled at Holly. "I volunteer at the Community Hospice. I take a painting class." She shrugged. "Being busy really helps. And I like Richmond. Have you seen all the dogwoods and azaleas?"

"Yay!" Patty handed Abby a carnation. "We're so glad you stuck with the group." She turned to face the circle. "Abby's going to join us as a leader in September. Isn't that great?"

****

Humming, Abby walked to the car. For some reason she couldn't get *Feelin' Groovy* out of her head. She inhaled the scent in the air. Blossoms, mulch, grass. She aimed her face to the sun, feeling the warmth, absorbing it all. She *was* feeling groovy.

Reflecting on the discussion this morning, she thought about how far she'd come since that first meeting, when she'd fled to her car. She'd recalled then that her life had unraveled like a sweater coming apart. It hadn't occurred to her that Peter losing his job was a springboard to something better, an opportunity for her to clarify who she was, to disentangle herself from everyone's expectations.

Her purse rang and she froze. Always when her cell phone rang, her first thought was of Ben. She looked at the call display. Peter.

"Hey, Abs. How are you? Was the brunch good?"

"It was great. What's up?" Peter seldom phoned during the day; he was always so busy.

"I got a call from a recruiter this morning. He told me about a job in Toronto I might be interested in."

Abby stood very still. Toronto. An opportunity to move back.

"Abs, did you hear me?"

Her heart thumped. "Yes, I did. What are you thinking? Do you want to pursue it?"

"I'm not sure. I wanted to pass it by you. It could be good, you know. Close to the kids. Your dad. You could work again."

All those things were running through her head too. "But is it a good job? Are you interested in it?"

"I could be. The pay's good. It's a VP position."

Abby remembered all she had gone through when they left Ontario. Imagine having an opportunity to move back there.

But what about her life here? She liked living in Richmond. She liked her new friends, her new pursuits. She liked the person she'd become here. And she was committed to being a leader for Lost in Transition.

"Peter?"

"Yeah, babe."

"I'm not sure I want you to go for it. I like our life here."

"Really? I thought you'd jump at the chance to go back."

Didn't Peter understand anything about her? She directed her gaze at the azalea bush ahead. An explosion of pink, spotlighted in the sun.

"No, I've kind of moved on from that. I'm happy here. I'm where I want to be right now."

"Well, we can talk about it tonight. Love you."

"You too."

She snapped her phone shut and unlocked the car.

Time to go home.

The End

Discussion Questions:

Why was Abby feeling both anxiety and excitement when considering the ramifications of Peter losing his job? Is hers an expected response? Would it be your response?

Abby's kids told her frequently to stop worrying. Did Abby worry too much about her young adult children?

Do you agree with the way Abby and Peter handled the situation with Ben? Should they have dealt with it differently?

How do Abby's reactions and behavior compare to those of her parents who also have to relocate because of circumstances beyond their control?

What are some earlier incidents that foreshadow or mirror how Abby reacts to her move?

What were the ways that the women in the *Lost in Transition* group responded to their situations? How do you account for the differences?

Abby struggles to think of Richmond as home. When she returns to Waterloo, her house no longer feels like home. What makes a home?

Was Abby fair to Peter? Was Peter fair to Abby? What aspects of their relationship helped them to survive the emotional upheaval of their relocation?

In what ways are friends important to Abby's adjustment? What impact do friends have on your life?

Relocating is as much about leaving behind familiar comforts as it is about moving ahead. Did Abby cling too much to what she left behind? How do you think you would respond to moving away from all you know to an unfamiliar environment? Would you be like Abby?

Sylvia May

Sylvia May was born in The Netherlands and has lived in Canada, the US, and currently resides in Bermuda. Her move from Ontario to Virginia inspired the writing *The Unraveling of Abby Settel*. Active in writers' groups wherever she calls home, her stories have placed in literary contests. A pianist and former music teacher, she is now delighted to call herself an author and is currently working on her second novel. She lives with her husband and has three grown children.

Please visit her website at www.sylviamay.com.

If you enjoyed Sylvia May's *The Unraveling of Abby Settel*,
you might also enjoy these women's fiction authors
published by Turquoise Morning Press:

Margaret Ethridge, author of *Contentment*

Mary O'Dell, author of *The Sweet Letting Go*

Grace Greene, author of *Beach Rental*

Thank you!

For purchasing this book from
Turquoise Morning Press.

We invite you to visit our Web site to learn more about
our
quality Trade Paperback and Ebook selections.

www.turquoisemorningpress.com
www.turquoisemorningpressbookstore.com

Turquoise Morning Press
Because every good beach deserves a book.
www.turquoisemorningpress.com

9233140R0

Made in the USA
Charleston, SC
22 August 2011